Mary Bishop

Jane Yunker

Published by Jane Yunker, 2020.

This is a work of fiction. Similarities to real people, places, or events are entirely coincidental.

MARY BISHOP

First edition. February 3, 2020.

ISBN: 978-1393571087

Written by Jane Yunker.

To my parents, who always believed in my dream to be a writer.

To my family and friends, who had to listen to me talk about my dream to be a writer.

And to those who helped me make it happen: all my beta and proof readers; my editor, Tina Susedik; my cover model photographer, Pam Eibs; and my cover designer, Jean Staral of Staral Ink.

I couldn't have done it without you.

CHAPTER 1

WISCONSIN: NOVEMBER 1880

The undertaker drove the team while the Reverend Elias Clark sat quietly next to him. Mary rode straight-backed on a bench next to Earl's casket, her hands folded over the Bible on her lap. An icy wind cut across the hilltops and whistled its discordant lament through the pines standing dark against the sky, releasing the last of the leaves to fall and crunch beneath the wagon wheels. It bit her cheeks, made her eyes water, and loosened the hair she had pinned so carefully beneath her hat.

She did not look away nor try to shelter herself from the coming storm. Instead, she welcomed the numbness that spread slowly but steadily to her core, as she imagined it must have spread through Earl's lifeless body swinging limp from the rope he'd thrown over the barn rafter.

Leaving her alone to cut him down. Leaving her alone to drag him into the house. Leaving her alone to wash and dress him for burial. Leaving her alone to ride into town and inform the Reverend of his sin. Leaving her alone.

If they had looked up from their business that November morning, the townspeople would have seen the distant silhouette of a wagon moving slowly along the hill's crest. They would have shaken their head and said, with a slight smile, *there goes Mary Bishop off to bury her husband*. Then they would have turned back to their day without a second thought. This Mary Bishop knew for a fact.

Graveside, Reverend Clark read from The Book of Psalms and led the three of them in a quick hymn as the first flakes fell from the sky and blew across the wretched fields to their miserable corner of the cemetery. In a singular act of kindness, the Reverend had agreed to bury Earl alongside the righteous founding citizens of Deer Creek despite the great sin of taking his own life, an act which should have banished him to unconsecrated ground. The last note of the hymn fast torn away on the wind, they stood for a moment of silence in that desolate place of Earl's last rest.

Oliver Polk stood farther back among the graves. Mary was pleased to see him there. He and his late wife, Irma, had been friends of theirs since she and Earl first moved to Deer Creek after the War.

When their eyes met, he hesitated then made his way slowly toward her, weaving a path between the leaning markers of the long, and not so long, dead.

"Thank you for coming, Oliver."

He looked down, his hands madly working the brim of the hat he held close to his chest. When a wind gust blew his gray hair into his eyes, he pushed it back with one hand.

"I didn't want to intrude." His eyes, a soft grayish-blue, misted over. "I'm sorry, Mary, so sorry. Please let me know if there's anything I can do, anything at all you need."

"Thank you. I will." Mary reached out and rested a hand on his arm. "You know there was nothing either one of us could have done to stop him. Once Earl made up his mind about something there was nothing anyone on God's green earth could say to change his mind."

Oliver nodded. "He was a stubborn one."

"Earl's pain went all the way back to his mother's death, the loss of our children, the War. The way these people treated him, treated both of us, was only the last straw."

She sighed. *A pain so great even our love couldn't overcome it.*

"There was nothing either one of us could have done," she repeated.

Reverend Clark took her arm. "We should be getting you home, Mrs. Bishop."

"Yes." She took her seat back in the wagon. The empty place where Earl's casket once rested tore at her heart with another reminder he was gone.

Oliver pushed his hair back again, this time holding it in place with his hat, and walked toward town. The wagon moved forward with a lurch. Mary, the Reverend, and the undertaker drove away to the howl of the growing storm and the scrape of the grave diggers' shovels.

MARY INVITED THE TWO men in for a cup of coffee and a slice of the cake the Reverend's young wife so generously sent with him that morning.

"Frances would have come to pay her respects in person but for the head cold she contracted last week at the Widow Johnson's funeral."

Mary remembered the widow's funeral well. She hadn't attended, wasn't welcome, but couldn't help noticing the crowded cemetery in passing. It seemed everyone in town must have come out to pay their respects. Azalea Johnson lost her son at the First Battle of Bull Run and was laid next to his grave. Mary had been happy for her but also a little jealous. Their Ander was buried in a mass Confederate grave somewhere at Gettysburg.

"Thank her for me. Tell her I hope she feels better soon." Mary handed him a plate.

"Mrs. Bishop, I hope you will feel free to call on me any time you need guidance during this trying time. Whenever I'm feeling alone or uncertain, I turn to the Good Book for comfort. I particularly like..." His voice faded into the background until it was nothing more than the buzz of an annoying fly.

Instead, Mary focused on the gluttonous manner in which the undertaker devoured his cake. He leaned over, his chin practically touching his plate, and shoveled the last bite into his mouth. He washed it all down with a final gulp of coffee, belched, and set the cup on the table with a clatter.

"Excuse me," he mumbled, red-faced, when he noticed Mary and the Reverend staring at him.

Mary set down her untouched coffee and turned her attention back to the Reverend. She managed a weak smile out of politeness, the way her mother had taught her. "Thank you, again, for all your kindness, but I think it best you both head home before the storm gets any worse."

The Reverend gazed out the window and nodded. Heavy clouds rolled and raced across the darkening sky. "Yes," he agreed.

Pulling a shawl tight around her shoulders, Mary followed them out into the snow. The Reverend returned to his place beside the undertaker. "My wife will be by to see you in a couple days, when she's feeling up to going out—and the weather allows, of course." Snapping the reins, they left her standing alone.

She went inside and closed the door, sliding the bolt with a click. Should she have been more hospitable, less in a hurry to see them gone, perhaps offered them a second cup? She wanted nothing more than to be rid of them and their polite condolences. *I'm sorry . . . if there's anything I can do . . . lean on the Good Book . . . God's will.* She especially hated that last one. Why would it be God's will to take her family from her?

Long shadows spilled from every corner of her little farmhouse, despite it being the middle of the day. She was cold but didn't stop to light a fire. She lay on her bed, still in her coat, and listened to the wind shriek and moan through the tiny chinks and cracks around the windows. She had never grown accustomed to the harsh winters in northern Wisconsin. They were long and bitter and isolating, not like back in Virginia. There they could have the occasional storm, cold snap, but nothing with the unending deep freeze of Wisconsin. Mary didn't know how she would stay warm without Earl to hold her close. She closed her eyes and slept.

WHEN SHE WOKE THE ROOM was completely dark. Mary jumped to her feet, stumbling when the toe of her shoe caught in her skirt hem. The material ripped free.

Her lips pinched together with a sigh. "What more?" It wasn't just the stitching that gave way but the material itself. Any attempt at repairs would have to wait.

What time was it? The cow must be crying for her milking. She sprang the cover on Earl's pocket watch, the one she'd given him as a wedding gift. She remembered that day and for a moment felt him standing next to her before God and her family. Mary's breath caught in her throat and tears filled her eyes.

"Oh, Earl. Why?" Her voice cracked, betraying her grief. A gulping sob burst free. She brushed her cheeks with the back of her hand and forced the pain back down deep. "Tears change nothing," she reminded herself. It was one of the many things she'd learned over years of loss and pain. Somehow life continued. They always found happiness again. But this time she expected the pain would follow her until it was time for the Reverend to lay her next to Earl.

She angled the watch face to catch the little bit of moonlight breaking through the clouds.

Six o'clock. She switched her shoes for barn boots, lit the lantern, and headed out to check on the animals. The snow wasn't so much falling as blowing, stinging her face. With only an inch or two covering the ground, though, walking was easy.

How long would it be before she could open those doors without seeing Earl hanging from the rafters? His body gently swinging, turning ever so slightly in the wind that blew in at her back. His face and neck a deep purplish red, dark as a beet washed fresh from the field. His empty eyes bloodshot and staring straight ahead. An empty whiskey bottle at his feet. Was it meant to be liquid courage or just one last unsuccessful attempt to dull the pain?

The frayed length of rope still hung from where she'd cut him down. She couldn't forget the thud of his body as it hit the hard dirt floor and the screams that could only be her own. She stood on the same stool he used and untied it.

What happened to the carefree boy I first saw standing over me in the field that summer afternoon so many years ago?

She dropped the rope on the burn pile for later and tended her animals in silence.

CHAPTER 2

VIRGINIA: SUMMER 1837

Mary stretched out as still as a stick in the tall grass, flat on her stomach, and pressed her chin as close to the ground as she could without eating dirt. Her cap slipped off her head to hang from one braid but she didn't mind. She wanted to see what the ants saw, see what the spiders and beetles saw. They scaled clumps of dirt barely big enough for her to feel beneath her bare feet as if those clumps were great mountains. She held her breath when a bumble bee flew past her head, lightly brushing her ear, stopping to inspect one clover flower after another in search of something sweet.

Most twelve-year-old girls would scream and squirm and thrash about. They would spend their afternoons inside, away from the bright sun their mothers warned would brown their skin like horse leather. Hours would be dedicated to needlepoint and French lessons. Not Mary. Unlike her older sister, Lucy, and much to their mother's chagrin, she hated all things girlish. She wanted to be out with the boys enjoying the summer sun, wading and fishing in the river that bordered their town. Their mother was beside herself every evening when Mary came home covered in dirt and bug bites, her hair so tangled a comb could barely pass through. And every evening Mary got a scolding.

"We can't have people see the minister's daughter running around dark as a field hand and dirty as a sharecropper. Think how your behavior reflects on your father. And where's your cap?" Mary would pull it out of her apron pocket where she had bunched it up earlier for safe keeping. It would be wrinkled and nowhere near the bright white it had been when her mother first pinned it to her hair that morning. The inevitable deep sigh reminded Mary of her mother's disappointment. This ritual repeated itself every summer evening until school started, when she could be kept indoors under the pretense of studying.

Footsteps approached, legs swishing through the grass. It was probably one of her brothers, Harlan or George, sent to find her. She wasn't ready to go home yet. Whoever it was stopped in front of her, his bare feet and legs muddy half way up the calf to the cuff of his rolled-up trousers. The sharp tang of fresh-caught fish tickled her nose.

"What do we have here?" the stranger asked. "Some kind of snake or over-sized beetle bug?"

It wasn't George or Harlan. It was someone Mary had never seen before. From where she lay, the sun formed a halo around his unruly curls that glowed the color of roasted chestnuts at Christmas. A string of dripping wet fish hung from one of his hands. The other held a pole balanced over his shoulder. She squinted to make out his face through the glare. He was undoubtedly the cutest boy she'd ever seen.

"Better close your mouth if you don't want bugs to crawl in." He plopped down beside her, laying his catch and pole on the ground. "What are you doing down here?"

"Watching a bumble bee in the clover."

"Sounds like as good a pastime as any for a hot summer afternoon." His deep brown eyes sparkled when he smiled.

"I think so." Mary, excited now that she knew he wasn't laughing at her, sat up beside him. He was taller than her, maybe as tall as Harlan. She guessed that would make him about fourteen. "I haven't seen you around before. Did your family just move here or are you visiting?"

"Earl Bishop," he introduced himself. "I'm going to be staying with my uncle now that my mother died. Uncle Jackson's the overseer for the Hollings Plantation."

She took the hand he offered. It was rough, warm, and the feel of it made her heart skip a beat. "Mary Smythe." She coughed to cover the catch in her voice, hoping he didn't notice. "What about your father? Can't he take care of you?"

"My father's a worthless drunk." Earl's face clouded over. "He's never been much interested in being a father so he shipped me off to live with his brother."

"Oh." Mary had never heard such a sad story before. What kind of man didn't want his own child?

"Smythe," he changed the subject. "As in Reverend Smythe?"

Mary nodded, worried he'd think less of her, as her mother warned, once he found out she wasn't behaving as a minister's daughter should.

"Well, Mary Smythe, then I guess I can expect to see you on Sunday." He smiled, stood, and strolled off whistling. His string of fish sparkling in the sun as they swung at his side.

"On Sunday," Mary whispered to herself, smiling and hugging her knees to her chest.

SUNDAY COULDN'T COME fast enough. Mary squirmed as her mother brushed and braided her hair.

"I want to wear my hair like Lucy's." She pulled away. "Braids are for little girls. I'm twelve now. I'm not a little girl anymore."

Mary's sister was fifteen and wore her long hair loose with just the sides tied back in a ribbon. All the boys wanted to spend time with Lucy, and Mary knew the other girls all envied her. She wanted Earl to notice her as a girl and not the dirty tomboy he found lying in the grass.

"Please, Mother?"

"Oh?" The corner of her mother's mouth turned up ever so slightly. "Would it be anyone in particular you're trying to impress? Anyone I know?"

Mary looked away, trying to hide her enthusiasm. "You're always saying it's time to start looking more like a young lady." She didn't want to tell her about Earl. Not yet.

"I'll never get a comb through it later if we don't braid it now."

"We're going to church. I'll be sitting in a pew not rolling around on the floor. I'll keep clean. I promise."

"Truly?" her mother hesitated. Mary gave the most innocent smile she could manage, hoping to convince her. "You won't run around before or after service no matter what the other children are doing?"

"I promise, and I'm not a child anymore."

Her mother undid the braids, brushing them out straight down Mary's back. "You really do have beautiful hair. If only you'd keep it neat." She picked up the white ribbon, hesitated, then put it back. "The green, I think."

"Yes," Mary agreed. It better suited her eyes.

"You never met my Grandma Colleen but her hair was auburn like yours, more red than brown. All the boys in her village back in Ireland were in love with her. It was her hair that captured their hearts. Grandpa Sean always said her temper was as fiery as her hair, and he wouldn't have it any other way. But—*glory be, she was a handful when riled*."

Mary loved it when her mother rolled out a thick Irish brogue in imitation.

"In that respect, you're a lot like her." She finished tying the ribbon and gave Mary a hug. "I pray whoever you have your eyes on appreciates you the way Grandpa Sean appreciated Grandma Colleen."

Mary hoped her mother was right. She studied her hair in the mirror. It glowed in the sunlight from her bedroom window and felt as soft as their neighbor's new kittens. How could Earl not notice?

SERVICE WAS OVER AND they were standing in the churchyard greeting parishioners when Mary finally caught Earl's eye. He must have come in late and sat in the back. Mary's family always sat in the front pew. She was not allowed to turn around no matter how curious she was about this or that sound coming from behind.

A rough looking man, unshaven, with a scowl that could curdle milk, pushed him forward. Jackson Bishop, she assumed.

"Reverend, Mrs. Smythe, this is my nephew Earl. He's come here from New York City. He's going to be staying with me, helping out at the plantation."

"I hope you are finding our little town to your liking, Earl. It's a big change from New York." Mary's father shook his hand.

"Yes, sir, so far everyone's been very nice." Earl winked at Mary. Her father didn't see it but her mother did. She gave Mary another long knowing look. A slight smile and nod and Mary's secret was out.

"So, what have you been doing with your time?" the Reverend asked.

"I mostly help Uncle Jackson with the field hands, but I like to fish when I have a little free time. In fact, I plan on doing some fishing this afternoon."

Earl smiled at Mary, and she knew he was telling her where she could find him later. She planned on being there waiting when he arrived.

CHAPTER 3

VIRGINIA: FALL 1837

Their first summer together quickly blazed into fall. The leaves on the hills burst into bright yellows and deep reds. Fishing on a lazy, hot afternoon was over as a new school year began. Apples ripened and soon filled baskets in cool, dark root cellars. Those that fell from the trees and bruised were gathered, mashed, and strained for cider. Pumpkins and squash grew large in the late season gardens. Hectic preparations for winter kept their little Virginia community busy. The only time Mary saw Earl was at Sunday service. Uncle Jackson didn't see a need for schooling for a boy Earl's age. He was of more use on the plantation.

One November afternoon, after the harvest was complete and everyone was settling in for the coming winter, Mary headed down to the river looking for somewhere quiet to read. The air was growing cold, but the sun was still warm on her face as she sat on the log where they liked to fish.

"What's that you're reading?"

Mary jumped. "Where'd you come from, Earl Bishop? I didn't see you anywhere."

"I was around the bend when I saw you walking across the field." He sat next to her and snatched away her father's book. "Aren't you a little young for Shakespeare?"

"No," she said defensively. Mary reached for her book, but he held it out of reach.

"You understand this sonnet stuff?" His brow wrinkled and lips moved silently as he read the words.

Mary took the book back. "Yes, well, some of it. I'm learning."

"Explain that one to me, then." He pointed to the page she'd been reading.

She slammed the book shut and stood to leave. He was treating her like a child, making fun of her the way her brothers always did, and she wasn't having any of it.

"Don't go. I'm serious. Explain it to me."

She studied him for a moment, waiting for him to start laughing or say something mean. When he didn't, she sat back down and opened to Sonnet 18. It was one of her favorites.

"All right, Father told me it's about a man professing his love to a young woman. He's telling her how beautiful she is, comparing her to a summer's day."

"So, you and your father read books like this together?"

"We read all kinds of books. He lets me borrow anything I want from his library. When I don't understand something I only have to ask, and he explains it to me." Mary knew it was unusual for a father to encourage his daughter to study, but her parents believed all children, even girls, should learn to read. "He said I'm the smartest girl he knows—aside from my mother."

"Well, you're certainly the smartest girl I've ever met." Earl turned back to the page in front of them. "Tell me more about this poem."

"He's telling her she's more beautiful than a summer's day, and unlike a summer's day, which can be too hot or too cloudy and always too short, her beauty will never fade. Not even in death."

"That's a lot of words just to tell a woman she's beautiful."

"I hope one day a man will find me beautiful."

Earl's eyes twinkled. His mouth turned up with a little laugh.

Oh, my! She blushed. *I can't believe I just said that out loud.* She'd never felt so mortified in all her life.

"I meant to say," she stammered, trying to back step and cover her embarrassment. "Every girl hopes one day a man will find her beautiful." Mary looked down and fiddled with the green ribbon she'd been using to mark her place, the same green ribbon she had worn in her hair that first Sunday he'd come to service.

"Read it to me," he said, and she did.

Shall I compare thee to a summer's day?

Thou art more lovely and more temperate:
Rough winds do shake the darling buds of May,
And summer's lease hath all too short a date:
Sometime too hot the eye of heaven shines,
And often is his gold complexion dimm'd,
And every fair from fair sometime declines,
By chance, or nature's changing course, untrimm'd;
But thy eternal summer shall not fade,
Nor lose possession of that fair though ow'st;
Nor shall Death brag thou wander'st in his shade,
When in eternal lines to time thou grow'st:

So long as men can breathe, or eyes can see,
So long lives this, and this gives life to thee.

Sitting there in the sun with Earl that November afternoon, the breeze rustling the dying leaves and rattling the bare branches, Mary read Shakespeare's 18th Sonnet aloud and for the first time truly appreciated Shakespeare's words.

She closed the book and waited to hear what Earl thought. His silence felt like an eternity before he finally spoke.

"Will you read some more to me another time?" He pushed a windblown strand of her hair back behind one ear. Mary's breath caught at the softness of his touch.

"If you'd like."

Earl's smile lit a flame in Mary's heart. He gave her a quick kiss on the cheek and was gone. Mary knew right then and there she would love him forever.

CHAPTER 4

VIRGINIA: CHRISTMAS Eve 1840

"Hurry along, Mary," her mother scolded. "Why must you always dawdle?"

Mary reluctantly pinned her cap in place. She hated paying calls on the congregation's shut-ins. In the past it was always Lucy who went with their mother. Then Lucy married Harold Wooten and moved to Arlington to be nearer the nation's fast-growing capital, Washington City. Now the chore of helping their mother with the visiting was left to her. And that's how she thought of it, a chore.

Lucy had enjoyed visiting with the old ladies, taking them fresh baked sweets, making them tea, listening to their long stories of woe and sadness. Mary despised the whole ritual of it. She found it boring and faintly disgusting. She had to learn how to breathe through her mouth, instead of her nose, to keep from gagging on the stench of camphor and other unmentionable, but definitely recognizable, odors trapped in the dark rooms. Why was it the elderly never opened a curtain, let alone a window, to partake of fresh air and sun light? She suspected such a move would go a long way toward dispelling their general melancholy.

"Who are we visiting today?" Mary asked. She wrapped a heavy wool shawl around her shoulders.

"Mrs. Hollings."

Mary stifled a groan. Mrs. Eugenia Hollings was the matriarch of Hollings Plantation. At eighty years, she was the oldest living person Mary had ever known and was as frightening as any witch or evil stepmother in the Brothers Grimm fairy tales her father gave her for her last birthday. It was said Eugenia Hollings once killed a slave woman for stealing a loaf of bread cooling in the kitchen. She reportedly gave the lashings herself, accusing her overseer of being too lenient. Then, as a warning to the others, she left the poor woman tethered to the tree half naked and bleeding in the heart of winter. The woman froze to death. Never mind the guilty dog was seen eating the bread behind the smokehouse.

And she wasn't the only slave to die at the hands of Mrs. Hollings, or so reported. People said God took home all her children and grandchildren at a young age, leaving Mrs. Hollings old and alone, as righteous punishment. Mary didn't know if the stories were true. This was long before she was born, but she didn't doubt the possibility. There was a look in Mrs. Hollings' eyes as cold and hard as river ice. The only thing that could make the afternoon bearable would be a glimpse of Earl.

Mary climbed into the buggy, and her mother handed her a basket of warm Christmas cake. A gift for Mrs. Hollings.

"I don't know why you take the time to bake for Mrs. Hollings when she has a house full of slaves who do for her every day. She's not the same as the other widows who need our care." Mary knew it was wrong, but she wished for nothing more than to be able to break off a bit of the lovely cinnamon-scented loaf resting in her lap.

"It's the gesture, Mary, not the gift, that matters." Her mother snapped the reins and turned the buggy down the road toward the Hollings Plantation.

Mary sulked but said not another word, instead concentrating on the passing empty tobacco fields. The plants harvested in September had long ago been cured, packed, and shipped to England. No row upon row of green plants standing taller than a man. No broad leaves rustling in the breeze. No sweet smell filling the air. Only the frozen earth resting until the time came to start the process all over again.

In the background were the long curing barns, empty now. Only the distant shapes of the field hands remained as they made the buildings ready for next year's harvest. There was never a time of rest on a plantation. They were either working the present crop or preparing to work the next.

Their buggy turned onto the tree-lined drive that led to the main house. Mary's stomach twisted with dread.

"Must we?"

"I am aware of the stories told about Mrs. Hollings. I do not like them, and I never want to hear you repeat them. It's time you over-came such childish fears. She is an old woman in need of companionship and spiritual guidance the same as any of the other widows. Someday you may find yourself sitting in the very same place Mrs. Hollings is now, and you'll be glad for the occasional visitor."

"But—"

"Mary!"

She bit her tongue and swallowed back all the words of protest running through her mind.

The Hollings house was white, two stories tall with dormer windows protruding from the roof for a partial third. Wide verandas and four grand Corinthian pillars topped with flourishes welcomed arriving guests. How wonderful it would be to live in such a large house where she could be alone whenever she wanted. Then she remembered Mrs. Hollings was always alone, except for her slaves. Maybe it wouldn't be so much fun after all. Mary's brothers were good for a game of dominoes or checkers, even cat's cradle, if she smiled and asked sweetly.

The house girl, Eliza, escorted them down the central hall and into the sitting room where the old lady waited by the fire. She sat with her back as straight as a board, her cane held tight in one hand, and her Bible open on her lap. There were no decorations, no hint that it was Christmas Eve.

Mrs. Hollings frowned when they entered the room. Her chin tucked down toward her chest, fingers caressing the knob of her cane, she appraised Mary's appearance from over top of her spectacles. Mary feared the old woman might reach out with that cane at any minute and bring it down on her head. Mrs. Hollings turned to where Eliza lingered in the shadows. She narrowed her eyes.

"Take Mrs. Smythe's basket to the kitchen and get back to work," she snapped, sending the girl scurrying with a violent thump of her cane against the floor.

Mary flinched. From somewhere in the back of the house came the sound of a sharp slap and a pain-filled squeal. She took a step closer to her mother. Mary's parents never slapped her, never slapped any of their children. Oh, Harlan and George had been at the wrong end of a switch a couple of times, but only for the most awful sins. Mostly a few stern words were all that were needed in the Smythe home.

Mrs. Hollings heard the slap, too, and smiled, her eyes locked on Mary's.

"Mrs. Smythe, I see you brought your other daughter with you this time. What's your name, child?"

Mary pulled her shawl tighter and attempted to dry her sweaty palms in the folds. Her heart beat rapidly. Her feet felt like they were nailed to the floor. Her mother poked a sharp finger into Mary's back.

"Mary, ma'am." She curtsied on wobbly knees. Her mouth was so dry her voice came out in a scratchy whisper.

"Louder, child!" Mrs. Hollings rapped her cane on the floor again. "A young lady needs to learn to speak up so she can be heard, but only when spoken to first, of course."

"Mary," she repeated, louder and with all the confidence she could muster, which wasn't much.

"Mary." The old lady mulled it over. "A good Christian name. Simple. Honest. No one I know has ever come to harm at the hands of a Mary. How old are you?"

"Fifteen on my last birthday, ma'am."

"Fifteen and not yet married?"

Mary's mother replied in defense. "We thought we might wait a couple more years. Now that our Lucy is gone, I don't know what I'd do without Mary's help."

"Nonsense. You could buy yourself a girl to help with your housework. I may even have an extra one around here I could sell you cheap, seeing as you're of limited means." She looked around, as if expecting someone to appear out of the shadows, then turned back to them. "After all, what worth is a well-raised girl of Mary's age to anyone but a husband?"

The old woman leaned forward, and Mary took a half step back. Her mother's hand closed firmly on her shoulder, keeping her still.

Mrs. Hollings continued with a smile. "I was married at fourteen and gave birth to my eldest son when I was fifteen." She turned back to Mary's mother. "Find a man of thirty or more years, a businessman well established in his community. He will be quite pleased to take on a wife of good moral character, someone to keep a Christian home and give him children. If you wish, I know a widower or two I might recommend, perhaps even make introductions for you. Of course, to do so I'd have to get better acquainted with your daughter to be certain it was the most advantageous match."

Mary panicked. She turned to her mother, mouth open, ready to argue against such a horrifying thought. Her mother stopped her with a warning glance.

"I thank you for the generous offer, but when the time comes to find Mary a husband, the Reverend and I will want to make that decision ourselves."

"What about a house girl, then? I could send Eliza back with you today, if you like. You can consider her a Christmas gift from me to you and the Reverend. She's a little lazy for my taste, but perhaps with a close eye and a ready switch she could be trained."

"No, thank you. That's kind of you, but I enjoy keeping my own house."

Mary knew her mother was merely being polite. Her parents abhorred slavery, and certainly Mrs. Hollings had to know that, even if she didn't understand it.

"Suit yourself." Mrs. Hollings shrugged. "Speaking of your oldest daughter and good marriages, how is Mrs. Wooten adjusting to her new life?" she asked, thankfully changing the subject.

"She writes she is happy in Arlington. Harold is now the proprietor of his own hotel and restaurant. Lucy spends much of her day overseeing the kitchen staff."

"And the child? I understand she had a child."

"Yes, a boy, Samuel. He's one year old and walking. She says he is already presenting himself as a highly intelligent and, I dare say, headstrong young man."

Mrs. Hollings laughed a single loud guffaw, like a dog's bark. "Then he will go far in this world. A man must be confident, committed in the attainment of all his life goals. Such a trait always presents itself early in life. Good for him." She shook her head, leaned forward, and spoke in a half whisper, "But God help the girl in the meantime. He will be a handful." She barked again.

A commotion rose outside the window. Mary craned her neck to see. It was Earl riding up fast. Several of the hands rushed forward to help him down from his horse. Earl was like a Greek god from legend, curls flying behind him, muscles straining his sleeves as he reined in his horse. He leapt to the ground with little effort and no assistance from the men. She imagined what it would be like if she were out there waiting for his return. He would sweep her into his arms for a long, lingering kiss, the whole world melting away around them. Her mother's voice drew her attention back to the room.

"Mary has formed a friendship with your overseer's nephew," she explained to Mrs. Hollings.

"Earl Bishop? I see, and no doubt she'd much rather be spending time with her young friend than with this old lady." Mrs. Hollings looked at Mary. "I've heard the stories."

Mary's face burned. "Oh, no, Mrs. Hollings. It's not . . . It's just . . ."

"For heaven's sakes, child, stop stammering. It's unbecoming of a young lady. Go wish your friend a happy Christmas while your mother has a seat, and we talk more about your future."

Mary's mother gave her a look and a nod that said not to worry. "Don't be long. Your father will be expecting a meal before the Christmas Eve service."

"Thank you." Mary kissed her mother on the cheek. With a quick curtsy and *Merry Christmas, ma'am* to Mrs. Hollings, she forced herself to walk slow and lady-like until out of sight. Only then did she allow herself to break into a run to catch up with Earl.

"Merry Christmas, Earl," she said, breathless in the cold air.

"Well, Merry Christmas, Mary. I thought I recognized the Reverend's horse and buggy out front. What brings you here?"

"Mother is visiting with Mrs. Hollings, and she thought it was time I came with to learn the proper way to make calls on the old and sick."

"I see. What have you learned?" he asked, leading the way toward the field hands' cabins.

"Mostly that old people are boring and smell bad, but not Mrs. Hollings. I imagine that's because she has help keeping clean."

He nodded.

"What's in the sack?" she asked, pointing at the bag the mercantile used for sweets.

"Candy for the children." He stopped and opened the bag for her to see all the brightly striped peppermint sticks.

"Mrs. Hollings gives the slave children Christmas candy?" Mary would never have guessed Mrs. Hollings to be generous in that way.

"It's from me. I figure every child deserves something special for Christmas, even slaves."

"I think that's wonderful."

"Do you want to come with me?" He closed the bag.

"I'd love to, but I can't be long. Mother will be looking for me to leave soon."

They hadn't gone far before Eliza caught up with them, the red slap mark still visible on her cheek. "Miss Mary, your mother would like to be heading home now."

"Another time," Earl said.

"Yes. Wish the children a Merry Christmas from me, too."

"I will." He studied her face for a moment. "You are a special girl, Mary Smythe."

Mary felt her cheeks warm. "Merry Christmas, Earl Bishop."

CHAPTER 5

VIRGINIA: CHRISTMAS Day 1840

The Smythe family Christmas feast got better every year, if that was possible. They all agreed their mother had outdone herself, again, their forks clattering on empty plates. Even Mary's brothers, whose stomachs, they joked, were bottomless, couldn't find room for one more candied walnut. The only thing missing that would have made for a perfect Christmas was Lucy and her new little family.

A racket in the yard stopped their cleanup. Fast hoof beats slid to a halt, feet stumbled up the stairs followed by a loud thud as something, or someone, fell against the back door.

Their father set down the dish he held in his hand and motioned for George and Harlan to follow. "Stay here," he said to Mary and her mother.

Mary hurried to the kitchen door and peeked around the edge. Her father was dragging an injured man into the house. George scanned the yard, and Harlan closed the door behind them after George declared it safe.

"Althea, come quick. I need your help," her father called.

"Who is it?" Her mother rushed to his side. Mary followed close behind.

"Earl," he said. "Looks like someone gave him a whipping."

Earl's bloodied shirt stuck to his back. He screamed and fainted when they peeled the torn remnants away to inspect his injuries. Deep gashes crisscrossed his back, just how many they couldn't tell. All the blood made it impossible to count.

"Help me lift him."

George, the oldest and strongest of her two brothers, helped their father carry Earl into the front room. They tried to be careful, but it was impossible to avoid his wounds. Earl cried out in pain.

"Mary, get a sheet to lay him on," her mother shouted. "I'll get something to clean and dress these wounds."

Mary pulled the sheets from her own bed, tossing blankets and pillow aside without care. One sheet she spread over the settee, folding it in layers to soak up the blood. The second she tore into strips for dressings. Her heart pounded with the fear Earl might be dying. He was so still and pale. There was so much blood.

"Harlan, take care of his horse. It's had a hard ride." Father never took his eyes from Earl. Harlan grabbed his coat and went out the back.

"Oh, John, who could have done such a thing? Who could be so cruel?" her mother asked.

"I don't know, but I intend to find out."

"Mrs. Hollings owns a big bull whip."

"Mary," her mother scolded. "I've told you not to repeat rumors."

"It's not a rumor if it's true, is it? Earl told me he's seen it, seen his uncle use it on the slaves."

Her parents exchanged a silent look that said they knew she was right.

"Do you think his uncle used it on Earl?" Mary asked in an almost whisper.

"Mary, it may not be a rumor if it's true, but it can quickly become a rumor if it's speculation. We don't know who did this and won't know until Earl can tell us." Her father shot her a hard look, stopping her from saying anything more, but he couldn't stop her from thinking what she knew in her heart must be the truth.

Her mother submerged a clean cloth in the basin of warm, soapy water and wrung out the extra. She blotted it gently against Earl's wounds, causing him to cry out.

"I know," she said quietly. "This is going to hurt, but it can't be helped."

"Talk to him, Mary." Her father's voice was low and calm. "Help take his mind from the pain."

Mary knelt beside his head, took Earl's hand in both of hers, and leaned in so she could get her face as close to his as possible. He cried out again.

"Hush, my love. Just look at me, listen to me, you're safe now. Mother's going to dress your wounds, and Harlan's taking care of your horse. Everything is going to be all right."

Earl squeezed her hand. His eyes teared-up as another pain stabbed through him.

"I'm right here." Mary gently kissed the back of his hand.

He managed a weak smile before passing out.

After her mother finished, Mary gently covered him with a blanket and waited for him to wake. It was an hour before his eyes finally fluttered open.

"Mary?"

She laid a hand on his shoulder when he tried to get up.

"Stay still." She rested her cheek in his hand. He brushed away her tears with his thumb. "Don't fear. I'm not going anywhere," she assured him.

"Can you tell us what happened?" her father asked. "Who did this to you?"

Earl shook his head.

"You don't know what happened, or you don't want to tell us?"

Earl hesitated, but then the story came spilling out.

"It was the Christmas candy I bought the slave children." He looked at Mary. "Mrs. Hollings thought one of the kitchen slaves stole money to pay for it because it was one of her children caught eating the sweets." Earl coughed. He gasped with renewed pain.

"Drink this." Mary held the glass of water to his lips. After, he closed his eyes for a moment before opening them again to continue.

"I went to the house to set things straight. Mrs. Hollings was beating the girl with her cane. She brought that cane down again and again while the girl screamed and cried and begged for mercy, insisting she hadn't done anything wrong." Tears streaked Earl's cheeks as he relived the girl's beating.

Mary turned to her father and gave him a look saying she knew the stories about that wicked old woman were true.

"What did you do?" Her father focused on Earl.

"I stepped up and told Mrs. Hollings I was the one who gave the children candy. *You,* she screamed at me. *I knew you were going to be trouble, but I let that man bring you here anyway.*" Earl gasped when another wave of pain shot through him.

"You need to rest," Mary said. "You don't have to say anything more, not now."

"Did she do this to you, son?" her father asked, ignoring Mary's pleas that he be allowed to rest.

"She told Uncle Jackson to take me out and teach me a lesson. I tried to run, but Uncle had Thomas and Cassias tie me to a tree. Thomas whispered, *just take it, Mr. Earl, don't scream cuz she likes that.* Mrs. Hollings gave Uncle that big bull whip of hers. I don't know how many lashes. I passed out after the first couple, but I didn't make a sound." He smiled at Mary. "I wouldn't give her the satisfaction."

"You were very brave." Mary held his hand to her lips.

"When I came to it was over. Uncle and Mrs. Hollings were gone. Cassias untied me and helped Thomas take me back to our cabin. That's when I got on my horse and came here." Earl closed his eyes.

"Sleep, my darling." She stroked his hair.

"Please, don't make me go back there," he whispered. "I can't go back there."

"Of course not," her father assured him. "You'll stay with us. You can have the room over the stables. It's not big, but we can make it comfortable. It was intended to be for a servant or hired man. We don't need either in our home. As soon as you're able, I'll help you find work in town."

"Thank you, sir."

The front door shook. Their mother jumped and let out a little scream.

"Reverend Smythe!" a man yelled from outside. More banging.

Earl tensed. "It's Uncle Jackson." He struggled to get up but couldn't.

"I'll send him away," her father said.

George and Harlan followed him. Mary and her mother stayed close by Earl and watched as her father opened the door only wide enough to face the man.

Jackson Bishop was clearly drunk, a nearly empty bottle in his hand. "Where's my boy, Reverend?" Uncle Jackson lost his balance and fell against the door jamb when he tried to push his way in. "I know he's here. He always comes sniffing around that girl of yours. She's like a bitch in heat he can't ignore." He laughed and took another drink.

Her father's face burned red, and his jaw set hard. She had never seen him so angry. He held back her brothers, their fists balled-up tight at their sides. Her mother gasped, buried her face in her hands, and cried.

"I'm sorry, Mary, Mrs. Smythe," Earl said, shame for his uncle's words clear in his voice.

"He's drunk," Mary whispered through her own tears. "Ignore him."

Her father wasn't a large man, but he used his body at full height to block the door. Her brothers stood ready to intervene.

"Mr. Bishop!" her father shouted. "Please lower your voice and keep your vulgarities to yourself." With a deep, calming breath, he lowered his own voice. "Your nephew showed up on our doorstep barely conscious, deep gashes cut across his back, he says at your hand. I ought to call the law and have you locked up for your brutality, but I won't if you leave and not return. Earl will be staying with us from now on. My sons and I will be by tomorrow to collect his belongings. I trust they will be packed and ready for us, nothing missing or damaged."

Jackson Bishop opened his mouth and raised a finger to press the matter. Hesitating, he decided, "Keep him." He drained the last of the golden liquid and threw the empty bottle against the side of the house with a crash. "He's been nothin' but trouble since the day he arrived. That's why your own father didn't want you, you know," he yelled, looking straight at Earl. "Nothin' but trouble. That's what he warned me, but I took you in anyway. I felt sorry for you, even, and look what that got me. Nothin' but trouble."

With those final cutting words, he left. Mary laid her head on Earl's chest. He wrapped his arms around her and they cried together.

"You'll always have me," she promised. "You'll always have me."

CHAPTER 6

VIRGINIA: MAY 1841

Mary ran through the trees, hiding behind one and then another, breath coming in short pants, and peeked around to spy if Earl was anywhere nearby. She hadn't heard him in a while and wondered if she'd managed to lose him back when she left the trail.

She screamed when he grabbed her from behind, lifting her off her feet. "Earl Bishop put me down!" She laughed as she struggled to free herself.

Earl did as he was told, spinning her around and back into his arms. He kissed her, first hard and quick, then soft and lingering.

Mary put up a half-hearted show of trying to push him away. "Stop," she mumbled between kisses.

"Do you really want me to stop?" he asked in a breathy whisper.

"No." She kissed him back and leaned into his chest as he held her tight. "Just think, tomorrow I'll be Mrs. Earl Bishop."

Earl brushed his lips against her neck and nipped at her earlobe. His hot breath raised goose flesh on her arms. He lifted her and laid her gently in the moss beneath the tree. His lips, his touch, every stroke was like a small flame running through her veins. Her heart raced. She was suffocating in her desire for him.

"We should stop," he said, breathless. His hands trembled as they trailed ever so lightly over her breasts. His eyes locked on hers, filled with a desire as strong as her own.

"No." She placed her hands on each side of his face and pulled him to her. She kissed him with all the heat coursing through her. "Don't stop."

They made love for the first time under the big old tree, sweeping her up in the sounds of their river flowing beside them. She welcomed his advances, encouraged them in every way she imagined. Part of her hoped a child would come of their first union under the spring sky. She'd loved him for so long she saw no reason to wait one more day to show him how much.

"You're not sorry, are you?" he asked after, as they watched the afternoon clouds drift in and out from behind the newly leafed-out branches.

"For what?" She pulled him on top of her and kissed him again. Her fingers traced the ridges that crisscrossed his back.

He rolled away from her, out of reach. She knew he didn't like to be reminded.

"Those are the marks of a man with heart, a good man. Never be ashamed. Be proud. I am." Mary curled into his side. "And, no, I'm not sorry for what we did. I'm happy." She nuzzled in a little closer, breathed deep the musky smell of his skin, and closed her eyes.

THEY SLEPT, AND WHEN they woke the shadows had grown long. "Hurry!" He pulled her to her feet. "We have to get back before your brothers come looking for us."

"It would not be good if they found us like this," she agreed and kissed him, slow and soft.

"Do not do that." He pushed her away with a laugh.

She kissed him again, this time on the neck and then behind the ear.

"Do not kiss me like some wanton barmaid or . . ."

"Or what?" She teased him with one more flash of skin before buttoning her blouse. "And, tell me, what do you know of wanton barmaids?"

"Straighten yourself and be quick about it." Earl picked the grass from her hair clean.

MARY'S MOTHER STOOD on the back steps. Her brothers approached through the yard when she and Earl strolled from the trees, leaving a chaste couple of feet between them. Mary carried a hastily picked handful of wildflowers as if they were merely returning from a lovely afternoon walk.

"There you are," her mother scolded. "I was ready to send your brothers out to look for you. I was afraid maybe you both fell in the river and drowned." She smiled at Mary. George and Harlan scowled suspiciously at Earl.

"I'm sorry, Mother. We lost track of time." Mary kissed her on the cheek.

"It's my fault, Mrs. Smythe." Earl blushed just enough for Mary to notice and jump in. She took his hand.

"Mine, too. Earl fell asleep while we were sitting by the river, and I didn't want to wake him. He's been working so hard getting our house ready I guess he wore himself out."

Mary's mother took the flowers from her daughter. "I'll put these in water while you two hurry and wash up. Dinner's waiting on the table." She went inside.

"You have a little grass in your hair, Mary." Harlan continued staring at Earl.

"I do?" Mary blushed as her fingers searched for the errant blades.

"You do," George said. "Now clean yourself up before our father knows what you two have been up to."

"And what would that be?" She stared at him, hands on hips. "I've heard the rumors about the two of you and the Boland sisters. Perhaps you should marry Mae and Isabel by choice before you are forced to by consequence."

"Enough, all of you." Earl stepped between the three of them. "Let's get inside before we draw even more attention to ourselves."

WHEN MARY WOKE THE next morning, she was certain the sun rose and the birds sang just for her. Her wedding dress, a bright sapphire blue with black lace and buttons up the bodice, was carefully hung from a peg in the corner. She would wear delicate fresh-picked white and purple flowers in her hair.

It would be a small wedding with only her family in attendance. Even Lucy had made the journey home. Samuel was a noisy, busy two-year-old who ran his mother to exhaustion, her belly growing large with another child. Everyone took their turn watching the boy so his mother could rest in hopes of carrying this one to term. She had lost another born too early, too small to survive, and they all shared her fear for this one. She often cradled her stomach and stroked it as if passing on her own strength and protection to the baby growing within. Harold promised as soon as they returned to Arlington Lucy would go into complete rest and seclusion for the remainder of her confinement, summers being so hot and humid in the city.

"I wish you had family here with us," Mary had said to Earl over coffee that morning.

"You are my family now," he explained. "You, your parents and your brothers and sister are all the family I need."

She couldn't blame him for the way he felt. He hadn't seen or talked to his Uncle Jackson in over a year.

The ceremony was perfect, and Mary would remember every moment for as long as she lived. They held it in the front room, rather than the church, so Lucy could put her feet up. When Mary opened her bedroom door and stepped out, she was greeted by the smiles of the people who mattered most. Samuel had helped his grandmother pick as many wildflowers as they could carry, although Mary suspected he was more hindrance than help. The scent filled the house. They could have been standing in the middle of a field, and she wouldn't have known any different.

Her father officiated as they stood before God and family, promising to love and honor until death they do part. When Earl took her hand, Mary's chest filled with the same hot rush and shortness of breath as the day before. Tears welled in Earl's eyes.

Her mother sniffled into her handkerchief, and everyone applauded when they were pronounced duly wed. The men shook Earl's hand and took turns slapping him on the back in official welcome to the family. The women kissed Mary. Samuel hugged them both after being given an encouraging push forward by his mother.

Earl swept her up into his arms and spun her around. "Are you happy, wife?"

"I've never been happier, husband." She kissed him.

Their wedding feast was like nothing she had seen before. There was honeyed ham, potatoes and vegetables, fresh baked bread, and for dessert, a two-tiered frosted spice cake with whipped cream. Mary could hardly eat with all the excitement, and for fear the buttons would pop off her dress if she wasn't careful.

Her father and brothers offered toasts to the newlyweds' future from a jug of hard cider that had been saved for just such a special occasion.

"To the happy couple!" Her father held his glass high.

"To Earl, our new brother!" George said.

Her mother handed Mary a Star of Bethlehem quilt stitched in grays and pinks and blues. "This is from me. May it keep you warm for years to come."

Mary wept when she saw the perfect little stitches. "When did you find the time?"

"Oh, a few minutes here, and a few minutes there. A mother can always find the time for her children."

Mary hugged her mother tight. "It's perfect."

A knock on the door interrupted their tears.

"Just in time," Lucy said, exchanging looks with Harold, George, and Harlan.

"What's just in time?" Mary asked.

"Our wedding gift to the two of you," her siblings said in unison.

Harold opened the door. "Come in, gentlemen. Welcome."

"Good to see you again, Mr. Wooten," said the one carrying a box he proceeded to set on a three-legged stand. The other, clearly his assistant, brought in several more of the large, rather heavy looking, boxes.

"Where would you like these?"

"Right there will do for now, Virgil."

Harold did the honor of introductions. "Mary, Earl, this is my friend, Mr. Artemus Hoffman, and his son, Virgil. They are here to take a daguerreotype of you in your wedding clothes so you might always remember this special day."

Mr. Hoffman extended his hand. "Mr. and Mrs. Bishop, pleasure to meet you, and my most sincere congratulations on your nuptials."

"I've heard of this." Her father's face lit up. He approached Mr. Hoffman's strange box but stopped short of touching it. "May I?" He gestured.

"Be my guest." Mr. Hoffman took a step back. "But I must ask that you be careful. It's a delicate piece of equipment."

"Of course." He walked around to the back and ducked his head under the black curtain. "Amazing!"

They all laughed at the muffled exclamation.

He popped back out. "It's a relatively new process wherein this box will imprint your reverse image on a glass plate, called a negative, and from that Mr. Hoffman will be able to print a life-like portrait of you. While the equipment is quite unwieldy, it's quickly becoming very popular. Truly amazing!"

"And you're here to take a portrait of me and Earl?"

"Yes, ma'am. In order to memorialize this most momentous occasion. And may I say, you are a lovely bride."

"Oh, Earl, how wonderful." Mary clasped her hands to her chest. "But everyone must be in our portrait. I could never remember this day without remembering all of you as you are right now."

Lucy gasped. "Looking like this?"

"You look beautiful, my darling." Harold reached for her hand. "We shall sit you in a chair with Samuel at your side and me standing proudly behind."

Mr. Hoffman jumped in. "The bride and groom will sit in the center with her brothers standing behind and her parents at her left, mother seated and father standing behind. On the right, the sister seated with her husband behind and this young man standing beside her, leaning into his mother's arm." He winked at Samuel.

The women stepped back. Lucy held young Samuel's hand tight to keep him from getting in the way as the men moved furniture aside and gathered four chairs for the front row. Virgil set-up tall clamps.

"These will hold your head still," Mr. Hoffman explained. "It's quite a prolonged exposure period, and you will have to keep perfectly still until I tell you to stop."

He carefully posed each one in turn, making slight adjustments until he was satisfied.

Lucy and Samuel were the last to pose, but the poor boy, tired after a long day of festivities, refused to stand still at his mother's side. He popped his thumb into his mouth and buried his head in her lap, whining and pulling away every time the unfortunate Virgil tried to take control. Mary wasn't sure who deserved the most pity, Samuel or the young Mr. Hoffman. Both were equally flustered with the situation.

Lucy tried to gently pry his fingers from her skirts. "Samuel, sweetheart, won't you stand nice and still for your mama?"

"No!" Samuel shook his head, put his thumb back in his mouth, and clung tight.

"That's quite all right," the senior Mr. Hoffman said. "The young master looks very sweet just like that." He stepped behind the box, with one final instruction. "Now, there will be a powder flash with smoke, but you must fight all instinct to react. I can't emphasize this enough."

Lucy brushed the curls away from Samuel's eyes. She held his head still on her lap with one gentle hand on the side, the other arm wrapped firmly around his arm and middle, while they waited for the powder flash and Mr. Hoffman's box to take their picture.

MARY STOOD IN THE DOORWAY of the little farmhouse Earl had bought for them with his wages from the lumber mill. It was perfect. She threw herself into his arms and wept.

"Is something wrong?" he asked. "Don't you like the house?"

"I love the house," she sobbed. "And I love you. Today was everything I could have ever hoped for and more. I'm just so very happy."

Earl laughed. "I'll never understand you. You cry at the oddest things. Now you're crying because you're happy."

"Yes, well, get accustomed to it because I'm going to be around for many years, and I expect I will cry tears of happiness many more times."

"Then perhaps I shouldn't give you your gift."

"Mine first." She set her carpet bag on the table, pulled out a small box, and handed it to him. He opened it, lifting out a shiny gold pocket watch.

"How could you ever afford it?"

"I put up extra jam and sold it in town. You know, everyone says I make the best jam in all of Virginia, even Mother."

"That you do, but you didn't have to do this, Mary. You already gave me the best gift of all, the promise of a long and happy life, and all I got you was this." He handed her a package in simple brown paper.

Mary eagerly tore off the wrapper. *Shakespeare's Sonnets.*

"I know how much you love reading your father's copy so I bought you one of your own. Look inside."

She turned to the first page. *To my eternal summer, Love, Earl.* Mary hugged the book to her chest and wept. She began to think perhaps Earl was right and she did cry at the oddest things.

Earl laughed and pulled her into his arms.

CHAPTER 7

VIRGINIA: OCTOBER 1846

Mary hadn't lied when she told Earl she would cry many more tears over time. There were happy tears when their son, Anderson John, Ander for short, was born. Then frightened, anxious tears when Lillian entered the world too early and sad tears when she left them as quickly as she arrived.

"Now, Mama?" Four-year-old Ander clutched a small bouquet of wildflowers in his hands. Mary pulled the last of the weeds from in front of the little stone and gathered up the wilted bouquet he'd placed there when they visited the week before.

"All right." She stepped aside to let him pass.

"I brought these flowers for you, Lillian. This one's a golden aster, this one's a blue mist, and this white one is boneset."

Mary held her breath and squeezed her eyes shut, trying to hold back the tears. It upset Ander when she cried. A small sob escaped as a hiccup. He looked up at her and then back at Lillian's grave.

"Mama still misses you. I do, too." He tucked his hand in hers. "Let's go home, Mama. I'm cold."

"Me, too."

They walked in silence for a while, kicking at the fallen leaves the wind collected along the side of the road. Ander laughed when she threw an armload in the air to drift over and around him. He stopped and looked at her far too solemnly for someone so young.

"Do you think Lillian is cold down there in the ground? Sometimes at night, when I'm all warm in my bed, I wonder if Lillian is cold."

Mary knelt and hugged her big-hearted boy. "Lillian is warm in Jesus' arms. She doesn't cry anymore or struggle to breathe. She's happy in heaven."

"Then why is Papa so angry all the time? Shouldn't we be happy for Lillian?"

"He is happy for Lillian, just sad for us," she said, kissing his cheek.

A spark lit in his eyes that meant he was thinking of something mischievous. "Race you home!" he shouted and took off at a sprint.

"Wait for me." She struggled to her feet, toes catching in her skirts. "No fair. You had a head start."

She ran after him, deliberately keeping a few paces behind. He laughed and looked back. "You run slow, Mama. Girls run slow."

As they came closer to the farm her mood shifted to dread. What would they find when they got there? Would Earl be home? Would he be drinking?

Ever since Lillian was born so small and sick, ever since her death, Earl was a different person. He started drinking. Some men were jolly drunks, singing and dancing. Not Earl. He was combative, taking out his anger on anyone who crossed him. His fights inevitably turned physical with the men in town. Fortunately, he never laid a hand on her or Ander, but his temper often left their soft-hearted son in tears. She knew Earl was hurting, but they all felt Lillian's loss.

Everything was quiet. Mary sent Ander to the house with strict instructions to rest while she went to the barn to collect eggs and fill a basket with apples from the barrel. A neighbor had brought them the day before in exchange for some help in repairing his barn. She would bake Earl his favorite apple cake for dinner.

Opening the front door of the house, Mary stopped to listen. "Earl?" she whispered, not wanting to wake Ander.

"Papa isn't here." Ander's small voice came from the back bedroom.

She poked her head in. Ander sat on his bed surrounded by tin soldiers. Colonists on one side and Red Coats on the other. The Colonists were clearly winning the battle as far more of them remained standing.

"Look, Mama. General Washington's army is winning." He made shooting noises and more of his Red Coats fell over. "Go home, King George! We don't want you here." More shooting noises, more English deaths. Mary wished her brothers hadn't filled Ander's head with stories of the glories of war.

"I thought I told you to rest."

"I am resting. I'm playing on my bed. That's resting."

"No, it's not. You may look at a book, if you like, but no more playing soldier." Mary gathered up both the survivors and the fallen and placed them on top of his bureau.

"But, Mama, I'm not tired," he complained as she spread a quilt over him.

"I'll get you a book to look at." She went to the parlor and returned with the book of botanicals her father had given her as a girl. Ander liked to look at the brightly penned drawings of wildflowers. He was learning to recognize them in the woods and fields around their farm and call them by name. He couldn't read the captions on his own, but she only had to tell him a couple times and he would remember. Mary imagined great things in her son's future. Perhaps he would study medicine, or read the law. He wouldn't have to be a farmer and rely on the fickle weather for either fortune or famine.

The afternoon crept by. Earl hadn't returned yet. Mary set dinner on the table and served Ander his plate. She had no appetite for her dinner. Every bite caught in her throat and settled like a rock sinking in the river. She pushed her plate away. The last time food made her feel this sick she was first pregnant with Lillian, but she knew that wasn't the case this time. They hadn't been intimate since before Lillian was born.

When dinner was over, the dishes washed, and still no Earl, Mary knew where he must be—in town drinking. Her stomach churned and the burn of bile rose in her throat. How easily Earl had gone from avoiding hard liquor to imbibing every day. How quickly he had forgotten what it was like to grow up first with his father and then his Uncle Jackson.

"I think it's time you were getting ready for bed, Ander."

"I want to wait up for Papa."

"Well, perhaps he will be here by the time you're ready to be tucked in. Otherwise, you'll see him in the morning." Ander pouted, then reluctantly agreed. Lying to their son made Mary even angrier at Earl.

She'd just gotten Ander into his nightshirt when they heard the front door open.

"Papa's home!" Ander ran from his room before she could stop him

Dear Lord, she prayed. *Please, let Earl be sober. Let me be wrong. Just let me be wrong this one time.*

She followed close behind, but it wasn't Earl waiting in their front room. It was her brother George and his wife Mae. Mary didn't know if she was more disappointed that it wasn't Earl, or more relieved it was George.

Ander threw himself into Mae's arms for a kiss. With no living children of their own, Mae had become a second mother to Ander, and he loved all the extra attention.

George removed his coat. "Mae, take Ander back to his room, tuck him in, maybe tell him a story. I need to talk to Mary alone for a few minutes."

"Of course." She lifted Ander and gave him another squeeze. "I can tell you all about the raccoon Blue caught trying to sneak into the hen house last night."

Ander gasped, already enthralled with the story. "Was it a big raccoon or a little one? Is Blue all right? The raccoon didn't hurt him, did he?"

"It was a big one, biggest raccoon I've ever seen, but Blue is just fine."

Mary waited until Mae carried Ander into his room and closed the door. She never loved her sister-in-law more than she did right then.

She took a deep breath. "What's wrong, George?" she asked, dreading the answer.

"It's Earl. He's in jail this time."

George's words hit her like a punch to the gut. Drunk, yes. Fighting, no doubt. But jail? She hadn't expected that.

"Jerome Webb stopped on his way home to let me know. Said he would have come and told you himself, but he wasn't headed this way, just thought someone in the family ought to know."

The room spun. Mary's knees buckled. She grabbed a kitchen chair and sat to keep from falling. Closing her eyes, tears slid down her cheeks.

"What happened?" she asked in a choked whisper.

"Earl got into it with Jed, again, over who caught the biggest fish. Jed says he did, but Earl insists it was him, and besides, Jed's fish don't count because . . ."

Mary stopped him with a wave of the hand. Why did men fight over the most ridiculous things? "I don't care about fish right now. Who threw the first punch?"

"Depends who you ask, but it really don't matter. They're both locked up. The sheriff isn't going to let either one out until someone sober comes to claim them."

Mary rose from her seat. She removed her hat from a peg by the door and tied it in place.

"You don't have to do this, Mary. I'll go fetch him if you want. Heck, if it was up to me, I'd say we let him sit there until morning."

"No." She shook her head. "As tempting as that is, I say we bring him home tonight."

"Then I'll go with you. Mae can stay with the boy."

"I'm sorry, Mary," Mae said.

Intent on the thought of Earl being in jail, Mary hadn't heard her come into the room. They hugged.

"People don't realize how hard it is on a man when a child is lost," Mae said. "Everyone worries about us mothers, but no one thinks about the fathers. They hurt, too."

Mae wasn't only talking about Earl. A person would have to be blind not to see the look in George's eyes whenever Ander brought him some newfound treasure to show off, or scooted in a little closer all anxious to hear about his uncle's adventures with his old hound dog Blue. Didn't matter if the stories were real or make believe, Ander hung on every word, and so did George. Ander might not have his father right now but at least he had his Uncle George.

Mary threw a shawl over her shoulders and checked there were enough coins in her reticule to pay whatever fine might be levied against Earl for his bad behavior. "Don't let me forget before you go home but I have a fresh-baked apple cake you can take with you for your troubles." The devil if she was going to let Earl have any of it now.

A door clicked shut behind them, followed by the soft footfalls and sobs of a little boy, the creak of his bed ropes and frame. Mary looked from George to Mae and her heart broke for her son.

"I've got this," Mae said. She went to Ander's side while George and Mary left to bail Earl out of jail.

CHAPTER 8

VIRGINIA: OCTOBER 1846

"Where do you want him, Mary?" George helped Earl out of the wagon bed, holding him up to keep him from falling face first into the dirt. Earl mumbled something and smiled, patting George on the chest. George took a couple steps toward the house.

"No! The barn." Mary pointed in the opposite direction. "He reeks of alcohol." She draped Earl's other arm over her shoulders and grabbed him around the waist. "I see no reason, whatsoever, that Ander and I should have our sleep disturbed."

They dumped him unceremoniously into a hay pile. Earl snorted, mumbled something else, but didn't move.

"You want me to come back in the morning and have a talk with him?"

"No, but thank you for all your help."

Mae waited by the wagon when they came out. She hugged Mary. "Ander's asleep. I think he'll be good until morning." George helped her onto the seat.

"Wait here and I'll get that apple cake for you to take with." Mary went into the house.

"Let us know if you need anything else," Mae said when Mary handed her the cake plate. "Anything."

Her words held down by the tears she fought to control, Mary waved until they were out of sight.

Mary dropped her shawl on the table next to her reticule. Exhaustion swept over her. She removed her shoes, but not her dress, and lay down on the bed. She was too tired to care but still she couldn't sleep.

It had been humiliating having to stand in front of the sheriff and plead Earl's case, having to vow she would keep her husband home and out of trouble if he were returned to her custody. The sheriff was not convinced she could uphold that promise, seeing as how this was not the first time Earl had started a drunken fist fight. George assured him he would also see to Earl's good behavior with Harlan's help.

Then there was the fine. Mary tried to hide that it would take almost all of her money. George must have suspected as much because he stepped forward and paid that, as well. On the ride home she promised she would pay back every last cent, but he whistled some nameless tune and acted as if he was deaf.

She hooked her arm in his and pulled him close. She thanked God every day for her brothers. While she couldn't count on her husband in his grief and pain, she could always count on her brothers. But she needed to learn to help herself. She was Ander's mother.

MARY TOOK CARE OF THE animals in the morning, not worrying if she was disturbing Earl's sleep. She wasn't. Even with all the noise he still didn't as much as roll over.

She stood over him, hands on hips. "This ends today, Earl Bishop." He didn't move. She shoved him with her foot. "Wake up!"

Earl jerked to life. "What . . . where . . . Mary? Why did you kick me?"

"Clean yourself up. You stink. It's a beautiful day and I'm taking our son for a picnic down by the river. I don't want him to see you like this. For some reason he thinks his father can do no wrong. I'd like to keep it that way. Although, after last night that might no longer be true." She never lied to Earl before. She saw how Ander watched his Papa, how he had learned to keep quiet when Earl was surly from drink. She just hoped it wasn't too late to get that all back. In no mood to debate his behavior, she stormed out of the barn before he could argue. She stopped outside the house and took a moment to calm herself.

Ander was sitting at the kitchen table with the little boat Earl had carved out of driftwood. "Are you ready to go yet, Mama?" He jumped to his feet.

"Yes, I am." She ruffled his hair and smiled at his excitement. She picked up the basket of food and her copy of *Walden* from the table.

"Is Papa coming with us?"

"Maybe later. He has chores to do in the barn first." She lied again, this time to Ander. Lying to protect Earl was getting to be a habit with her.

"I'll carry the blanket," he offered.

Mary held Ander's hand and they were off for an afternoon of adventure by the river.

IT WAS AN UNUSUALLY mild October day. The sun shone bright in a cloudless blue sky. The warm breeze kept the insects at bay. Soon winter would come. The sky would turn gray and the wind cold. Mary was content to while away what might be the last summer-like afternoon hours sitting on a log with her bare feet tickling the river's surface and a book on her lap. His shoes off and pant legs rolled up, Ander chased his boat up and down the water's edge. He stopped periodically to watch a fish slip back and forth between his legs, laughing when a tail tickled his ankles or toes.

"I wish we'd brought my fishing pole. I could have caught us some dinner," he said.

"Fish dinner sounds tasty. Good thing I brought my pole," Earl said as he appeared at Mary's side.

"Papa!" Ander rushed to his side.

Mary had been so engrossed watching Ander play she didn't hear Earl come through the trees. She jumped to her feet, slipped on the wet rocks, and fell into the water. She gasped at the sudden icy bath and clamored to right herself. Ander laughed at the sight of his mother sitting in the cold river.

Earl dropped his fishing gear and rushed to her rescue, pulling her to her feet. He had done what he could to clean himself up from when she'd last seen him sprawled and stinking on the barn floor, but it was plain to see he was still a little green around the gills.

"Mary, your book." He retrieved it from the water.

Mary groaned and snatched the ruined book from him. It was just another irritation, another disappointment. She turned on him, angry as a bear caught in a swarm of bees after enjoying the stolen honey.

"What were you thinking by sneaking up on us like that?"

Earl's face crumbled, and his shoulders slumped in defeat. "I'm sorry, I haven't been much of a husband lately."

She regretted her harsh words as soon as she heard the break in his voice. She never could stay mad at Earl for long. Besides, no one was hurt and a book was only a book.

"Should I get my fishing pole, too, Papa?" Ander jumped up and down. "I can run really fast and be back before you know I'm gone. I know the way. I won't get lost."

"I think it's time we were all headed home," Mary said. "Ander, collect your things and start out ahead. Your father and I will catch up."

"We'll go fishing another time real soon, little man, I promise."

"But—" Disappointment hung heavy in the air.

"Go along," Earl said quietly. "Do as your mother says."

"Yes, sir." Ander picked up his stockings, shoes, and boat. He stopped to look at the fish. "I'll be back for you later."

They waited for Ander to skip out of earshot. "Talk to me, Earl. What's happening with you? Losing Lillian's been hard on all of us, but . . . drinking and fighting? That's your answer?"

Earl looked down at his fishing pole still lying on the ground. "I don't know what to say, other than I'm sorry. I'm sorry for the drinking. I'm sorry for the fighting. I'm sorry I haven't been here for you and Ander these last few months. And then getting arrested last night. I just . . ." He raked his fingers through his hair. "She was so tiny. I was her father and supposed to protect her. But I couldn't. I couldn't do anything to help her."

Mary took his face in her hands and looked into his eyes. A single tear ran down his cheek. She brushed it away.

"There was nothing anyone could do to help Lillian. You said it yourself, she was too small. She was too sick." She picked up the blanket. Earl took one end and helped her fold it. Holding it to her chest, she continued. "Don't you think I miss her, too? Every day I find myself wishing she was still here with us. My arms ache to hold her again. Sometimes I even catch myself heading to the bedroom to check on her, only to remember she isn't there. Then it's like she's died all over again." Mary picked up the lunch basket. "I lost a piece of my heart that day. Don't you break off another piece by turning your back on me and Ander."

"You two are everything to me," he said. "Never forget that, no matter what, never forget." He pulled her close and kissed her. It had been a long time since she felt his lips on hers. A familiar flame lit in her heart.

"You're wet," he laughed.

"I know."

"And you're shivering. Let's get you home." He kissed her again, long and deep. She knew tonight she would welcome him back into their bed and into her arms.

"The river's cold."

Earl laughed. "I imagine it is. Sorry, again, about your book. I'll buy you a new one."

"No hurry. I have plenty of others I can read in the meantime."

Earl nodded. "That you do."

They held hands and walked silently back to the house. An easy peace fell over them once more.

THEY STEPPED FROM THE tree line and into the open. There, Ander stood still, wide-eyed, starring at the door that led to the root cellar under the barn.

"Ander? What's wrong, son?" Earl squatted down and put his arm around the boy.

Ander's shoulders trembled. Mary took his hand.

"There's something in the root cellar," Ander replied in a tiny voice. "I heard it."

There was a muffled crash, one of Mary's preserve jars falling from the shelf and breaking on the hard dirt floor. Ander sucked in his breath and his body stiffened. "Hear that?"

"Yes, I did." Earl set down his fishing gear and pushed Ander toward her. "Take the boy into the house and bring me my gun."

Mary didn't need to coax Ander. He was already at a full run in front of her. She caught up to him on the porch. "Get under the bed and stay there until we tell you."

He nodded, his lower lip quivering.

"And not a sound."

He pursed his lips tight and pulled himself back into the shadows against the wall.

Mary took Earl's gun from the wall, along with a bag of shot and his powder flask. She looked about, desperate for something to arm herself. She remembered her garden hoe leaning against the side of the house. She grabbed it on her way out and stumbled back across the yard to Earl, trying to ignore the wet skirts clinging to her legs, threatening to pull her down.

Earl loaded his gun. "You stay out here in case something, or someone, gets by me."

Mary raised the hoe over her head, ready to swing. Earl opened the door and aimed his gun.

"Who's there? You'd better come out before I'm forced to come in after you."

There was a scuffling noise, then silence.

Earl hesitated halfway down the stairs. "I have a gun," he said from the shadows below.

"Don't shoot, Mr. Earl."

Mary lowered the hoe. The voice was familiar, but she couldn't quite place it.

"Come down here, Mary," Earl called up to her.

It took a moment for her eyes to adjust to the dim interior. Then she saw them, three adults and one child huddled below. She recognized the two men and the woman from the Hollings Plantation. She assumed the child belonged to the woman holding her close. Perhaps one of the men was the girl's father.

"You remember Cassias, Thomas, and Eliza. And the little one . . ." Earl looked to the three adults.

"She our daughter, Mr. Earl. Mine and Eliza's." Thomas put his arm around Eliza, who pulled the little girl tighter.

"Her name's Annabelle," Eliza said.

"Hello, Annabelle," Mary said to the frightened little girl.

Annabelle hid her face in her mother's skirts.

Earl and Mary looked at each other, clearly thinking the same thing.

What do we do now?

CHAPTER 9

VIRGINIA: OCTOBER 1846

The six of them stared at each other for what felt like an eternity. Earl cautiously lowered his gun when it was clear the runaways weren't armed.

"What are you doing here, Thomas?" he asked. "Uncle Jackson know you've left the plantation?"

"No, sir," Thomas replied. "Don't tell him and don't take us back there, either. We'll only run off again, first chance we get."

Mary glanced at Earl, then back at the runaways. What they should do as Christians was clear, but what they had to do legally was also clear.

"He'll have to kill us to keep us there." Cassias' voice was deep, his words slow and ominous. "Unless I kill him first."

Annabelle sobbed at all the talk of killing. Eliza held her daughter tight to comfort her. "Please help us, Mr. Earl, Mrs. Mary," she pleaded.

Mary pulled Earl aside. "You have to send them away. If anyone finds them here, we're . . ." The thought of the consequences was too frightening to even contemplate. That was as much a risk as she was willing to take. Not return them, not report them, but let them find their own way.

Eliza trembled, attempting to calm Annabelle. Thomas' hands clenched and unclenched at his side. But it was Cassias who scared Mary the most. His feet were planted at shoulder width, his thick, muscled arms held tight across his chest.

"Well, Mr. Earl? You gonna help us, or not?" he growled

He was the dangerous one.

"No one's killing anyone," Earl said, taking charge of the situation. "Thomas, tell me what happened."

"We ran away, that's what happened," Cassias answered. "You gonna help us, or not?"

"I heard that part," Earl said. He turned back to the other man. "Thomas, tell me from the beginning."

"The old lady, she died," Thomas said. "Last night."

"About time, too," Cassias said. "She older than Methuselah and meaner than the devil!"

"Your Uncle Jackson, he tells us this mornin'," Thomas continued. "He tells us cuz she ain't got no kin we're all gonna be sold off to the highest bidder."

"They gonna separate us, Mr. Earl. I know it!" Eliza was beginning to panic, making Annabelle wail even louder.

Mary gave Earl a pleading look. It was clear he was thinking about getting involved. She felt bad for them, but there was Ander to consider.

"Keep that child quiet!" Earl snapped at Eliza. "Mary, go up and watch. Tell me if you see anyone coming."

Mary went to the top of the stairs. From there she had a full view of the yard but was still close enough to hear what was going on below. If Earl was planning to do what she suspected, she had to do everything she could to protect them from discovery.

"Why'd you come here?" Earl asked.

"This was the only place we could think to come. You gotta help us, Mr. Earl," Thomas pleaded. "We helped you that time she had you whipped, remember? That Christmas you gave our little ones the candy."

"Now it's your turn to help us," Cassias finished for his brother.

Earl joined Mary at the top of the stairs.

"Send them away," she said again.

"We can't send them out there alone, and we certainly can't send them back." He handed Mary his gun. "Go back to the house and see to Ander before he comes looking for us."

"Ander. That your boy's name, Mrs. Mary?" Eliza asked. She'd come forward to stand at the bottom of the stairs. "He a real sweet lookin' boy. We saw you two down by the river. Him with his little boat playin' in the water. Real sweet."

Mary's heart skipped a beat. They'd been right there watching, and she hadn't even known.

"We just want to go where our Annabelle can play, like your Ander. Not have to work all day," she continued.

"If Ander asks, just tell him it was possums," Earl told her. "Whole family of them, but they're gone now."

Mary went back down into the cellar, grabbed a basket, and filled it with dinner supplies—sweet potatoes, green beans, and apples. "I'll make extra. Biscuits, too," she told the frightened fugitives. She forced herself to not look at their desperate faces. She was afraid of what more she might say if she didn't distance herself from the situation. Earl had made his decision, and there would be no changing his mind.

Crossing the yard with her basket of food, she tried to look as calm and everyday as possible, but her stomach churned, her heart raced, and she feared she might be sick. Sweat ran down her forehead. She wiped her eyes with her sleeve, forgetting it was still wet from her fall in the river.

Men could be watching from anywhere right now, looking for those slaves. She scanned the trees for movement, for the flash of sunlight on a gun barrel. What if they already knew the runaways were here? What if she was shot dead right where Ander could hear and come out to see? What if they then shot Earl and those people hiding in the root cellar, including that terrified little girl? They could shoot Ander. Every shadow, every rustle of a squirrel in the leaves, made Mary jump. She tried not to run so she wouldn't look guilty, but she couldn't help herself. She hiked her skirts and sprinted the last few yards, stopping at the front door to catch her breath.

"Ander?" She called out cheerfully, smiling, as she came in the door. "You can come out now." She heard him scuttle out from under the bed.

"Was it a bad man, Mama? Is he gone? Did Papa have to shoot him?"

"Heavens, no." She laughed, maybe a little too loud. "It was just a mama possum and her babies. They knocked over one of my jam jars, made a mess. Your father's cleaning up the glass right now." Mary's hands shook as she unloaded the fruit and vegetables from her basket.

Ander was wide-eyed at the thought of possums in their root cellar. "Did he shoot them, Mama? I hope he didn't shoot them, being just babies."

"No, he didn't shoot them," she assured the relieved little boy. "He chased them out. Last I saw, they were scurrying off into the trees, their little faces smeared with my raspberry jam."

Ander laughed and clapped his hands. "I wish I was there to see them."

"Besides, shooting a gun in the root cellar guarantees more broken jam jars, and you know how your father loves my jam too much to risk that." Mary turned away so he wouldn't see her close her eyes and take a deep breath to slow her heart.

"That he does," Earl said, walking in the door. He hung his rifle, shot, and powder back on the wall. "Your mother makes the best jam in all of Virginia. Even one broken jar makes me want to cry." He slipped an arm around his wife and whispered, "Everything's going to be all right." She wished she believed him.

"Makes me want to cry, too, Mama." Ander hugged her. "Sorry about your jam."

"Thank you, sweet boy, but there's still plenty left for all winter."

Ander was still thinking about the possums during dinner. "Papa, you know what we need? A dog like Uncle George's Blue. Did you know he chased a big raccoon out of their barn before it could get even one chicken egg?"

"I did not know that," Earl said, smiling at Mary.

"It's true. Aunt Mae told me all about it. If we had a dog, Papa, do you know what I'd name it?"

"What?"

"Boone. I think Boone's a fine name for a dog. Don't you?"

"That it is, little man," Earl agreed.

"And if we had a dog, there'd be no possums getting into our root cellar and breaking Mama's jam jars."

Mary thought about the people sitting in the root cellar. How was Earl planning on helping them?

"Can we get a dog, Papa?" Ander tugged at his father's sleeve to get his attention.

"I don't know. I'll have to think about it," Earl answered absent-mindedly.

Ander was quiet for a moment. Mary could see he was thinking hard, working out the possibilities in his head. Then Ander smiled. "I hope you say yes. I'll pray on it in church Sunday."

AFTER DINNER WAS DONE, dishes washed, and Ander finally asleep, Mary packed the leftover food for Earl to take to the runaways. She didn't like the situation, but she couldn't let them starve to death while seeking their freedom.

"They must be hungry waiting all this time."

"Mary, they're in a root cellar full of food. I doubt they sat there without eating something."

Mary stopped what she was doing, a napkin full of biscuits in her hands. "You think they came here for our help and then stole our food?"

"I gave them a jar of ham hocks to share and each an apple to hold them over. Told them I couldn't come back until after dark."

"What are we going to do with them? They can't stay here and, you're right, they can't go back."

"No, they can't," he agreed. "If they haven't already been missed, they soon will be. Uncle Jackson will have the dogs and half the men in the county looking for them." He armed himself and picked up the basket of food.

Mary knew then what he was planning to do. She'd heard stories about people who helped runaway slaves escape. There was a whole network of hiding places all the way to Canada. She also heard the stories of what happened to those who were caught.

"I'll see you when I get back," he said, kissing her good-bye.

"When will that be?" She grabbed his arm.

"Don't know, sooner than later, I hope."

"What do you want me to tell Ander? What do I tell the search teams if—correction—when they come asking?"

"Tell them I've gone hunting. I'll bring back something so I don't make a liar out of you." He hesitated. "Mary, I have to do this. I owe them this much."

She knew he was right. She let out a slow breath, nodded, and smoothed her apron to compose herself. This was not the time to panic.

"Where will you take them?" she asked.

Mary waited for Earl to say something. His silence was louder than any words he might say. Maybe it was best if he didn't tell her.

"I just want to know in what direction you're headed in case you don't come home, and I have to go looking for you."

"West. I'll take them to the Quakers. I hear they know what to do."

Mary knew the farm he was talking about. They had bought cheese from them many times.

"If you know about them, you can bet so does your uncle."

"I'll have to take the long way, stay off the roads. I found an old overgrown Indian trail while out hunting some years back. I don't think it's been used by anything more than deer in ages."

She held him and kissed him again, this time long and slow. His familiar musky scent made her as light-headed as apple cider when it turned. She pressed her face into his chest and said a silent prayer for his safe return. This was the old Earl she loved, and she was terrified she'd never see him again. Why did he have to choose this moment to find his strength?

"I have to go, Mary," he whispered. He turned, hesitated, then came back into her arms, giving her a quick kiss before leaving.

Mary rested against the closed door. "Be careful."

"I will," he said from the other side, followed by the thud of his footsteps down the stairs, fading as he crossed the yard.

She waited, listened to the return of the night sounds—crickets, an owl in the distance, a light breeze through the trees. They were gone.

ANDER WAS FINISHING his breakfast the next morning when Mary heard the dogs.

"Go to your room and play," she told him. He looked from his mother to the door and obeyed without argument.

She took a moment to calm her breathing and waited for the knock.

"Good morning, Uncle," she said with the most convincing smile she could muster. "Earl's not here." She stepped outside and closed the door behind her.

"Where is he, Mary?"

"Hunting. You just missed him."

Uncle Jackson's men, all of whom she recognized from town, rode about the yard as their hounds sniffed the ground in front of them.

"Is there a problem?" Mary quelled her fear that they might pick-up a trail. She thanked God it had rained during the night, hopefully washing away any scent of the runaways, buying Earl much needed time. Just in case, she broke a jar of pickled pigs' feet in the root cellar. It was going to stink down there for a long time, but she saw no other way should Uncle Jackson bring his dogs around.

"Eugenia Hollings died."

"I'm sorry to hear that, but she led a long life and earned her rest."

"Problem is, some of her slaves ran off after hearing. You see anything unusual lately? Missing food? Laundry gone from the line?"

She shook her head. "No, nothing like that. It's been really quiet."

"We tracked them heading this way. Are you sure you didn't see anything?"

Mary returned Uncle Jackson's stare. She didn't allow her gaze to wander from his. "I am."

He hesitated, his eyes scanning their surroundings one more time. "When do you expect him back?"

"Don't know exactly. When he's done, I imagine."

"Done with what?"

Was he trying to trip her up? "Done with hunting. Now, if you gentlemen will excuse me, I have some dishes need washing."

"Mind if I have a look in the house while my men search the other buildings? I'd hate to learn later they were hiding here all along. Would be really sad if something happened to you and your boy while your man was away."

"Only if you leave that gun outside and don't make a mess. I don't need you scaring Ander."

Mary stood her ground. He questioned the smell in the root cellar, and she said, *possums*. She didn't know if he believed her, but he had no proof otherwise.

He mounted his horse, leaned over, and looked her in the eyes. "There are serious consequences for stealing another man's property, Mrs. Bishop."

"They're people, not horses," she replied.

He sat up straight. "On the contrary, they're much more valuable than a horse." Uncle Jackson motioned for his men to head out. "The penalty for aiding runaways is hanging. You know that?" he added.

"I do."

"Make sure your husband knows it, as well."

Mary locked her knees and forced a smile as they rode away. After the last man disappeared, she dropped to the ground and gulped air until the shaking stopped.

A week later, Earl returned with a sack full of rabbits. They had stew and biscuits for dinner that night, and after Ander fell asleep Mary gave Earl a proper wife's welcome home.

She'd wait until morning to tell him about Uncle Jackson's warning.

CHAPTER 10

VIRGINIA: SPRING 1847

"You're going to get caught. One of these times you're going to get caught, and they're going to hang you right in the center of town for all to watch. A warning to others. Is that what you want?" Mary threw her wet dish towel and apron in a heap on the table. "Your uncle promised as much. The law requires it."

Helping Cassias, Thomas, Eliza, and little Annabelle escape had only been the beginning for Earl. Word spread fast through the slave community that first winter. Every month or so a new group of runaways huddled in their root cellar, begging for a ride to freedom. And Uncle Jackson, his men, and their dogs always showed up shortly after, following their trail.

"How long do you think we can keep him from finding the proof he needs?"

It was an old argument, and Earl wouldn't listen. He'd found strength in this new purpose, had even stopped drinking. Despite her joy in seeing the old Earl, the return of the man she'd fallen in love with, her fear of discovery caused her to wake in a cold sweat many nights.

"I'm not going to get caught." Earl continued to clean his muzzle loader, paying little mind to what she was saying. He pulled the lantern closer to better see what he was doing. "Now keep your voice down. You're going to wake the boy."

Mary leaned in so he could hear. "You're going to get caught," she repeated in a strained whisper. "You're going to get caught, you're going to be hung, and then what's to become of me and Ander? We need you more than they do. If they want to run away, let them find their own way to freedom."

"You don't mean that, Mary. You hate slavery as much as I do."

"Yes, you're right. I do hate it. It's a sin against God. But the risks are too great. There has to be a better way."

Earl set down his gun, stood, and took her gently by the shoulders. She was crying and knew how much that upset him, but she didn't care. The knot in her stomach was as big as a pumpkin, and it grew larger whenever he left on one of his midnight runs.

"Do you hear yourself? You know they'll never find their way safely north on their own. I can't wonder whether or not I could have helped every time I hear one of them has been found swinging from a tree, or chained naked and bleeding on the auction block."

"I know." She hated losing control, crying like a child, but she couldn't stop. "You're going to get caught, and you're going to be hung." He held her as she sobbed into his shoulder.

"Come with me." He picked up the lantern and gun, now clean, reassembled, and loaded. "I'll show you why I won't get caught."

Earl led her out to the barn. The lantern swung at his side, throwing a moving pool of light around their feet, reminding her of the young boy walking through the field with his string of fish glittering wet in the sun.

Earl set the lantern and gun on his workbench. The wagon was parked in the middle of the barn, but the load of lumber he'd brought home was now stacked neatly to one side.

"You can't tell a soul, not even your family, what I'm about to show you. Promise me."

"I promise," she whispered, uncertain what she was about to see, realizing this was all much bigger than she ever imagined.

Earl took a crowbar from under the wagon seat, stepped up into the freight bed, and lifted a square in the floor. The hatch fit so well she hadn't noticed it was there.

Mary moved closer and looked inside. The compartment was the size of the wagon but very shallow.

"Are you saying you hide them in this . . . this . . . coffin?" She didn't know how else to describe the close-fitting space. The smell of sweat and fear rose up from the dark confines. "How do they breathe?" She couldn't take her eyes off the forbidding hole, imagining dead Negro men, women, and children trapped inside.

He jumped down and walked around to the front of the wagon, sliding back a board that acted as a false front. Small fingers of light reached into the far corners of the box.

"I've cut holes under my seat large enough to let in air. No one can see them unless they climb under and look closely. My passengers just have to lie still and quiet with their heads toward the front."

"Aren't they afraid? Do they ever refuse to get in?"

"Of course, they're afraid. Think what they're doing. Sometimes one of the women or children will refuse, but the men always squeeze in and, in the end, their families follow. What choice do they have, really?"

He was right, there was no alternative. She would do it in a heartbeat to save her family.

"It's completely safe," he said again.

"Not completely," she said to herself and turned away, unable to watch as he set the hatch back into place. She closed her eyes to the frightened faces she imagined disappearing inside. Eyeing the pile of lumber off to one side, she wondered why he didn't leave it in the wagon until morning, and why he brought it home at all.

"Does Mr. Lund know you have this lumber here?"

"Yes."

"Why didn't you deliver it on your way home?"

Earl hesitated, and she realized there was still more to all of this. "Remember, you promised not to say a word to anyone. There are more lives at stake here than just mine and the runaways."

The implications behind what he said began to sink in.

"That's how I know to expect passengers. Clay sends me home with a load of lumber and a delivery slip for somewhere in a neighboring county. I come home, unload the lumber, and wait."

So, Clay Lund was a part of this, too.

"Sometime during the night they'll slip into the root cellar, and I'll bring them up before dawn."

"Tonight?"

"Tonight."

"But how do you unload and load this—?" Oh, Sweet Lord Almighty! Mary covered her face with both hands. Earl wasn't alone when he'd come home from the mill earlier. He never seemed to be alone on the nights he brought an order home with him, and he wasn't alone when he left the next morning.

"George?" Shock pushed the air from her lungs, and she began to shake. Her voice rose, hands fisted at her side. "You dragged my brother into this? It's bad enough you put your own life on the line, now you tell me you've endangered my brother, as well?"

"Mary, you promised. I told you there are more lives at risk here than you know. You can't say a word to anyone."

"Does Mae know you've gotten her husband involved in such dangerous work?"

"All she knows is George helps me with some of the deliveries. She doesn't know it's anything other than lumber and a little extra money in his pocket."

"But George knows the truth?"

"Yes, I would never involve him without his agreement."

Mary ran her fingers through her hair and closed her eyes. She opened her mouth to speak, but the words weren't there. She paced the barn floor in front of him. She wanted to scream, to throw things, to vomit with fear. On the one hand, she loved that the old Earl was back—strong Earl, sober Earl. But on the other, this old Earl was likely to get himself killed. And George. Then what?

Earl reached for her, but she pulled away. "I have to get back to the house."

She grabbed the lantern and fled. Earl's footsteps sounded behind her, running to catch up. She didn't look back.

"Mary, wait."

She didn't slow down. She was too angry, too frightened, to speak.

He grabbed her arm and spun her around. "Talk to me."

"Let go." She pulled and twisted, trying to free herself from his grip. "Ow!" she squealed when he tightened his hold, pinching her. He let go, and she rubbed her wrist.

"Talk to me," he said again, softer, pleading.

"I can't, not right now. There's too much . . ." She hesitated, searching for the right words, but there were none.

Earl took the lantern from her and set it on the ground along with his gun.

"I have a lot to think about," she said. "I can't talk about it. Not now."

"Then we won't talk." He pulled her into his arms and kissed her.

She pushed him away and slapped him, hard. How dare he try to quiet her worries with a kiss. He touched his cheek and stared.

She covered her mouth with her hand, then slowly let it drop. She had never hit him before. "I'm sorry," she whispered.

Earl smiled. "Did I ever tell you you're beautiful when you're all fired up? I've always thought so." He kissed her again. His lips lingered on hers.

"I shouldn't have . . . I mean . . . I was just so angry . . . but I shouldn't have . . ." Mary's apology came in short bursts. Her breath caught as he kissed her again and again. His fingers fumbled with her shirt buttons. She responded with growing passion.

"I think it's the spark in your eyes," he said. Earl exposed her breasts to the moonlight. He cupped them and gently squeezed, his thumbs tracing circles around her nipples, all the time staring into her eyes. "There it is again, that spark."

Her lips hungry for his, her body aching for his possession, she didn't resist when he eased her down into the grass. He extinguished the lantern and made love to her, a sea of stars floating above them. Everything, everyone, vanished. His hands, his lips, their soft moans growing urgent in their need for each other. Their love was all that mattered.

After, Earl leaned on one elbow and watched, smiling, as she buttoned her shirt front and straightened her skirts. "I love your hair the best when it's all mussed and full of grass and bits of leaves." He laughed. "Remember the time your brothers caught you looking like this, the day before our wedding?"

"I remember. I thought for sure they'd give you a beating."

"Probably would have, if your mother hadn't stepped in. Do you think she knew?"

"Of course, she knew. Nothing got past Mother."

Earl plucked a leaf from her hair and smoothed some stray strands behind her ear. "There are big changes coming, Mary. I can feel it. Just know I'll always be here for you and Ander, no matter what."

She reached up and ran her fingers over his cheek and into his curls. His gaze was deep, his eyes glowed dark as molasses in the moonlight. Earl was right. Big changes were coming. She'd sensed it, too. They were as heavy in the air as the promise of winter in November. Earl truly believed he'd always be there for them, but she knew that odds were they would eventually be caught on one of their runs. Then she'd lose both her husband and her brother forever, and Ander would lose his father and favorite uncle.

"It's getting cold," she finally said after a long silence. "We'd better go inside."

They found Ander awake and standing in the parlor, rubbing his eyes. "I had a bad dream," he said. "Where were you, Mama? I called for you, but you didn't come."

"Sorry, sweet boy." She swept him up into her arms. "Your father and I went out to the barn to check on the animals one last time before bed."

"If we had a dog you wouldn't have to worry so much about the animals. Boone would protect them."

"I already told you, son, no dog. Now, I don't want to hear about it again."

Ander sniffled. He was tired and that made him weepy.

"We'll talk about it." She hugged him.

"Mary—"

She gave Earl a warning look. She knew his reason for not wanting a dog was a sound one—their secret night visitors. A barking dog could give them away to search teams. But those runaways were the very reason she needed a good dog. If Earl was going to continue being gone a lot, she needed a dog to help her protect Ander.

"Let's get you back to bed. Mama will sing you a song and sit with you until you're asleep. Would you like that?"

Ander nodded and laid his head on her shoulder.

CHAPTER 11

VIRGINIA: SEPTEMBER 1848

Ander raced down the center of the road toward town, his lunch pail in one hand, slate in the other, and a brand-new piece of chalk tucked safely into his shirt pocket. He was growing so fast Mary was afraid if she blinked, he'd be a man and gone.

"Hurry, Mother! We'll be late for school. I can't be late on my first day."

"Slow down before you fall and rip the knees out of your pants. You won't be late. We have plenty of time."

A handful of other early arrivals played in the schoolyard. Ander's excitement died. Mary squeezed his shoulder as he clung silently to her skirts. Older children rushed past them, greeting friends they probably hadn't seen since school let out in the spring.

Mr. Nichols kept an eye on his young charges from the front steps. His bell waited on the railing while he periodically checked the time on the pocket watch he pulled from his coat. Tall and ramrod straight, not even a hint of a smile, Mr. Nichols looked every bit the strict schoolmaster. Mary remembered Mr. Braunmeister and his willow switch. She hoped Mr. Nichols would be more patient with his students, but she doubted it.

"Why don't you go join the other children?" Mary tousled her son's unruly curls.

Ander turned his face to her, a hint of tears in the corners of his eyes. "I don't know anybody, Mama," he said in a soft voice, shifting his weight from foot to foot as his glance darted from one child to the next. She knew he was scared when he reverted to calling her Mama. It had been Mother and Father ever since they told him he was old enough to start school.

"Yes, you do. There's Amy Lynn Young from church. I recognize a few others, too."

"But they're not my friends."

She leaned over, slid her arm around him, and held him close. "Pick someone and go say hello. Then you will know one person," she whispered in his ear. "That person will introduce you to his friends and soon you will know the names of everyone in the school, and they will all be your friends."

"But who should I say hello to first? Who should I pick?"

Mary saw a lone boy standing on the far side of the schoolyard. He looked to be the same age as Ander and just as lost.

"Him," she said. "Do you see the boy all alone by the tree? He looks nice."

Ander nodded. "All right, I'll say hello to him, and then we can be friends."

Mr. Nichols snapped his watch shut, cleared his throat, and rang his bell loud and hard. The children stopped what they were doing and hurried to line up at the bottom of the stairs. Ander gave her a panicked look.

"Now I can't say hello to the boy."

"You can talk to him during lunch."

Ander hesitated.

"Master Bishop! We are waiting!"

Ander's eyes flew open wide and his back stiffened.

"Hurry," she said. "I'll meet you right here after school."

He looked ready to run the other way.

"I promise." She gave him a gentle push forward.

Ander took his place at the back of the line, and the children marched up the stairs into the school. He gave her one last frightened look over his shoulder as Mr. Nichols closed the doors behind them.

MARY CHECKED THE WATCH that hung on a chain around her neck. It was only a half hour later than the last time she looked. She tried to keep busy working in her garden, hoping to make the time go by more quickly, but instead it seemed to creep along even slower. She worried about Ander adjusting to the classroom, and if he'd been able to make friends with that other boy. She couldn't forget the look on his face when Mr. Nichols closed the schoolhouse doors.

When she returned the schoolyard was empty. Mary spun around, expecting to catch him peeking at her from behind a tree. No children played or waited. She listened for his mischievous laugh. Silence.

"Ander?"

Where was he? Had Mr. Nichols dismissed them early? She would have seen him on the road if he'd started home on his own, unless he became confused and took a wrong turn.

"Ander!" Her voice cracked, fear catching in her throat.

The school doors opened. Mr. Nichols stepped out. When he looked at her over the top of his pince-nez her heart skipped a beat. For the second time that day he reminded her of Mr. Braunmeister.

"Mrs. Bishop, your son is inside." Mary followed as he strode back into the classroom. It was the same feeling she had so long ago when she misbehaved. She knew how frightened Ander must be. He'd been so excited to start school. She hoped this wouldn't make him feel differently.

Ander sat at the front of the room. His head hung low, and his shoulders trembled with each breath. The boy from the playground sat next to him, but he held his head high, his shoulders set back defiantly. A woman, no doubt his mother, stood at his side. Mary walked up behind Ander and rested her hand on his shoulder. He looked up at her. His cheek was scraped and a bruise bloomed beneath one eye. The other boy made them a matched pair. They'd been fighting. Her heart sank. Was this what he'd learned from his father's recent behavior?

Mr. Nichols stood before them, hands clutched behind his back, rocking heel to toe as he stared at one boy, then the other, and then up at the two mothers. The five of them stayed that way, silent, for what felt like a lifetime.

The other mother spoke first. "Mr. Nichols, why are we here? Boys will have the occasional schoolyard fight. I don't see why this should warrant a meeting." Her voice cracked at the end, the only indication perhaps she wasn't as brave as she tried to appear.

"Yes, Mr. Nichols," Mary spoke up. "Let's proceed so we can all get back to our day. I'm sure you have as many things to accomplish before nightfall as we do."

"Indeed, Mrs. Bishop, and it displeases me all the more when I have to interrupt my very busy schedule to deal with some of the backwoods savages forced upon me by this school board. There is no room in my classroom for two such truculent boys, and I will bring an end to it right now. If that is not possible, then you can believe me when I say your boys will not be returning to my school any time soon."

The women gasped in unison to hear their sons referred to in such a disrespectful manner. Truculent backwoods savages, indeed! They were just two little boys doing what boys unfortunately do best—fighting. Mary's eyes narrowed. She pulled herself up to full height.

"We will leave you, Mr. Nichols, with our assurances this will not happen again. Come along, boys."

She led the way out of the school, down the stairs, and across the yard to the road home. Mr. Nichols slammed the door with a resounding bang, as if to have the last word. No doubt he was not accustomed to being so heartily dismissed, and by a woman, no less.

It was then she squatted down in front of Ander, smiled, and wiped the tears from his cheeks. "Let me see that eye." She touched it lightly and he winced. "Yes, well, I imagine that's going to hurt for a while, but it will heal in time."

She straightened up, folded her arms across her chest, and scowled down at the two boys. "Ander, what do you have to say for yourself?"

"Robert?" His mother took a stance next to Mary. "Why did you hit this boy?"

"He pushed me first. He knocked me down and ripped my shirt." Robert held out his arm so his mother could see the tear in his sleeve.

"Robert was picking on Amy Lynn." Ander was quick to defend himself.

"I was not!" Robert pushed Ander.

"Were, too!" Ander pushed back.

Their mothers pulled them apart.

Mr. Nichols watched from the school steps, a smug smile on his face. They each took their boy by the arm and marched him down the road, not stopping until they were well out of Mr. Nichols' sight.

"Let's try this again," Mary said. "Ander, start at the beginning."

"We were playing outside after lunch when Robert told Amy Lynn her freckles were ugly. Then he pulled her hair."

"Did not! And her freckles are ugly." Robert lunged for Ander, who jumped out of his reach. Robert's mother pulled him back.

"He made Amy Lynn cry," Ander continued, "so I pushed him. That's when he punched me."

Amy Lynn Young, the storekeeper's daughter, was a pretty little thing with blond braids and a fair complexion riddled with freckles.

"Robert Shaw!" His mother grabbed him by the ear, and the boy cried out. "Is that true? Were you picking on a little girl? I thought your father and I taught you better than that."

"I was just having some fun. I didn't know she was going to cry."

"How did Robert get all those scrapes and bruises from one little push?" Mary asked her son.

"After he punched me, I jumped him," Ander answered, clearly proud of himself. "I heard when father told you sometimes a man has to fight back. I was fighting back."

Mary took in a deep breath and let it out slowly. She closed her eyes and tried to keep her temper in check. She would have words with Earl, out in the barn, *after* Ander went to sleep.

"That's when Mr. Nichols came running out of the schoolhouse," Robert said. "You should have seen him, Mother." He giggled. "He was all frog-eyed, like this." He opened his eyes wide and tried to make them bulge like Mr. Nichols'.

Ander laughed at Robert's impersonation. "Yes. His face turned all red, and his neck stuck out."

By then both boys were laughing, each trying to do a better imitation of Mr. Nichols' rage. Mary took Robert's mother aside before they, too, started laughing. She didn't want the boys to think their mothers approved of such behavior.

"Mary Bishop," she said by way of introduction. "I don't believe I've seen you in town before."

"Sarah Shaw. We moved here from Tennessee only a couple months ago. Lucas works for Clay Lund at the mill."

"So does my Earl." Mary looked back at the boys. They were rolling around on the ground, but this time it was clearly all in fun. "I see Ander and Robert have made their amends."

"Do you think they're done fighting, then?" Sarah asked, her tone hopeful.

"I seriously doubt it. Having two older brothers, I can attest that boys are like puppies, scrapping all the time. Sometimes it's hard to tell if they're biting for real, or just nipping in fun."

It was their turn to laugh.

"I promise, they will fight again and make good again, but I can tell they will be friends for life." She looked at Sarah. "And I believe, so shall we."

CHAPTER 12

VIRGINIA: SEPTEMBER 1848

"Mary, tell me what all this is about." Earl stood firm with his legs apart and his arms folded tight across his chest. After putting Ander to bed, she had dragged him out to the barn without explanation.

"Our son has been fighting in the schoolyard." She waited for his response. When there was none, she continued. "You did notice the black eye at dinner, didn't you?"

"Oh, yes." He chuckled and leaned against a post.

"And where did you think he got it?"

"Well, I didn't think he gave it to himself. Of course, he got it fighting with another boy. That's what boys do. You should know that, having two brothers."

She ignored him. He was right, but that wasn't the point. "And who do you think gave him the idea it's all right to fight?"

That question took some of the air out of him. His shoulders sank, and he stuck his hands in pockets.

"Oh."

"Yes, oh. When I asked Ander why he hit the other boy he said it was because he heard his father say it was all right to fight sometimes."

"Well, it is . . . sometimes." Some of Earl's bravado came back. "Did he explain why he was fighting? Did he tell you who the other boy was?"

"Robert Shaw."

"Lucas' boy." He nodded. "Met him once in town. He struck me as a boy who could hold his own in a fight."

"Yes, Lucas and Sarah's boy. Apparently, Robert teased Amy Lynn Young at lunch, and our son felt it was his duty to defend her honor. That meant the two of them were kept after school. Sarah and I had to have a meeting with Mr. Nichols, a very disagreeable man, I might add. Would you believe he called our boys truculent backwoods savages?"

"What does truculent mean?"

"Hostile, mean."

"Well, I don't know enough about this Robert, but our Ander is not . . . what's the word?"

"Truculent."

"Ander is not truculent." Earl paced the barn floor, making the horses and cows nervous. The chickens squawked and flapped about in their coop. "I'll have a word with this Mr. Nichols tomorrow."

"No, you won't. I'll handle Mr. Nichols." Mary was afraid Earl might only prove the schoolmaster's opinion of them by showing *his* truculent side. "My point, Earl, is our son thinks fighting is how a man solves his problems. That's not how I want to raise him."

"And how do you want to raise him?" he asked, arms folded across his chest.

If she wasn't careful, she was going to lose this argument, and the possibilities from there were worrisome. When Earl got angry, Earl drank. Things had been going well. She wanted to keep it that way.

"Answer me. How do you want to raise Ander? Do you want him to be a scared little bookworm?" The bad mood in the barn was quickly escalating. "Because sometimes a man does have to fight to be a man."

"Of course. But Ander needs to learn when it's the appropriate time to throw a punch and when it's not. When he's in the schoolyard and another little boy tells a little girl she has ugly freckles, that is not the time."

Earl roared and slapped his leg. "So that's what all this was about? I hate to be the one to tell you, but our son has taken a shine to a certain Amy Lynn Young."

Mary laughed with him. "I think there are two little boys who have taken a shine to Amy Lynn."

"I'll talk to him tomorrow. I promise." Earl hugged her. They walked back to the house with his arm around her shoulders. She wrapped her arm around his waist and leaned in close.

THE NEXT MORNING, EARL looked across the breakfast table and past Mary to their son's scraped and bruised face. "Your mother told me about yesterday." He stared at Ander, waiting for a reply. Ander sunk down in his chair.

"I'm sorry, Father, but you said sometimes a man has to fight."

"Yes, well, you're not a man. Not yet, anyway. I don't want to hear about any more fighting at school. Understand?"

Ander nodded. "Yes, sir." He hesitated. "Are you going to punish me?"

"Not this time." Earl looked at the visibly relieved Ander. He took another bite of his biscuits and gravy. "Isn't it time you were off to school? Don't want to be late."

"Yes, sir." Ander jumped to his feet, stuffed a couple biscuits in his pocket, and grabbed his lunch pail and slate on the way out the door.

"Stop!" Earl turned. Ander stopped in his tracks, his back straight and stiff. "What's with the biscuits?"

"What biscuits?"

"Don't sass me, son, you know what biscuits. The ones you just stuffed in your pocket."

Ander's small body shook just enough for a mother to notice. "Ander," Mary stood behind him and rested a hand on the back of his neck, "why did you put those biscuits in your pocket?"

"I'm still hungry. I thought I'd eat them on the way to school."

Mary looked at Earl. She didn't believe Ander. Did Earl also see through the boy's story? "Do you need me to walk with you?"

"No, Mother. I know the way."

"How about after school? Do you need me to come for you?"

"No." Ander remained standing with his back to them, clearly anxious to be out and on to whatever he had planned.

"Go ahead, then, but behave yourself today. No more fighting."

"Yes, Mother." He ran out the door.

"It's not the first time he's taken food," she told Earl. "I saw him pocket a chicken leg the other night when he thought I wasn't looking."

"That boy's up to something. And I intend to find out what."

She tossed her dish towel on the table and followed Earl out the door in time to see Ander disappear around the side of the house.

"That's not the way to school," Earl said.

They stepped off the porch and watched as Ander slipped into the woods, heading toward the river. He was so intent on his mission he didn't notice them following.

"There you are," Ander said to someone in the brush alongside the clearing. "I brought you something to eat." He dug in his pocket and placed the two biscuits on the ground, stepping back.

"Who's he talking to?" Earl whispered.

Mary peered around a tree. "And why is he putting their food on the ground? You don't think it's one of those runaway slaves, do you?"

"I don't know."

A large stray dog, more bone than flesh, edged into the open. Dirty, mangy, gray fur with a hungry gleam in his eyes they could see even from a distance. He sniffed at the biscuits, never taking his eyes from their son. Mary wanted to rush the beast but feared he'd attack, rather than flee.

"Go ahead, eat." Ander encouraged the animal.

Earl grabbed a large branch from the ground near his feet and ran at the animal. He swung the limb at the dog's head. Mary threw the closest rock she could get her hands on.

"Don't hurt him!" Ander cried, frantic. "Stop! You're scaring him!"

Mary grabbed her son up into her arms. "Is this why you've been stealing food?"

"He's hungry and doesn't have anyone to feed him."

Earl returned, red-faced and breathing hard. "I don't want to see you near that dog again." He threw the stick to the ground. "He's dangerous. If I see him again, I'll shoot him." Earl continued home without turning around.

"I'll take you to school in the wagon so you're not late," he called back, not stopping. "I have to go to town anyway."

"I'll go with," Mary told her frightened son. "I have to pick up a few things at the store and can walk home after."

She held Ander's hand tight in hers. "What were you thinking?" But she knew what he was thinking. He was thinking he could tame that creature and make it his own.

CHAPTER 13

VIRGINIA: OCTOBER 1848

"Fishing and a picnic were wonderful ideas." Sarah shifted the heavy basket from one hand to the other.

"Do you want to switch?" Mary held the fishing gear out to her friend. "I can carry that, if you like. After all, I am the one who probably packed too much food."

Sarah laughed. "No, I'm fine." She stopped in a pool of light where the sun shone through the colored leaves. "Won't be too many more of these days before winter sets in," she said, lifting her face skyward.

Mary nodded.

"I hope the men can finish their delivery in time to join us."

Mary wondered if Sarah knew what kind of *delivery* their husbands were sent on so early that morning. When Earl told her Lucas would be joining him, she suspected Lucas had not told Sarah the true details.

"Earl thought maybe later this afternoon. I sent food with them for their lunch."

Robert and Ander ran ahead down the path to the river and out of sight, but their voices still rang clear as they argued over who was the greater national hero, George Washington or Paul Revere. Robert thought it was Washington, after all he had been named their first president for a reason. Ander was convinced it was Paul Revere, because he had been the one to spread that all important warning.

"Can you tell the boys have been studying the Revolution?"

"Oh, I know. It's all Ander talks about at the dinner table each night."

"I didn't realize how much I'd forgotten from my studies until Robert told me."

The river sparkled in the mid-day sun. Not a breeze disturbed the grass bordering the meandering ribbon of water. By the time Sarah and Mary arrived, Robert and Ander had stripped off their shoes and stockings, rolled up their pant legs, and were kicking river water on each other. The two women sat on the rocks dangling their bare feet in the water as they watched the boys play.

"You should see all the fish," Ander called to them on shore.

Robert laughed. "They're tickling my feet."

"Well, you're going to scare them away if you're not careful," Mary warned.

The boys stopped splashing and stood still. They looked at each other, hands pressed to their mouths, stifling more giggles.

"How about some lunch?" Mary only had to ask once before the boys appeared at her side as quick as a summer breeze.

"What's in the basket, Mother?" Ander pulled the cloth from the top to sneak a peek.

"I'm starving." Robert helped Ander remove one goodie after another.

"There's buttered bread, cold chicken, apples, and sugar cookies. Fresh cider to drink."

"Mmmpff pmmff" Ander tried to speak through a mouthful of bread. Mary took the cookies from him before he could shove one into his mouth and risk choking.

"We'll save these for later."

"And slow down, both of you," Sarah scolded. The boys licked butter from their fingers, then wiped them on their pant legs before grabbing chicken legs. Sarah and Mary helped themselves before there was nothing left.

Sarah shook her head. "I don't know where they put it all."

"There are days Ander almost out eats his father, and that's saying a lot."

"We have to eat a lot to grow big and strong, Mother," Ander said between bites of his apple. "I want to grow up to be a soldier someday and fight Red Coats."

"We already beat the Red Coats, stupid!" Robert punched Ander in the arm. Ander punched him back.

"Robert! We don't call others stupid." Sarah gave him a scathing look that wilted the boy's bravado. "And we don't hit."

"Sorry, we already beat the Red Coats, *silly*." Robert looked at his mother for approval. "We'll have to find someone else to fight."

"Yeah," Ander agreed. "We'll have to find someone else to fight."

Their stomachs full, and the sun warm on their faces, the four of them dozed under the trees.

WHEN EARL AND LUCAS woke them, the sky had grown heavy with dark, threatening storm clouds. The river was no longer sparkling glass, but a muddy fast-moving torrent stirred by a stiff wind.

"Wake up, sleepy heads." Earl shook Mary lightly by the shoulder. "We need to get home before the rain starts."

They gathered their belongings. The boys grumbled that they'd never gotten to go fishing. "Another day," Mary assured them.

A sudden gust of wind lifted the women's hats and sent them spiraling toward the river's edge. Mary caught Sarah's, but hers tumbled out of reach.

"I'll get it for you, Mother!" Ander ran close behind but couldn't catch Mary's hat as it rolled and leaped until it landed in the water.

"Let it go, Ander," Mary called. Either he couldn't hear her over the growing storm, or his stubborn streak had taken over all sense of reason.

Ander ran into the water and dove for the hat. His hand closed on the brim, but he couldn't find his footing on the slippery river bottom.

"Ander!" Mary's heart raced as the current pulled her son farther and farther downstream.

Earl was already running along the river's edge with Lucas one step behind, trying to get ahead of the boy.

Sarah held Mary back as she fought to go in after him. "The men will get him."

Mary had to believe her friend. The alternative was unimaginable.

Over and over, she lost sight of Ander when his head disappeared under water, only to reappear downriver, sputtering, panic in his eyes. He thrashed, struggling to swim to shore. His arms slowed. He was tiring. Her hat, forgotten in the struggle, was swept out of sight.

Mama, he mouthed, his eyes locked with hers.

Mary broke free of Sarah's hold. She stumbled after the men, praying and crying, certain her sweet boy would be taken from them. Trying to be heard over the wind and water, she screamed his name until she was hoarse. She couldn't lose him. She couldn't bear it, not again.

Out of nowhere, a dog crashed through the brush and into the water. It was the same wild dog they'd caught Ander feeding. They hadn't seen him, nor heard anything of him, since that day. He must have been hiding nearby. Ander had probably continued feeding him the entire time.

The animal was big, and despite his lean hungry look, strong. He grabbed Ander's shirt sleeve in his teeth and swam toward shore. The sleeve tore under the force of the water, and Ander was swept away from the dog. The animal did not give up. He managed to grip Ander's shirt once more. This time Ander wrapped his arms around the dog's neck. Mary could see the animal was tiring, losing his battle against the strong current as he fought to make the last few feet to shore. It looked like the river might claim them both.

Earl lay down on the rocks and stretched his arm out, trying to get hold of anything to pull them to shore. He snagged Ander's arm. The power of the water threatened to pull him off the smooth, wet surface, and into the churning water. Down river, Lucas hung onto a tree limb with one hand and leaned out to catch Ander with the other.

Mary reached them as the two men pulled Ander and the dog from the water. She swept Ander up into her arms and wept.

"It was just a hat. It was just a hat."

Earl gathered them close. He was out of breath. His entire body shook with sobs. Sarah ran to Lucas. Mary looked up at them and mouthed a thank you to Lucas.

"Is he all right?" Sarah asked.

"Yes. I think so." Mary inspected every inch of her son's body.

"I'm sorry, Mama," he sniffled, and held her skirts tight in his fists, refusing to let go.

A whimper reminded them the real hero was still there, lying wet and exhausted in the grass.

"He saved my life." Ander crawled over to the dog and stroked his head.

"Don't!" Earl pulled him back. "He's a wild animal. We don't know what he's capable of."

"But he saved my life."

"And for that reason, I won't shoot him—this time. But I can't have him around."

The sky lit up with another flash of lightening, followed almost immediately by a crash of thunder. The storm was closer. The dog looked up, stumbled to his feet, and limped off into the woods.

"See," Earl said. "He'll be fine. He's used to taking care of himself."

Sarah looked around. "Where's Robert?"

In all the commotion, they'd forgotten about Robert.

"Robert?" Lucas called. No answer.

"You don't think he went into the water after Ander, do you?" Sarah asked, spinning toward the river, then back again. "Robert!" she screamed.

They found him sitting under the tree where they'd left him, knees pulled close to his chest, his face buried in his arms.

"Robert?" Sarah knelt by her son.

"Is he drowned?" Robert sobbed. "Is Ander drowned?"

"No. He's right here."

Robert scrambled to his feet and threw his arms around his friend. "Sorry I called you stupid and silly. You're really brave." He wiped his nose on his shirt sleeve.

A second crack of thunder sent them running for home while Ander told an incredulous Robert all about the huge wild dog that saved his life.

EARL AND MARY SAT QUIETLY in front of the fire, trying to make sense of all that happened, all they could have lost. The storm continued to blow outside, but Ander, exhausted from his fight with the river, slept peacefully in the other room. Robert refused to leave his friend and slept at his side.

Lucas and Sarah brought cups of coffee from the kitchen.

"Dishes are done and put away." Sarah handed Mary a cup. "I still can't get over the way that dog came running out of nowhere."

"I will be forever grateful to him." Mary stared into the flames. "I hope he's all right out in this storm."

Earl took a cup from Lucas. "He's a wild dog, Mary. He's used to living outside and probably has some hole or cave where he hides when the weather gets bad."

It was just like Earl to not give an inch, no matter what.

As if on cue, a bark outside the door, a scratching on the porch, made them turn their heads. Earl took down his gun, cautiously opened the door, and stepped outside.

"Earl!" Mary raced after him.

The dog backed away, hung his head, and whimpered. He was wet and shivering in the cold rain. Earl raised his gun.

"Don't you dare shoot that animal, Earl!" Mary screamed. "He saved our son's life." She stood between Earl and the animal, blocking his aim.

Earl lowered the gun. "Fine, I won't kill him, but he can't stay here."

"Yes, he can. I'm putting my foot down on the subject, and that's that." Mary held her shawl over her head, poor protection from the rain, and went to coax the animal inside.

Sarah pushed the men aside and crouched in the doorway. The dog stretched his neck and sniffed at the cookie she held. He crept forward on his belly until he was eating it out of her hand. Only then did he enter the house, lay in front of the fire, and fall asleep.

"Boone looks quite comfortable there, like he belongs," Mary said with a smile.

"Boone?" Sarah asked.

"Boone," Earl replied with a huff, hung his gun back on the wall, and went to bed.

CHAPTER 14

VIRGINIA: OCTOBER 1848

"Here, Boone! Here, boy!"

Boone's head popped up from where he'd been napping on the porch. Mary looked down at the dog and sighed, hands on hips. "Go on! What are you waiting for?"

Boone jumped from the porch and crossed the yard at a full run, meeting Ander halfway. Robert wasn't far behind. A tentative Amy Lynn followed at a distance.

Ander dropped his lunch pail in the grass, wrapped his arms around Boone's neck, and scratched him behind his ears. Boone licked Ander's face. Mary sat on the edge of the porch and watched her happy son play with the dog he'd wanted for so long.

"Isn't he great, Amy Lynn?" Robert knelt beside Ander and pet Boone with long strokes down his back. Boone licked him in return, knocking him over. The boys laughed. Boone barked and danced around them.

Amy Lynn hung back. "He's so big," she said quietly. "Will he bite? He looks mean."

"No, he won't bite. He's a real friendly dog." Robert took Amy Lynn's hand and tried to lead her over to where Boone sat watching.

Amy Lynn pulled away, tucking both hands behind her, and took a step back. "You didn't tell me he was so big, Ander. I thought he was a puppy."

Ander stood next to her. "I told you how he saved my life, remember? A puppy couldn't do that."

"I suppose not." She took a step forward and hesitated before patting the top of the dog's head. Boone barked. Amy Lynn jumped back behind Ander.

"Don't be such a girl, Amy Lynn." Robert laughed. "I'll protect you." He tried to take Amy Lynn's hand again, but she wouldn't let him. Instead, she stayed by Ander's side.

"Here, let me." Ander squatted and called Boone closer. He grasped the collar Earl had fashioned. "Sit! Stay! Good boy." He took Amy Lynn's hand and set it on Boone's head.

"He's softer than he looks." Boone licked her hand. She yanked it back, held it close to her chest, and giggled.

"See, he likes you," Ander said.

Amy Lynn smiled at him. Mary recognized that smile. It was the same one she used to give Earl when he offered to take the fish off her line, even though she was quite capable of doing it herself. Robert stood off to the side, hands in his pockets, and kicked at the stones by his feet. She hoped the boys wouldn't let the girl come between them.

She picked up her laundry basket as the children, Boone trotting at Ander's side, walked to the house.

"Hello, Mrs. Bishop," Amy Lynn said. "Ander invited us to come see his new dog. I hope you don't mind."

"No, that's fine. As long as your mother knows where you are."

"She does, Mrs. Bishop. She said it was all right to come over."

"Do we have any more cookies, Mother? We're hungry after a long day of learning how to cipher."

"I think we still have a few in the tin. I'll see what I can find." Mary left the children and Boone sitting on the porch.

"Did I hear Ander brought some friends home with him?" Earl sat at the table sharpening Mary's kitchen knives.

"Robert and Amy Lynn came to see Boone." She left the basket on the floor and checked the cookie tin. Good, Earl managed to leave enough for each child to have one.

"Don't know why everyone makes such a big deal out of that animal. It's just a dog." He grumbled as he checked the newly-honed edge of a large blade.

"It's never just a dog when it comes to little boys. You know that."

He grunted again.

Outside, Mary held the tin out to the children. "One each, then it's time for Ander to do his chores before dinner."

Amy Lynn slid a little closer to him. He moved away. "I was hoping you could walk me home, Ander."

"Sorry," Mary said, "but I know Robert passes right by your house on his way home. I'm certain he wouldn't mind walking with you. Would you, Robert?"

"Of course, Mrs. Bishop. I could walk you home, Amy Lynn."

"I suppose," the girl sighed. "Thank you, Robert. And thank you, Mrs. Bishop, for the cookie. It was delicious."

"You're welcome."

After they left, Mary studied Ander's face, trying to read what he might be thinking.

"What are you smiling about, Mother?" he asked, looking away.

"Amy Lynn is quite smitten with you. You do know that, don't you?"

Ander's cheeks turned bright red. He stood and brushed cookie crumbs from the front of his shirt. Boone lapped them up, sniffing around for more. "I have stalls to clean." Before heading to the barn, he asked, "Mother, why do girls have to act so silly?"

She laughed. "Because they're girls, sweet boy. Because they're girls. Someday you'll learn to appreciate them."

Ander rolled his eyes. "I just wish she'd stop acting so silly around me." He turned. "Come on, Boone. We have chores to do."

"What was that all about?" Earl stood behind her in the doorway.

"Amy Lynn has a crush on our Ander. He might have a crush on her, but Robert most definitely does."

"Sounds like trouble to me." Earl smiled. "Schoolgirl crushes never come to any good by my experience."

"Oh, get out of my way. I have clothes to fold and you're blocking the door." She gave him a little push, but he stood firm. Reaching around, he pulled her in close and kissed her.

"Nope, those schoolgirl crushes never come to anything but trouble. Next thing you know she'll be asking him to take fish off her line because they're too wet and slippery. What was the word you used? Oh, yes, *icky*."

"You offered. I was perfectly capable of taking those fish off my own line."

"But you never refused my offer, did you?"

She kissed him back then nudged him out of her way. He laughed so hard she couldn't help but laugh with him.

"Earl Bishop, you're impossible."

"But you love me anyway."

Mary pretended to think about it. "Yes, I love you anyway."

"And I love you even when you're trying to trap me with your wily woman ways."

"Oh, I wasn't *trying* to trap you. I didn't need to. I had you wrapped around my little finger from the day we first met. Admit it."

"That you did." He gathered her in his arms and walked her toward their bedroom, each kiss pulling her in closer.

"What about Ander?" Mary half-heartedly argued.

"He's going to be busy for a while. The stalls were awful dirty last I checked. Why do you think I left that chore for him?" He closed the bedroom door behind them.

CHAPTER 15

VIRGINIA: JULY 1858

Mary dreamt of violence, of guns and blood and screaming. She woke fighting the bed covers, drenched in sweat. Earl grabbed her in his arms, melting her screams away. Ander's bare feet thumped to the floor as he jumped from his bed and ran to theirs. His hair mussed and standing on end, his new baseball bat held over his head, he rushed into their room like a wild man, Boone tight behind, growling, ready for a fight.

"What's wrong? What is it?" Ander spun from side to side trying to find the danger. At sixteen he was slender, gangly, nearly as tall as his father. Boone sniffed at the corners and under the bed.

"Your mother had a bad dream. Now, put that thing down before you hurt someone."

"Earl, it was so real." Sweat trickled down the side of Mary's face. Despite the early hour, it was already hot. The sticky July air, mixed with fear, made it hard to catch her breath.

"But it wasn't." Earl hugged her tight and kissed her damp hair. Ander lowered his bat and shook his head.

"Then I'm going back to bed," he announced.

"No, you're not. Sun's coming up, might as well get a start on your chores. You're going to want to leave early for the festivities, and no one's going anywhere until the chores are done."

"Yes, sir." Ander dragged himself back to his room, scratching his stomach and yawning.

"Earl, something bad is going to happen today. I can feel it."

"It's the 4th of July. The worst that could happen is someone twists an ankle in the potato sack race, or gets knocked on the head with a baseball." He patted her shoulder and got out of bed.

"I suppose you're right, but—"

"No buts about it. I know I'm right." Earl tucked in his shirt and slipped on his boots. "I'll be out in the barn with Ander, if you need me."

Mary's hands shook as she attempted to button her dress, taking several tries for each one. Her head told her Earl was right, but she had never had such a strong sense of dread about anything before. She closed her eyes and took a couple of deep breaths, letting them out slowly, steading her hands and clearing her mind before heading to the kitchen. She tied on her apron and grabbed the coffee pot from the shelf.

By the time Earl and Ander came in from the barn the coffee was ready. Platters of eggs and bacon waited on the table. Earl grabbed a slice of bread and slathered it with a thick layer of jam.

Ander snatched the jar from his father. "Hey, leave some of that for me."

"Gotta work hard to eat here, boy."

"I work hard. Harder than you."

"Ha!" Earl nodded toward the baseball bat Ander left standing in the corner. "You work harder at learning how to play that game than you do at your chores."

"Isn't she a beauty?" Ander smiled with pride at his creation. He'd spent many hours carving and sanding to make it look just like the one in the catalog, right down to the exact measurements.

"I have to admit, you did a fine job." Earl got up from the table and held the bat in his hand. He looked like he might take a swing.

Mary knocked her chair over making a grab for it. "Not in the house."

"You should join us, Father. I'd bet real money you could hit that ball farther than anyone."

"I don't know." Earl ran his hand over the smooth surface. "And where would you get *real money*?" He laughed.

"Will you at least promise to watch us play? You'll see how much fun it is."

"Of course, we'll watch you and your friends play," Mary said, setting her chair right and dishing herself a plate. "Is Amy Lynn bringing a picnic basket for the bidding?"

"I should think so. That's all the girls in school are talking about, who they want to have buy their basket." He stuffed a forkful of eggs into his mouth.

Earl looked across the table. "Are you going to bid on a basket? Amy Lynn's basket, perhaps?" he asked between mouthfuls.

Ander blushed. "Oh, I'll probably bid on a basket, depending what's in it. But you know, we don't get to know which basket belongs to which girl until after the bidding's over."

"What I do know," Earl said with a wink and smile toward Mary, "is that the girls are not above telling their favorite young man which basket is theirs, marking it easy to find. Your mother used to tie a big red ribbon on the handle of hers and filled it with all my favorites. Made certain I knew it, too."

Ander stared at his plate as he shoveled more eggs into his mouth.

"So, how'd Amy Lynn mark hers?" Earl continued to push.

Mary gave him a look that said enough was enough.

Ander didn't answer. Earl leaned forward and looked at Ander's downturned face.

"A ribbon, maybe? Something special only you'd recognize?"

"A bouquet of wildflowers," Ander said, grinning. His cheeks bloomed an even deeper red than Mary thought possible.

"Wildflowers?" Earl chuckled.

"Yes, she's going to lay a bouquet of wildflowers on top of the basket." Ander dropped his fork on the table and stood. "I'm done with my chores. Can I go now? I told Robert I'd meet him early to warm up, throw a few balls."

"Of course," Mary said before his father could say otherwise. "Have fun and good luck on the game. And the basket."

EARL AND MARY HELD hands as they walked into town. Earl carried their lunch in a basket decorated with a big red bow. They had debated taking the wagon but decided it was too nice a day. Besides, the horses would be frightened by all the people and noise.

Life had been kind to them the last ten years. Earl was earning a good living at the mill and had found his purpose helping the runaway slaves find their way to freedom. Mary still feared he would one day get caught and hung for his crime, but she accepted this was something he had to do. Every time he left with his special cargo she went down on her knees and prayed to God to watch over him and Lucas.

She filled her days with gardening, canning, and watching Ander grow into a fine young man. Sarah and Mary often talked about the day when their sons would marry and give them grandchildren. They even argued over who would make the better grandmother.

They had made it through the bad times and come out the other side smiling. There was still a tear or two shed for their lost Lillian, but there was no more drinking or fighting. Earl had come to accept her death was not his fault.

Yet, Mary couldn't shake her feeling of dread, that fear something horrible was about to happen.

They'd had a late start and the baseball game was in its final inning when they arrived. The bases were full, with Robert on second. It was Ander's turn at bat.

"Who's winning?" Mary asked Sarah after they made their way through the crowd to stand by the Shaws.

"The other team's up one. If Ander strikes out the game is over."

Ander struck a pose at home plate. His teammates shouted words of encouragement while the other team tried to make him lose his confidence with jeers and boos. The first pitch crossed the plate too low, but he swung anyway.

"Strike one!"

Ander grimaced. He wiped his forehead with his sleeve and looked over to where they were seated. Earl gave him a nod. Mary waved. Ander smiled and nodded back. He raised his bat.

The pitcher threw again. This time it came across the plate at the perfect height. Ander swung. The bat connected with a tremendous crack and the ball went flying out over the players' heads. Ander froze, mouth open, arms hanging limp at his side.

"Run!" Robert yelled.

Ander sprinted around the bases, pushing first one teammate, then another, across home plate. He was met by them and lifted onto their shoulders as he crossed, cinching the win for his team. Amy Lynn jumped up and down, clapping and waving when he was carried past. Mary noticed at least one or two other girls looking wistfully after her handsome and victorious son.

"I'd say by the envious looks on all the fathers' faces that maybe the men should consider putting together a couple teams for next year," she said to Earl.

"Could be fun," he admitted.

"Could be," Lucas agreed.

The boys put Ander down and they all wandered over to check out the girls' picnic baskets. Ander ran ahead with Robert to get a close-up look before the bidding started. Amy Lynn's basket was on the far end. They stopped when they saw the bouquet of wildflowers. Perhaps this was the reason for her sense of dread. Ander and Robert wouldn't fight over a girl. Well, if they did it wouldn't be the first time. Sarah and Mary looked at each other and sighed.

"What's the money for this year?" Sarah asked.

"New chalk board for Mr. Nichols."

"What's wrong with the old chalk board?"

Mary shrugged. "Nothing. Guess he just wants a new one." They shook their heads and laughed.

There was lively bidding and squeals from each girl as a winner for her basket was announced. All the colored ribbons, combined with the girls' delighted responses, told Mary there were no surprises involved. The boys knew who they were bidding on, with the appropriate suitor claiming his prize.

When Amy Lynn's basket came up for bidding, both Robert and Ander rushed to the front of the crowd. By the pleased look on Amy Lynn's face, this was exactly what she had hoped would happen. By the way Robert and Ander glared at each other, perhaps they didn't.

"Oh, dear," Sarah said.

"They're nearly grown men," Mary reminded her. "Neither one is such a fool that he didn't know they were competing for the same girl. Look at them. They're enjoying this."

Sarah craned her neck to see around the man in front of her. The boys were making a bigger challenge of this bidding war than they were on the ball game. Problem was, each one expected to come out the winner. What would happen when one of them had to lose?

As it turned out, no one would find out. Uncle Jackson stumbled his way through the crowd, pushing people aside, then stopping in front of Earl.

"I know what you've been up to." He poked his finger hard into Earl's chest, pushing him back a step. "You and your friend." He spun around to look at Lucas and nearly fell over. The crowd went deathly silent.

"Not here." Earl grabbed his uncle by the arm and dragged him away. Lucas followed, making certain Uncle Jackson couldn't stop or turn back.

"What's that all about?" Sarah asked Mary as the people crowded in between them and their husbands.

"He's drunk," Mary said. "Come on."

They made their way to the three men. Uncle Jackson was still shouting and pointing while their husbands forced him backward, farther away from the crowd.

"What does he think they've done?"

"I don't know," Mary lied.

Uncle Jackson was shouting now. "I know it's you two been helping the Negroes run away at night."

Mary's heart sank.

Sarah turned. "What's he talking about?"

Earl held up a hand to keep his distance. "Go home, Uncle Jackson. Sleep it off. You don't know what you're talking about."

"You'd like that, wouldn't you?" Uncle Jackson pulled the cork from his liquor bottle and tipped it back for another swig. It was empty. He tossed it over his shoulder in disgust.

"You're making a fool of yourself. Look at these people." Earl stepped back so Uncle Jackson could get a good look at the crowd. "They're laughing at you."

It was true. For most people, the initial shock had worn off and they were starting to whisper and snicker.

"You think this is funny?" he shouted. He grabbed a gun from the waistband of his pants and pointed it at Lucas' chest. "Is this funny?"

A few women screamed. No one laughed. Mary caught Sarah as her knees buckled.

Violence. Guns. Blood. It was all rushing back to her.

He waved the gun back and forth between Earl and Lucas. "Huh? I don't hear anyone laughing now."

Robert and Ander burst from the crowd.

"You boys a part of this, too?" Uncle Jackson pointed the gun at them. They froze.

Ander looked to his mother. She shook her head, holding out a hand telling them to stay where they were.

"Smart boy. Do as your mama says." Uncle Jackson almost lost his footing as he turned the gun back to their husbands.

Earl grabbed for the gun. Uncle Jackson jerked his arm. The gun went off. Lucas flew backward. Women screamed. Earl dropped to his knees. Several men tackled Uncle Jackson. Sarah fainted in Mary's arms.

Lucas was dead.

CHAPTER 16

VIRGINIA: JULY 1858

The celebration was over. The crowd milled about, whispering, waiting to learn something new. Some voiced hopes of a hanging. One group gleefully speculated about a possible double hanging. Didn't seem to matter if it was Jackson Bishop, Earl Bishop, or both who might swing from a rope. Mary shielded Sarah from the talk.

Lucas' body was moved to the doctor's surgery until the undertaker could claim him. Uncle Jackson was locked up, and the sheriff had Earl come in for questioning. Mary wanted to go with him. In his state of mind, she was afraid he might confess to everything.

"Stay with her until I get back," she told Ander. Robert and Amy Lynn helped Sarah to a bench before she fainted again.

Mary fought her way through the crowd and pulled Clay Lund aside.

"Go with him," she urged. "Be sure he doesn't say the wrong thing or we'll all hang." He nodded and hurried to join the men gathering in front of the jail house.

"Sheriff, I saw and heard everything," she heard him say as she turned to leave. "Perhaps I can be of some assistance here." The sheriff closed his office door and pulled the curtains against prying eyes. An armed deputy stood watch outside to be sure no one tried to intrude.

Mary used the Shaw's wagon to take Sarah and Robert home. Ander drove the team. Robert sat beside him, silently staring at the road ahead. Amy Lynn and Mary road in back where Sarah lay on a horse blanket.

Ander laid a hand on his friend's shoulder. Robert silently shrugged it away.

Mary held Sarah's head in her lap and stroked her hair. "Hush, now. I'm here. Robert's here. We're taking you home."

"Lucas," she sobbed.

"They've taken him to the surgery."

She pushed herself up to sit. Hope lit her eyes.

"No." Mary shook her head. "It's just temporary until Mr. Preston can come for him."

A new round of sobbing shook Sarah's body. She fell back into Mary's lap. "Why?" she wailed.

"I don't know." It wasn't a lie. Not really. Mary knew the truth of what Uncle Jackson was accusing Earl and Lucas, but she didn't know why a good man had to die.

Amy Lynn hugged her knees and cried. Ander's and Robert's sobs came from the front of the wagon. Mary could no longer hold back her tears. Thankfully, the horses knew the way home because she didn't think any one of them was capable of keeping the team on the road.

MARY STAYED BY SARAH'S side through the following week. Other than attending Lucas' funeral, Sarah never left her room, rarely getting out of bed. Mary sat with her, making small talk and bringing her food she barely touched.

"Why are you still here, Mary? You should be home taking care of your husband and son." Sarah stared out the window.

"Except for when he goes home to feed the animals, Ander's been here with Robert. Even Boone has stopped by from time to time." Mary leaned over and touched Sarah's hand. "I believe they're here right now if you'd like to see them."

"No, thank you. I'm not seeing anyone."

Mary patted Sarah's hand and sat back in her chair. She had hoped Sarah would agree to see Ander. It would be a good first step to getting her back into the world outside her bedroom. It wasn't healthy staying cooped up.

"What about Earl? What's he been up to with you gone so long?"

"He's been helping the sheriff deal with his uncle." Mary lied. Earl had been on a seven-day drunk, managing to stay barely sober long enough to be presentable at Lucas' funeral. Ander had reported his father passed out somewhere on their property nearly every day. Maybe if she spent more time with him, he'd stop drinking.

No, Sarah needed her more. There was nothing she could do for Earl when he was drinking. At least he wasn't fighting or he'd be locked up in the cell next to Uncle Jackson.

Sarah turned away from the window to stare at her. "Why are you still here?" she asked again.

"Because we're family, and family takes care of family."

Sarah smiled for the first time since the shooting. Not her usual big grin but a small glimmer of hope. "I think it's time I started taking care of my family and you went home to take care of yours. I know you lied about Earl. I heard you and Ander talking."

"Perhaps you're right."

"I know I am. Now go. Earl needs a good tongue-lashing only you can give to put him back on the straight and narrow."

Mary hugged her friend and made her promise she'd send for them anytime, day or night.

RATHER THAN GO STRAIGHT home, Mary decided to head into town and have a talk with Uncle Jackson herself. Word was he still insisted it was a righteous shooting. That he was justified in taking Lucas' life. He said he welcomed a court trial so the whole town could hear his evidence of Earl's and Lucas' guilt. Mary didn't know what his proof was, but she knew it couldn't be good. And sharing it with anyone else would be disastrous.

Clay Lund and the deputy were sitting with their feet up on the sheriff's desk, drinking coffee, and laughing. They jumped to their feet and removed their hats when they saw her standing in the door.

"Mary, I don't think you should be here." Clay took her arm gently in hand and tried to steer her back out into the street.

"On the contrary." Mary released herself from his grip and turned to face the jail cell. "I want to hear for myself what Uncle Jackson thinks he has against my husband, what he thought he had against Lucas before he killed him in cold blood."

Uncle Jackson rose from his cot where he appeared to be napping. His smile sent a chill through Mary's core. She tried hiding her fear, but it pushed up from deep in her gut, tasting like blood. She cleared her throat and took a deep breath.

His eyes locked with hers. His grin was worthy of the devil himself. "Good morning to you, Mary. I hope you are enjoying this sunny summer day. Such glorious weather for July, don't you think? Not too hot. Not too rainy. Bugs ain't even all that bad. Enjoy it while there's still breath in you to do so." He spit through the bars, the disgusting wad landing at her feet. She stepped over it to stand closer to the vile man she loathed to recognize as family.

"Why are you doing this to us? Why are you spreading these lies about Earl?"

"You know, for a preacher's daughter you sure find it easy to live on the wrong side of the law."

"Lucas Shaw was an honorable man, a family man. He didn't deserve to be shot down like that."

He laughed. "Oh, but he did! If anything, he deserved to be hung, strung up right there in front of his friends and family." A snarl rolled from his curled lips, and he leaned as close to Mary as he could through the bars. "Tell me, who's going to take care of that son of yours when you and Earl are convicted and hung for stealin' another man's rightful property? Perhaps I'll take in the boy myself. Teach him the true ways of Virginia law." Uncle Jackson chuckled.

Mary couldn't hold in her anger any longer and lunged for him. Clay grabbed her around the waist and pulled her back. "You stay away from Ander you drunken immoral animal!"

"Judge ought to be here by the end of the week. Time to make your peace with the Lord and say good-bye to your boy, Mary." Uncle Jackson stretched out on his cot and placed his hat over his eyes.

Mary shook with rage and fear. Clay held her up as he walked her to the door.

"Go home, Mary, and don't worry. Jackson Bishop won't see the inside of a court room. There isn't going to be any trial." The deputy gave a slight nod in agreement.

MARY COULDN'T SLEEP that night. Every time she closed her eyes Uncle Jackson leered at her, laughing, leading Ander away as she and Earl struggled against the ropes lifting their feet above the ground. When the sun finally peeked over the trees, she walked to Sarah's to see how they were getting along. Ander and Boone followed.

Sarah and Robert were on the porch talking with Clay. Mary could tell by Sarah's face something had happened.

"Morning, Mary, Ander." Clay nodded, hat in hand. "I was just telling Mrs. Shaw there isn't going be a trial. Jackson Bishop hung himself in his cell overnight. He left a note confessing it was all a lie."

"Well, I hope he burns in hell!" Sarah snapped.

Mary had never heard such venom from her normally gracious friend. Sarah was easily the kindest woman she knew.

"I'm sorry." Sarah sighed and gave Mary a hug. "I know he was family of yours, but he was an evil man."

"You won't get an argument from me. Now we can put all this behind us and go forward."

Clay mounted his horse and tipped his hat. "You ever need anything, Mrs. Shaw, just let me know. You or your son."

"Thank you."

They stood together on Sarah's porch as Clay rode away. She knew for a fact Uncle Jackson would never confess to a lie, even a true lie, let alone take his own life. Not when he had the opportunity to ruin a few others first.

She squeezed Sarah's hand. "I need to go home and tell Earl it's all over."

CHAPTER 17

VIRGINIA: APRIL 1861

Time moved through a slow haze after Lucas' death. At first it was one day at a time, then week to week, month to month, until years passed and their lives gradually reached a new normal. Sarah found work with a local seamstress. Shortly after, Robert announced he was leaving school to work at the dry goods store.

"What about your studies?" his mother asked as they sat on the Bishop's porch enjoying a warm autumn afternoon.

Mary handed them a glass of lemonade before taking a seat. "Your mother's right."

Robert shook his head. "Thank you, Mrs. Bishop." He took a sip. "But I'm the man of the house now, and it's not right that my mother should have to go out to work while I spend my days in a schoolhouse surrounded by children."

Nothing they said that afternoon, the next, or the one after that, changed his mind.

"Leave him alone," Earl told them one day. "Without his father, he has to learn to make his own way in the world."

They reluctantly agreed, and the subject was dropped.

Mary was relieved when Clay said he would no longer help runaways. It was too dangerous after Uncle Jackson's public accusations. They would have to wait until the whispers and rumors died down.

"But," he warned Earl, "you're going to be out a job if you don't stop drinking."

Even though he did, Earl was never the same. He grew quiet, spent a lot of his time hunting or fishing or walking alone in the woods. He spoke little and laughed even less.

Ander didn't last long in school after Robert left, now being the lone target of Mr. Nichol's wrath.

"Mr. Smead's looking for a young man to mentor and one day take over his law practice," Ander said during dinner one night. "And I told him I know just the person for the job." He scooped himself a second helping of potatoes.

Earl reached for the bowl. "I thought Robert was happy working at the dry goods. I understand they got him doing their bookwork now." He swapped the potato bowl for the black-eyed peas.

"Not Robert. Me."

Mary's fork clattered against her plate. "What does Mr. Nichols say about it?"

"I don't give a fig what Mr. Nichols thinks."

"Ander!" Earl slammed a fist against the table.

"Sorry, Father, but Mr. Nichols can't teach me half what Mr. Smead can. I spend most of my day listening to the little ones recite their reading and arithmetic lessons."

"He has a point, Earl."

The next day, Mary withdrew Ander from school with no argument from Mr. Nichols, and Mr. Smead found himself an eager new clerk.

IT WAS A TIME OF GROWING legal debate over the future of the southern way of life. Unfortunately, Ander's young mind thrived on the heated discussions in town, many of which took place in Mr. Smead's office as the local men sought out his opinion.

Ander brought legal texts home to read late into the night, taking copious notes to question his employer on the next day. Then he'd bring home all his new-found knowledge to try and bring his father around to his way of thinking.

"It's the only answer. First South Carolina, then Mississippi, Florida, Alabama, Georgia, Louisiana, and now Texas. All the rest of the southern states will have to follow." Yet again, Ander went through his argument on why Virginia should secede from the Union. "If we don't do something now, the north is going to outnumber us in Washington, and then all is lost."

"All what is lost?" Earl asked, paying little attention to Ander's oft repeated argument.

Mary concentrated on the sock she was darning. They were proud of Ander and his interest in politics. He had a keen mind, was smarter than most anyone they knew. One day he would make a worthy attorney. Unfortunately, at barely nineteen he was overly susceptible to the angry voices raised in every town, and on every farm, across the south. He often came home in the evening all riled up, spouting new ideas about a separate southern nation without a thought to the consequences.

"Our whole way of life. Living off the land, growing things, cotton, tobacco. Next thing you know, we'll all be living in big noisy cities, working in factories, never just sitting back watching the grass grow or our children catch lightening bugs in a jar on a hot summer night."

Ander stretched out in the grass, arms resting behind his head as a pillow. It was a mild spring evening, and they had moved outside to enjoy what little time remained before bed. He rolled onto his side.

"Mother, do you really want all this to be taken away from your grandchildren? Tell Father we have to act now or it will be too late."

"Grandchildren!" she laughed. "Are you trying to tell me something? Are you and Amy Lynn making plans I should know about?" Lately Amy Lynn appeared to have given up on regaining Robert's interest and had turned her sights back to Ander. Mary wished that girl would make up her mind. She played those two boys to distraction.

"No, Mother. I have to focus on my studies. I don't have time for a wife and family right now. But you know what I mean. Tell him." He pointed at his father.

"Your son's afraid we're going to have to move to the big city," she said to Earl with a wink and a smile, trying to pull him into the conversation.

"Now you're just making fun." Ander dropped onto his back and stared up at the darkening sky. "I hear in the city you can't even see the stars because of all the fancy streetlights and the smoke coming from those big factories. Is that what you want? Not me."

"Of course not." Mary looked down at their boy stretched out in the grass. When had he gotten to be so tall? She knew every mother must feel that way, but she still wondered where her sweet boy had gone. His curls were as unruly as ever. He'd inherited those from his father, only Earl's were turning gray around the edges while Ander's were that beautiful chestnut brown. He'd become a man when she wasn't looking.

"Son, don't you think there are farms up north?" Earl asked. "I know for a fact not everyone lives in a big city."

Ander sat up, eager to hear more. "I forgot you lived in New York for a while. Am I right? Was it awful?"

"Well, it wasn't Virginia, that's for sure."

"That's what I'm talking about. They want us to have our big plantations. They want us to keep growing our cotton and tobacco and shipping it north to their big factories. Tell me, how are we supposed to grow all that cotton and tobacco without field hands for help?"

Mary set side her mending, the light too dim to continue. Ander was treading on uncertain ground. They had somehow succeeded in keeping him from learning about Earl's secret passengers over the years, even after Uncle Jackson's accusations. She'd answered his questions as truthfully as she dared and prayed that would suffice.

But now Ander was older and full of big ideas, a lot more questions, just when Clay announced he was restarting their night runs. George refused to go with Earl any longer, said he'd had enough, wasn't risking his neck. Let them free themselves, he shouted before storming off. Mary had begged Clay not to do it, at least not to include Earl, but Clay said it was even more important with all the talk of secession and war. Earl agreed.

In fact, they were expecting passengers that night, their first in three years. Were they already waiting in the woods? She looked over Ander's head and strained to see into the dark but couldn't make out anything more than the silhouette of the barn and the trees beyond.

"I don't know, Ander." Earl sighed. "I have to believe there's a better way than slavery."

Ander threw up his hands. "I wish there was, too. But shouldn't that be for individual states to decide? Besides, we give these people a job, a roof over their heads, clothes to wear, and food to eat."

"No freedom to come and go as they please." Earl's voice grew tense, his jaw clenched in anger.

Ander pushed. "How can they take care of themselves when they can't even read or write?"

"More than half the people living in these parts can't read or write beyond their own name. Some not even that!" A lively political debate was fast becoming an argument. "But they don't live in fear of being sold, separated from their families, or the next whipping."

Ander turned away, silent. He'd seen the scars on his father's back many times. "I just think maybe they should let individual states make up their own minds on matters that affect them," he said quietly. "That's all I'm saying."

Had they done Ander a disservice by sheltering him from the dark side of slavery? All he'd ever seen were the men and women hard at work in the fields. Everyone he knew worked hard at something. He never saw the beatings, the meager rations, the disgraceful shacks. They'd kept him from town whenever there was an auction, so he never saw the pain of a family torn apart. His father never told him the story behind his whipping. She wished they'd exposed him to the ugliness, leaving out the details of their dangerous secret.

Mary jumped in to change the subject. A dark cloud hung over their heads. What she had hoped would be a nice evening had turned sour. "So, Ander, are you planning on taking Amy Lynn to the spring social at church on Sunday?"

"I haven't decided yet if I'm going."

"Does that mean you haven't even asked her? You'd better get right over there first thing tomorrow if you don't want her to accept another invitation. Sarah tells me Amy Lynn's been by their place on more than one occasion asking after Robert. If you're at all serious about that girl you'd better start to show a little more interest or you'll lose her to your friend."

"If she wants to marry Robert, then she should go ahead and marry Robert." His voice rose. "I told you, I don't have time for courting right now, and if she can't understand that and wait, then . . ." He broke off and jumped to his feet. "It's late. I'm going to bed." He strode into the house, sulking.

Mary shook her head. Sometimes he was still her sweet boy hidden inside the body of a grown man.

Earl shook his head. "That boy doesn't know what he's talking about, coming home spouting all that secession nonsense. Does he think those men in Washington are going to just let us go our separate way with a wave and a smile and their good wishes? We're going to have to fight our way to freedom, like our founding fathers. A lot of men will die, and we won't win. No one will win." He placed his hands on his thighs, and with a groan, stood. "There is one thing he's right about, though."

"What's that?"

"It's time we were heading to bed. Morning will be here before we know it."

Earl went inside. Mary followed, but stopped to poke her head into Ander's room.

"Is Father angry with me?" he asked from the darkness.

"No," she said in a half-whisper. "He isn't angry. He's afraid. Good night my sweet boy."

"Good night, Mother." The bed creaked as Ander rolled over.

She closed the door to his room and went to join Earl in theirs.

EARL WAS UP AND GONE with his load of *freight* before she woke the next morning. Ander sulked over his breakfast. Setting down his cup, he looked up at her.

"Do you think Father will ever understand?"

"Understand why we have to tear our nation in two? A nation we fought so hard to build barely a hundred years ago? No. You'll never make him understand." Mary finished her coffee and went to the kitchen to pour another. "There has to be a way we can all learn to get along without one half forced to give up their ways."

"It's never going to happen, Mother. Not as long as the north continues to look the other way when it comes to the Fugitive Slave Act. As long as they only impose nominal fines and jail time, we are left with no choice but to secede. If you ask me, anyone who helps slaves escape should be hung on the spot. Then maybe the next guy will think twice."

Mary dropped her cup. Coffee splattered around the porcelain shards at her feet. She grabbed the edge of the table to keep from falling. Ander had no idea what he was saying.

"Are you all right?" He put his arm around her shoulders and helped her sit.

"You'd better go or you'll be late." Mary's voice quivered. He didn't move. "Go! I'm fine."

Ander hesitated, then left. She covered her mouth to muffle the sobs. *You're going to get caught. You're going to hang.* How many times had she said that to Earl over the years? She couldn't forget how close he'd come to a rope. He could have been shot along with Lucas, or instead of him. She could be the widow going to bed alone every night. She buried her face in her arms and wept.

MARY WIPED THE SWEAT from her brow with her apron. She'd been breaking clods of winter dirt and hoeing rows to plant when Ander appeared from the trees, his face red, eyes big with excitement.

"Is Father home?" he asked, winded.

"Did you run all the way from town?"

"Is Father home?" he asked again.

"No. Your father had a delivery for a man two counties over. He won't be home until tomorrow night. What's happened?"

"It's Fort Sumter!" He grabbed her shoulders and held her close. "We captured Fort Sumter yesterday. It took three days, but we sent Lincoln's soldiers packing." He let her go, looked to the sky and then back again, laughing. "It's ours now. Fort Sumter belongs to the Confederacy!"

"Oh, Dear God." Light-headed, she fell to her knees. "This means—"

"Yes. War. But it won't last long. I guarantee you we will soon show those men in Washington we mean business. Then it will all be over."

No. Wars are never short. War is never quick with everyone shaking hands and happily going their own way as soon as the smoke clears.

"No," she said. "It won't be. War never is."

But Ander wasn't listening. He was too caught up in the excitement of his dreams presumably coming true. His dreams of an autonomous Confederate nation free from northern control.

"I quit my job," he continued. "I just came home to pack my things and say good-bye." He knelt down in front of her. "Robert and I leave for Richmond tomorrow. We're going to enlist."

She stared at him. What did he want her to say? Congratulations? Good luck?

"Did you hear me? I'm joining the Confederate Army. I leave tomorrow."

"I heard you," she whispered, her throat almost too tight, her tongue too dry, to speak. "What about your studies?"

"I'm putting them on hold. I'll be back before you know it, I promise. Mr. Smead says we're at a great turning point in our nation and its laws, the formation of a new country. He said I must be a part of it to truly appreciate its significance. It will make me a better lawyer, maybe even a senator, one day. In fact, he wishes he was younger so he could go, too."

She stared into his eyes as he made promises he had no ability to keep. There was so much she wanted to say, but the words wouldn't come. She couldn't stop him. He was like his father once he set his mind to something so she said nothing. She left him standing in silence and went back to her garden.

ANDER WAS GONE. HE slipped out while she was sleeping. He left a note saying good-bye, don't worry, he'd be home soon.

She was sitting at the table when Earl returned home that evening. She held up the note.

He took it from her. "What's this?" He read Ander's words.

"He's gone," was all she said.

Earl set the note down on the table, his face blank. "I have chores to do," he said, walking out the door.

Mary put her face in her hands. Her heart crumbled. She wanted to scream, to cry, but there were no tears left.

Later, dinner cold on the table, she found Earl stretched out in the hay, a half empty whiskey bottle beside him. She sat and took a big swallow of the amber liquid. Gasping, coughing, unable to breathe, the burn was like nothing she'd ever experienced.

"Mary?" Earl pushed himself onto his elbows. "What are you doing?"

She looked at the liquor bottle still in her hand. "I thought maybe I'd give it a try. It's what you do whenever there's trouble or heartache. Thought it might help."

"Give me that!" He took the bottle from her. "Did it? Did it help?"

"No. Does it help you?"

"No," he admitted.

"So, maybe I should take up drinking, too. We both admit it won't change anything, but at least it's something we can do together."

"Don't be a fool, Mary." Earl struggled to his feet and dumped the remaining liquid outside the barn door.

"No, being the fool is your job, Earl," she said under her breath. "And, apparently, our son's."

She helped him stumble back to the house where he collapsed onto their bed, snoring before his head even hit the pillow. Sitting in her rocking chair in front of the cold hearth, she cradled the picture of Ander and Lillian to her chest. Would she have to say good-bye to her son, too?

CHAPTER 18

VIRGINIA: APRIL 1861

Every day was the same after Ander left. Earl went to town early each morning, not returning until almost dark. At night he ate his dinner in silence and then went out to tend the animals, or so he said. He wasn't drinking every night. But he was drinking.

There were nights he didn't come back to their bed at all, instead spending it in the barn. Mary told herself it was for the best, but she longed for the days when he chose her over whiskey.

She threw herself into spring planting, trying not to fret over the *what ifs* playing out in her head. Whether or not there was a war, whether or not Ander ever came home again, they would always need to eat. But nothing she did lessened the sense of dread that hung in the air thick as pond water in August.

The boys had been gone two weeks when Mary and Earl were jolted from their sleep by someone pounding on the front door. Earl grabbed his shotgun from under the bed. Mary rose to follow him.

"Stay here! Be ready to go out the window, if necessary."

"Earl, you don't think—"

"I don't know what to think." He closed the bedroom door behind him.

Easing the door open a crack to see what was happening, she said a little prayer of thanks Earl wasn't passed out drunk in the barn.

He stood to one side of the door. Gun ready. "Who's there?"

"Let us in!"

Mary recognized Clay's voice. Who else was with him?

"What's wrong?" Earl stepped back to let his boss pass. Two young slave girls cowered in the doorway. They clung to each other, shaking, eyes as wide as dinner plates. Clay pulled the girls inside and closed the door.

Mary flew out of hiding. "Why'd you bring them here?"

Earl lowered his gun. "I told you to stay in the bedroom," he snapped, jaw tight, eyes flashing.

She pushed past him, not caring if he was angry. Clay had promised no more runs. He was going back on his word. And why did he bring the girls into their home?

"I tried leaving them in your root cellar, but they wouldn't stay alone."

Earl combed his hand through his hair and sighed.

"This is the last," Clay added.

Mary rushed him, hitting him in the chest with the flat of her hands. He landed back against the door with a thud. "You promised!" she screamed.

The girls flinched and hugged each other. The younger one started to cry.

"I'm sorry, Mary. I wouldn't ask if there was any other way."

"There is another way. You take them. Your risk, your life. Let *your* wife worry whether or not you're coming home or hanging from a tree. You do it!"

Earl pulled her away from Clay and into the bedroom.

"I'll handle this," he said, closing the door behind him.

"No more!" she hollered through the closed door.

She pressed her ear against the wood but couldn't make out what the men were saying. The front door closed.

Earl returned to the bedroom. He pulled off his nightshirt and picked up the trousers hanging over the back of the chair.

"Well?" she asked. He wouldn't look her in the eye. She spun him around.

"Well, what, Mary? Am I going?" He buttoned his shirt and tucked it in. "What do you think?" He headed for the door.

She threw her hairbrush at him. It hit the wall and clattered to the floor.

He turned back and reached out for her.

"You promised!" she yelled, pacing, looking for something else to throw. "And it's even more dangerous now that we're at war." She grabbed one of her shoes. This time it bounced off the side of his head.

He hollered and rubbed the spot. "Damn it, Mary! Stop throwing things." Earl held her tight until she stopped struggling. "I have no choice. Their owner was going to take them with to the fighting. Make them cook, sew, and . . ." he paused, looked down at the floor, "for him and the other officers."

She stopped crying and stared, mouth open. "They're barely grown. I doubt the one's even had her first blood yet."

"That's why I have to help them."

She stepped back and thought about it for a moment. "No. They're not our problem. Let Clay take them or let them find their own way."

"You know they'd never make it on their own. And Clay, well . . ."

"Clay's a coward. Oh, he's brave enough when it's someone else's neck at risk, but not if it means his own." She went back to pacing. Could she ever forgive Earl if he went? But because of the two young girls, she'd never forgive herself if he didn't.

"Then I'm going with you." She stood, hands on hips, daring him to stop her. He wasn't going to change her mind. She was going.

"No, you're not. I need you to stay here and keep watch over our things, keep the soldiers from requisitioning anything."

"Do you really think they'd do that? Take our food, our animals?"

"I don't know. Maybe not with you here. But if they found the place empty, they might declare it abandoned and take everything. It's war, Mary. Besides, I'm not going far this time. I'll be back by sundown."

"Then I'm going with you." She repeated and pulled off her nightgown to get dressed. "I'll pack a basket lunch, enough for the four of us. If we're questioned, we'll just say we're on our way to visit family."

"I said—"

She stopped him with a single look. "I heard what you said." She retrieved her thrown shoe. "And I said I'm going with. We'll be back by sundown. You said so yourself. Boone can watch the place until then. He'll tear apart anyone who tries to steal so much as a loaf of bread."

"They'll shoot him if he does."

She hesitated. "Probably, so we'd better get moving. The sooner we leave, the sooner we return."

THEY LEFT SHORTLY AFTER first light. Clay had taken the girls to the root cellar and sat with them the rest of the night. There wasn't time to arrange a load of lumber, so they would have to take the girls hidden under the wagon bed without any freight to cover the trap door. She was still amazed at how well the edges blended. At least there were only the two, and they were small. There should be plenty of room and enough air through the holes under Earl's seat. If only the youngest one would stop crying, Mary would feel more confident.

The sun rose bright and warm. A light breeze tousled the new young leaves like a mother might tousle a child's curls. Bees hummed in and out of the flowers along the roadside. Mary closed her eyes and listened to nothing other than the horses' hooves against the dry road, the creak of their leather harness, the birds singing in the trees, almost believing they were off on a picnic. There was no war, and no dark-skinned contraband hidden under the boards of their wagon bed. It was just her and Earl on the front seat, and Ander stretched out in back chewing on a long stalk of grass while staring up at the clouds. She could even imagine Lillian at his side. She'd have curly hair like her brother's, and they'd tease and poke each other in fun.

"Wake up, Mary." Earl nudged her.

"I'm not sleeping," she responded with a smile. "I'm just pretending."

"Good, keep pretending then, because we've got company."

There was an edge to his voice that alarmed her. She opened her eyes. A young Confederate officer, barely older than Ander, approached on horseback. Not some farm animal fresh from the plow, either. His mount was a thoroughbred accustomed to being raced. Mary's throat went dry.

"Smile," Earl said under his breath. "Good morning!" he called out.

"Good morning, sir." The young officer removed his hat and bowed his head in her direction. "Good morning, ma'am." His diction was as crisp as his uniform. He came from money. His daddy no doubt bought his commission.

"Good morning," she replied, as happy and relaxed as she could manage. "A beautiful day, isn't it?"

"Yes, a glorious day for the Confederacy." He stopped his horse in front of their team, forcing Earl to yank back on the reins. "And where might the two of you be headed, if I may ask? It's not safe out here. There's a war going on, you know."

"We're going to visit my aunt," Earl said, his voice calm. "She's old and feeling poorly. My wife and I thought we'd bring her some food and some company." Mary held up the basket in her lap.

"How far is it to your aunt's house?"

His questions made her stomach churn. He was detaining them too long. The sooner they could put some distance between them, the better she would feel.

"Not far," Earl pointed beyond the officer. "Just over the county line a short way."

"Well, like I said, it's not safe to be riding around out here. Could be Union soldiers in the area. I suggest you turn around and head back home, visit your aunt another day after the fighting is over. I assure you it won't be long before we have the Yankee scum turning tail and running back home to their mothers. Pardon my language, ma'am." He tipped his hat to Mary.

She put a hand over her mouth and turned away, trying for a proper look of shock and embarrassment. "You sound like our son," she said. There was a sniffle from the air vent below their bench. She raised her voice. "He's about your age, too. He and a friend went off to Richmond not long ago to enlist. Perhaps you know of him. Anderson Bishop."

Why did she just tell him their name? Mary wished she could eat her words. She was talking too much.

"No, ma'am, I don't. But if I do happen to meet up with him, I'll tell him his mother sends her regards."

"Oh, I'd much appreciate that. Now, if you'd let us pass, I promise you we'll drop off this food, say our hellos and good-byes and then head straight back home. We just want to see that she's well and getting along with all the fighting so close."

Earl raised the reins and gave them a snap across the horses' rumps. The officer moved his horse sideways, blocking their passage.

"I can't let you do that. Rest assured your aunt will be fine. We are watching over all civilians living near our encampments."

Encampments, of course, there would be more where he came from.

"Earl, I think the young man is right. Perhaps we should turn around and head back toward home."

Earl nodded. "Very well." One of the girls sneezed and the other started to cry. Mary's heart skipped. Sweat ran down the back of her neck. She held the basket tighter to keep her hands from shaking.

The officer pulled his gun. "Get down from the wagon." He pointed his weapon at them. Earl raised his hands and stepped down, keeping his eyes on the officer. Mary clutched the basket to her chest and stared at his weapon.

Would Ander ever know what became of them, and why? Or would he merely return to an empty house one day and think they'd abandoned him?

"Set the basket on the seat, ma'am, and get down from the wagon."

His words were as cold as the steel in his hands. Shaking, she did as she was told. Everything was quiet except for the songbirds and the sniffling girl.

"Where are they?" he asked.

The sniffling stopped.

"Who?" Earl asked.

It was over. Mary had planned on dying in her own bed, old and surrounded by her grandchildren, not dangling from a rope at the side of the road.

Keeping his gun trained on Earl's chest, the officer dismounted and walked around the side of the wagon. "Awful shallow wagon bed for such deep sides." He knocked on one side and the girls screamed.

"Come out of there!" He moved the gun from Earl to the wagon bed. The girls pushed the loose panel aside and pulled themselves up out of their hiding place. "Get down!"

With the officer's attention now trained on the girls, Earl reached for the shotgun he'd hidden under the bench.

"Well, what do we have here? These two belong to you?"

Earl's fingers closed around the stock.

"I wouldn't do that if I were you." The officer pointed his gun back at them. Earl froze, one hand still on the shotgun.

Sweat beaded up on the young officer's forehead. His eyes darted back and forth between the two runaways huddled together on one side and the grown man with a shotgun on the other. He was outnumbered, nervous, and clearly uncertain what to do next. It was a dangerous combination of emotions.

Mary stepped forward. The officer pointed the gun at her chest.

"Stay right there."

Earl raised a hand and shook his head at her.

"Please put your gun down," she continued, ignoring Earl. "They're just girls. You're frightening them."

"They're property," he countered. "And they're not yours or you wouldn't be keeping them trapped under your wagon bed like that."

"You're right," she continued, inching forward. "They're not ours, but they're just children."

Why hadn't they thought of that? They could have traveled with the girls in the open, claimed them as their property, and convinced him their paperwork was merely misplaced.

The officer's eyes darted back to the girls. His arm relaxed a little. "Where are you taking them?"

"Away." Mary took another step. He looked back at her. "Where they don't have to be afraid anymore."

He hesitated.

"Their owner had immoral plans for them. Look, they're so young."

His jaw set, and his arm came up again. "They're coming with me."

Earl screamed at the girls. "Run!"

The older one grabbed the younger one's hand, and they bolted for the brush. Earl lunged for the officer, but not before he swung around and got off two clean shots, killing the girls. Mary screamed. Earl knocked the young man to the ground.

Mary's ears rang. Gun powder burned her nose. She fought to stay on her feet.

Their horses reared at the noise, threatening to bolt. Mary grabbed the reins and led them a short distance to where they were distracted by the tall sweet grasses growing along the roadside. She ran back, Earl's shotgun at the ready.

Earl lay unconscious, a bloody rock next to him. The officer, winded and bloodied, stood over Earl, rope in hand. He tossed one end over a tree limb and tied it to his saddle. Earl moaned. His head rolled to the side, but his eyes didn't open.

"First you, then your wife," the officer said.

The blast from Earl's shotgun threw Mary off her feet, crashing to the road. It took a minute to get her bearings, but when she pushed herself up, Earl was stumbling toward her, holding his side, blood dripping from his head. The officer lay sprawled on his face, a fast-spreading pool of blood flowing from his body.

So much blood!

Mary struggled to breathe. She'd shot him. He was barely a man. He was some other woman's son, and she killed him.

So much blood!

Her hands shook.

"Mary." Earl knelt beside her and pulled her close. "Are you hurt?"

"I just got the wind knocked out of me. That gun of yours has quite a kick."

Earl went back to the fallen officer. He retrieved the revolver and handed it to her. "I'll teach you to shoot it, and then I want you to keep it on you at all times." It was heavy, but without all the extra length it would be easier to handle.

"All right." she nodded, attempting to tuck the gun into her waistband, but she couldn't stop her hands from shaking.

Earl took the gun back. "I don't want you accidentally shooting yourself. Or me." He helped her to her feet. The officer's horse was nearby. A well-trained Army mount, it hadn't run at the sound of her shot. Earl rummaged through the officer's sack and pulled out the powder and shot. "You'll need this until I can get more." A quick search came up with a cleaning kit. He took that, too.

Squatting by the officer's body, he rolled him over. The boy gasped, coughed. He grabbed Earl's sleeve.

"Help me," he whispered.

Earl took his hand. "Only God can help you now, son."

"Then pray for me."

Earl went through the boy's pockets, pulling out anything he could find.

"Earl, you wouldn't rob a dying man!"

"No." He tucked the money back where he found it and held up a letter. "This from your girl?"

The dying man nodded. He fumbled with the collar of his shirt and pulled out a locket. With an easy tug the chain broke, and he pressed it into Earl's hand. "Return this to her, along with what little money I have. Tell her I loved her and spoke kindly of her in the end." He drew his last breath.

Earl dropped to the ground and stared at the locket in his hand. Mary took it from him, along with the letter. She glanced at the address before tucking them carefully in her skirt pocket. Charleston. He was a long way from home. Earl handed her the boy's money. She put it safe with his other valuables.

"Come," she said. "We have to get out of here before someone finds us. There are bound to be more men in the area who could have heard the shot."

Earl stood. "What about the girls? We can't leave them here like this." She pulled him back and looked away from the poor young things lying face-down in the brush.

"We have no choice," she whispered.

Earl's shoulders sagged. "I'm sorry, Mary. It wasn't supposed to happen this way. I could have gotten us both killed."

There was nothing she could say. It was true, but it was over now. The girls were dead, and she had killed a young man no older than their Ander.

Mary took over the reins. They rode back in silence, the horses leading by memory. Thankfully, the road was dry so their wheel tracks wouldn't be visible. No search party should be able to follow. And the only one who knew their names was dead.

WHEN THEY ARRIVED HOME, Boone met them in the yard. He followed the wagon into the barn, whimpering. She patted him on the head and unhitched the horses. They went straight for their stalls where fresh hay and water waited. She'd let them eat and rest while she took care of Earl, give them a good rub down later.

She stepped back onto the wagon seat where Earl remained, staring, eyes blank. He turned when she touched his shoulder. His face was cut and bruised. One eye had swollen shut. Dried blood matted his hair and formed trails down the side of his face. She checked his hands. He'd gotten a few good punches in before the officer hit him with the rock.

"Can you get to the house on your own?" she asked.

He looked from her to the house and back again. He nodded.

"Good, because I sure as hell can't carry you."

"Where did you learn to cuss?" he asked in a hoarse whisper.

"Where do you think?" She looked him in the eyes.

He hung his head. "Well, I don't like it."

Getting him down from the wagon took a bit of doing. She let him lean on her as they walked through the yard, stopping whenever a spasm of pain caused him to stumble and cry out. She suspected at least one broken rib.

"I want my sweet girl back," he said. "The one who doesn't cuss and yell at me," he said between painful steps

"And I want that curly haired young man back who didn't drink and get into fist fights," she replied, knowing those two people no longer existed.

"I still love you," he said.

"And I still love you."

Earl set the gun down on the bureau and practically fell into bed. He was asleep by the time she returned with a basin of water, soap, and a washcloth. She dabbed his cuts. He stirred but didn't wake.

"Oh, Lord, Earl."

Mary rung out the cloth and wiped her hands on her skirt. She stopped. The officer's belongings were still in her pocket. The money, locket, and letter went into her box of treasures under the bed. She would write a suitable letter to his sweetheart later. Sitting next to Earl, she picked up the revolver. Shiny and new, its cold weight was heavy in her hands.

"It's a .45 caliber Army Colt," he said. "Cap and ball, newest model out there. And be careful, it's still loaded."

She set it down again. "How do you feel?"

"Like I got run over by a team of horses."

"Did you?" she joked.

"I wish," he said with a little chuckle. "It probably wouldn't hurt nearly so much."

She stayed with him until he fell back to sleep before going out to the barn to rub down the horses. Then she took a crowbar and pulled out the false bottom in the wagon, yanking on the boards and throwing the pieces aside. By the time she was done, her hair had come unpinned and stuck to her head and neck. Her skirts were in tatters from catching on the broken edges. Her hands were blistered and bleeding. She sat down on the end of the wagon bed, pulled a sliver from her thumb, and cried. No amount of hard work would ever remove the image of that boy dying by the side of the road.

CHAPTER 19

VIRGINIA: APRIL 1861

Clay sat across the table from Earl. Mary poured cups of coffee before joining them. She had gone into town the day before to tell him what happened on the road. She told him in no uncertain terms there wouldn't be any more runs, and that she had dismantled the hiding place in their wagon. He was heartbroken at the way things had turned out, apologized for what he'd put them through, and agreed they were done. It was too dangerous.

But he'd said that before.

"You heard what happened?" Earl winced as he lifted his coffee cup to his lips.

"Mary told me."

Earl nodded. "No more," he said after a long silence.

"No more," Clay agreed.

More silence. Boone whimpered. Mary let him out, then sat down with the men.

Earl slammed his cup on the table, breaking it.

"Earl!" Mary jumped to her feet, grabbing a towel to mop up the mess. Clay flinched.

"Mary was forced to kill a man!" Wincing and holding his side, Earl added, "And those two girls are dead."

"I know. I'm sorry. Mary." Clay hung his head.

"These are hard times for all of us." She put her hand on his shoulder for a moment before getting Earl a fresh cup.

After Clay rode away, the house became unbearably quiet. Mary fidgeted with her coffee cup, then rose to clear the table.

"How's your rib?" she asked, returning from the kitchen. With Earl in one of his dark moods, the question seemed safe enough.

Earl went into their bedroom. She thought he'd gone to rest, but he returned with the Colt he'd taken from the dead officer.

"Sit down."

He set the gun on the table. Even though she'd held it in her hands just two days earlier, she was reluctant to touch it.

"Pick it up. Feel how heavy it is."

She weighed the gun in one hand, then the other. The cold metal against her skin, like death, was familiar. She set it down. Earl handed it back to her.

"Remember, it's still loaded so keep your finger off the trigger."

She slid it across the table to him, but he wouldn't take it. He walked around to stand behind her.

"Hold it in your right hand, wrap your left underneath your wrist to help balance, then extend your arms out in front of you."

"Shouldn't we be doing this outside? What if it goes off in the house?"

"It's not cocked. Keep your finger off the trigger and pointed away from me and the dog, and you'll be all right. For now, I just want you to get the feel of it. Then we'll go outside and actually shoot."

She extended her arms, holding the gun as Earl instructed.

"Use your dominant eye to site down the barrel."

Mary went back and forth, closing one eye, then the other, to determine her dominant eye. She settled on her right. Her shoulders shook from the weight.

"Set it down."

"How do you know it's loaded?"

"I'm guessing there are still three shots left in the chamber, maybe four. He got off two, the ones that killed the girls. There's room for six, but generally in the field they'll load five and leave the hammer on the sixth empty chamber so it can't go off accidentally while riding. If you're uncertain, this is how you check. They call this the cylinder and it has six chambers." Earl spun the cylinder one chamber at a time. "You can see there are one, two, three empty chambers and one, two, three loaded chambers." He angled the gun to show each chamber as he turned the cylinder another full rotation. "Now, we're going outside and shoot off these three. See how you do."

Earl set an empty liquor bottle on a stump. She smiled. She would enjoy shooting at those.

"We'll start with this one. If you hit it, I'll get another."

Yes, there were always more where that one came from.

He handed her the gun. "Feet slightly apart, right one a little forward. You need to balance or you'll throw yourself over backwards. This gun is smaller than my shotgun, but it still packs a heavy kick."

She nodded and set her feet.

"Loosen your knees a little to absorb the shock and lean in. Now aim like I showed you. Do you see the bottle in your site?"

"Yes."

"Good. Use your thumb to slowly pull back the hammer. Did you hear it click?"

"Yes."

"Pull it a little farther. Did you hear a second click?"

"Yes."

"First click is for loading, second click for shooting. Now, put your finger on the trigger and squeeze, don't pull."

A flash and black smoke erupted from the muzzle. Mary's arms flew up. Earl caught her as she fell backwards. Her ears rang, and there was a heavy smell of sulfur in the air.

Earl held his breath, then groaned. It must have hurt him terribly when she fell against him.

"Are you all right?"

She let her gun hand hang loose at her side and reached out to him with the other. Earl turned her back around to face her target.

"Now you know what to expect," he said.

"Did I hit it?"

"Not even close. Try again."

Mary nodded, disappointed but determined.

"Remember your balance."

She took her time, tested her balance, prepared for the kick. This time when she squeezed the trigger she stayed upright and the bullet nicked the neck of the bottle, knocking it over to break in two on a rock below.

"That's better." Earl took the gun from her and set it on the ground while he retrieved the broken bottle. He set the larger bottom piece back on the stump. "You have one shot left," he said when he returned. "Pick up the gun and aim a little farther down this time and you should hit it square."

The bottle shattered. Mary was ecstatic, but when she turned to Earl all she saw was sadness in his eyes.

Confused, she asked, "What's wrong? I hit it. I thought you'd be happy."

"I didn't expect to have to teach my wife how to shoot to protect herself. That's supposed to be my job."

"And you do. This is only for when you're not here. We're a country at war. None of us expected this."

"Yes, well . . ." He took the gun from her. "Tomorrow I'll teach you how to load and clean your weapon." Without another word, he limped away to the barn. Without a doubt, there'd be an extra target in the morning.

THAT NIGHT MARY SAT down and wrote a letter to Miss Caroline Henshaw of Charleston, South Carolina, saying how they'd come across her young man injured at the side of the road. They didn't know who or how or why, but he'd been shot. In his dying breath he asked that they write her and tell her how much he loved her and to return her locket and all the money he had on him. Mary signed it Someone Who Cares. She would give the package to Clay and ask him to post it from another town on his next delivery. It was the least he could do.

CHAPTER 20

VIRGINIA: JUNE 1862

The War did not end quickly, as their loyal Confederate leaders promised, as Ander promised, but dragged on into a darker future. Union blockades led to food shortages. Coffee was replaced by chicory, ground acorns or tree bark, or a combination thereof, each an almost unpalatable substitute for the real thing. Hunger had become as everyday as the sun rising in the morning and setting at night.

Ander wrote as often as he could to let them know he was well. She read his letters over and over, keeping them safe in the box with her few other keepsakes. At least she knew he was alive. Every day in her head she would plan for his homecoming. The favorite foods she would prepare, the hot bath she would draw, allowing him to soak as long as he wanted, the fresh clothes she would lay out and last, the clean sheets and mattress he would sleep on.

"What do you think, Earl?" she asked one night after dinner while he cleaned his gun and she mended yet another pair of socks.

"About what?" he mumbled.

"I can't decide what to make for Ander's first night home. Ham and corn bread, sweet potatoes, stew and biscuits? Real coffee or sweet tea? Both, I think. Or maybe I should let him decide. And should I bake him an apple cake for dessert? Then again, he does love peach pie."

Earl closed his eyes, sighed, then turned to her. "We don't know if he's ever coming home."

"Don't say that!" she snapped. "Don't ever say that again." She worked her needle furiously in and out. "You're wrong. He is coming home."

Earl put his gun away and kissed her on the forehead. "I pray you're right. I'm going to bed. You coming?"

"Shortly."

He turned back to her before closing the bedroom door. "How about we decide when he gets here. Might not be anything more than grits left in the pantry."

She looked up at him and smiled. "I won't be long."

"I'll wait up for you." Earl closed the door with a soft click.

He was right about the food. The soldiers regularly came through. First the Confederates, then the Union, then the Confederates again, and each time they took everything they could find, especially food, but also anything of value they might use, sell, trade, or send home to their wives. They said the soldiers needed these things more than anyone else, needed sustenance to fight. If anyone tried to stop them, tried to hold anything back, they would beat, even kill, them. So, most gave without argument.

Mary insisted Earl bury their few valuables. Her father's books, her mother's silver and good china, disappeared in small caches under the root cellar, the barn, and the floorboards of the house. He hid food, too. Not all of it so as not to raise suspicion, but enough to assure they wouldn't starve. You had to have something to give the soldiers or they'd tear the place apart, take it all, maybe burn your house down.

Earl continued to work at Clay's lumber mill, and for that they were grateful. When Earl was busy, he was less likely to be drinking, but even with work he wasn't always busy.

He never got over the death of the two slave girls, or her being forced to kill the officer. Sometimes he woke in the middle of the night in a cold sweat, fighting as if to save his life. He'd stop, stare at her with blank eyes, then turn his back to face the wall.

"It's all right," she'd say. "I'm here." She didn't tell him the boy's dead eyes haunted her sleep, as well.

Earl and Clay kept their word, though, and there were no more runs. For that Mary felt blessed. She had enough to worry about with Ander.

MARY HANDED SARAH A cup of weak chicory. "Sorry I can't offer you better, but it's all we have." Her hope of making real coffee for Ander was long gone.

"Well, you shouldn't have, but I thank you." Sarah took a sip.

"Have you had any new sewing jobs?" Mary asked, knowing full well no one had the money for new clothes.

Sarah shook her head. "Things are so bad Mrs. Preston's decided to close shop and move to her brother's in New York. She suggested I come with, but I told her I could never leave here with Robert off fighting. How would he find me?"

"I know what you mean. But, the two of us need something to fill our days while we wait for this war to end and our boys to return. I've been giving it a lot of thought, and I know just the thing."

"Oh?"

"Meet me here after breakfast tomorrow."

MARY WALKED WITH SARAH down the long tree-lined drive to the old Hollings Plantation. The Confederate Army had confiscated the abandoned property early in the fighting and turned it into yet another convalescent hospital for the constant flow of wounded. The grounds were no longer manicured. The gardens long overgrown. No crops waited to be harvested, and the slaves' quarters, visible in the distance, were falling down.

Ahead of them was the main house. Paint peeling, windows grimy with dirt and smoke, some shuttered, probably broken, Mary barely recognized it. The lavish rooms would be crowded with the injured and dying, filled with the smell of festering wounds and filthy bodies. Her heart ached to see how this grand home that once buzzed with life now sat crumbling into a slow death.

"You should have seen this place when Old Lady Hollings was alive. All the people, the animals, fields of tobacco rustling in the breeze. And the house! You rode down this lane and in front of you was this big house gleaming white in the sun. In my eyes, it was as grand as any fairy tale castle."

"You must have loved coming here."

"On the contrary, I hated coming here, but my mother made me. She said it was our Christian duty to visit shut-ins. Mrs. Hollings was a mean woman. People in town said that's why God took away all her family, left her alone but for her slaves, as a punishment for being so mean. It's because of her Earl has those scars on his back. She's the one who ordered him whipped, and it was his Uncle Jackson who followed that order. Earl was seventeen and I was fifteen." She sighed and looked around. "It feels like a lifetime ago."

Sarah put her arm around Mary's waist and leaned her head on her shoulder as they continued to walk closer to all those old memories. "Lucas asked me once if I knew the story behind Earl's scars. I said I didn't. We decided not to ask."

"He doesn't like to talk about them. My parents took him in after that and we never visited Mrs. Hollings again. Mother and I nursed Earl's wounds. Father helped get him the job with Clay Lund. You know the rest."

"You and Earl fell in love, got married, and lived happily ever after."

"Oh, I loved Earl long before then. I've loved Earl since the first time I laid eyes on him. I was only twelve at the time, Earl was fourteen, but I knew I'd marry him one day. All those curls, the way his eyes lit up when he smiled, the way he laughed . . ." She trailed off. "He doesn't laugh anymore. Where did that happy young man go, Sarah?"

"These are hard times for all of us. One day this war will be over, our boys will come home to us, get married, and give us grandchildren. Then you'll see that happy smiling young man Earl used to be. He will laugh again someday."

"Promise?"

"Promise."

So many promises made they both knew no one could guarantee, but they needed to believe to survive.

They went up the front walk, stopping at the veranda. The steps were broken.

"Can't go in that way no more, Misses. Gotta go 'round back." A black man with an armload of wood came around the side of the house. "Gotta go 'round back," he said again. "Not safe."

"Yes, I see. Thank you." Mary smiled, nodded, and he rushed off.

They walked around to the double doors that once opened into the dining room but were now the main entrance to the hospital. The room had been converted into a sitting area where sweethearts, sisters, wives, and mothers, desperate for word of a loved one, waited to be granted entrance to the wards. The room was quiet, but Mary suspected that was not always the case. Today only two women, one older and one younger, sat wringing their hands, leaning on each other

"Are you hungry, Mama?" the younger one asked. "There's one biscuit left from last night." She pulled a small napkin-wrapped bundle from her pocket.

"I'm not hungry, dear. You go ahead."

"But you haven't eaten a bite since yesterday." The girl tried to put it in her mother's hands. "Well, all right," she said when her mother refused it again. "I'll save it for later." She slipped it back into her pocket.

A nurse approached carrying a small bundle in her hands. The women stood, tentative, fearful.

"Mrs. Huston," the nurse said in a flat and not so quiet voice. "I'm afraid your son was with us, but he passed away from his injuries a couple weeks back. He had these few belongings with him." She held the bundle out to the sobbing woman. "I'm sorry for your loss." When the mother didn't take it, the nurse handed it to the sister, then turned and walked back into the ward without another word.

Mary stopped them as the two walked slowly toward the doors. "I couldn't help but overhear. I'm terribly sorry for your loss."

"Thank you," the young one said.

"Would you like a drink of water?" Sarah asked. "I'm certain I can find a cup somewhere." She scanned the room for a pitcher, bucket, anything.

"No, thank you, ma'am. We got what we came for. At least we now know. We'll be headed home to Kentucky to tell the others."

Kentucky. They'd traveled so far. How many hospitals had they visited, only to be turned away in the end?

The older woman took the bundle from the younger and held it tightly to her chest. She looked up and stopped crying long enough to ask, "You here looking for your boy?"

"No," Mary said. "We just came to offer a helping hand."

She nodded. "God bless you both." They left.

How many times had the same scene played out in that room? How many times had a mother come looking for her son only to be sent away with a small bundle of his meager last effects?

The nurse returned and looked about, relieved. "Oh, good, they're gone," she said.

"You could have shown a little more compassion." Mary's voice was harsh, even to her own ears. The woman stared back at her with blank eyes. "Their loved one died, and you said it like you were telling them you were all out of bread, come back tomorrow."

"You don't understand how many times a day we have to do this. Tell them their boy is dead or dying, or we don't have their husband here and send them away after they've already been sent away by a dozen other hospitals. After a while there's just no compassion left, only work."

There were no words to respond.

"If there's nothing else you ladies need from me, I have work to do."

Sarah stepped forward. "That's why we're here. We want to help."

They were put to work that afternoon. Sarah was assigned to the never-ending laundry. They led her back outside where bedding boiled in great kettles over roaring fires. Row upon row of hopelessly gray sheets hung to dry. Some had been washed so many times you could see through.

It was Mary's job to go from bed to bed and help the men any way she could. Some wanted to be read to, others wanted to dictate letters, some just wanted to talk. She listened to stories of wives and babies left behind, sometimes knowing that man wasn't going to live long enough to go home. But they always talked as if they were going home tomorrow. She held their hands when they told her about their mama's apple fritters or their sweetheart's award-winning cornbread recipe. They'd tell her about their dogs and their best friends. If they carried a trinket, a picture or a lock of hair, they always showed it to her before putting it safely back in a pocket or under their pillow. Every night she walked home with a prayer on her lips and a tear in her eye for those that had died that day.

"Tell me about the young man from Tennessee," Sarah said on their way home. Sometimes it was the Captain from Kentucky, or the young drummer from Carolina who should have stayed in school but lied about his age to run away and enlist. There was always someone on Mary's mind, and Sarah never failed to ask so she wouldn't have to carry the burden alone.

"They had to take his leg today. I had to help hold him down while the surgeon cut."

"Oh, Mary." Sarah stopped. She turned to block Mary so she was forced to look at her. "How awful for you. Are you all right?"

"I'll be fine. Jeb died. I get to go home to my husband. Jeb's young wife will only have a letter and the small bundle of his belongings I put together for his friend to take to her. We gave him whiskey to dull the pain. I put a stick in his mouth to bite down on. I prayed aloud to distract him and give him peace, but it wasn't enough. He screamed until he passed out, and then he died. The surgeon said sometimes it happens that way. The heart just gives up under the shock."

"I don't know where you find the strength to do this. How you are able to watch these young men suffer, die such slow agonizing deaths, and yet keep a smile on your face and the confidence of God's love in your heart." Sarah turned and they continued walking. "I'm happy to be in the laundry. I can handle the smells and the heat, but I could never sit with a young man and listen to him call out for his mother as he lay dying. Knowing that could be my Robert in another hospital somewhere. Knowing that could be your Ander."

"It's that confidence in God's love that gives me the strength. That and knowing I have a friend who will walk with me, who I know will never let me bear these troubles and sorrows alone."

They linked arms and walked home in silence.

THAT NIGHT, MARY SAT in the dark and relived Captain Jeb Walker's screams, the sound of the surgeon's blade as it cut through soft rotting tissue and then healthy hard bone. Her shoulders ached from holding him down as he thrashed and pulled against his restraints. She smelled the putrid flesh of his wound and then the fetid rank of his bowels letting loose when he stopped moving and the room grew quiet.

CHAPTER 21

VIRGINIA: AUGUST 1863

They hadn't heard from Ander in months. Mary knew this wasn't unusual, but a sense of dread hung over her. Sarah hadn't heard from Robert, either, and they both prayed long and hard before they slept each night.

During the day they kept busy at the hospital. The stream of injured and dying never ended. There weren't enough beds so many were forced to sleep on the floor. Luckily, there were plenty of rooms to at least keep them indoors and dry.

The wives and mothers and sisters who came to ask about their loved ones were also unending. They crowded the reception area. The wails of the bereaved mixed with the cries of the injured in the wards until Mary had to sneak off and hide in one of the old slave shacks to find some peace.

That's where Sarah found her one day, seated on a ragged abandoned mattress, staring down at her hands. Not even the rat chewing on an old blanket in the corner bothered her.

"The matron saw you leave. She sent me to say we can go home for the night."

"There are so many of them. Sometimes I wonder if we're any help at all." Mary looked up at her.

"I know. We can hardly keep up with the laundry." Sarah picked up a broken table leg and used it to kill the rat and push its body out the front door. "Come on. Let's go home." She tossed the table leg aside and reached out her hand.

"I had to give at least a dozen mothers their son's personal belongings today. Then there were those men who left nothing behind. No trinket to remember them by."

The rat's brother joined them, scratching and gnawing at a wooden crate, heedless of their presence. Mary didn't want to think what he might smell in it after all these years.

"Do you know what kind of sound comes from a woman when they hear their son has died?"

Sarah shook her head.

"I do."

They stepped into the fading sunlight. The clouds were as fluffy as cotton. The evening bird songs filled her heart with hope. The late summer heat would have been stifling, if not for the light breeze.

"It's other-worldly, Sarah, almost frightening in the way it makes you feel their pain. Not merely their sadness but actual pain."

They strolled down the front drive, away from the death and chaos that engulfed the once grand mansion.

"I got a letter from Robert yesterday," Sarah said after a long silence.

Mary grabbed her hands. "Did he say anything about Ander?"

"No. It was short. All he said was he was injured at Gettysburg and has been in a Pennsylvania hospital ever since. He didn't even say what those injuries were but hopes to be home soon. It was dated two weeks ago."

She pulled the letter from her pocket. Mary scanned it for the slightest hint about Ander.

"I've read it so many times the creases have begun to come apart."

Mary folded it gently and handed it back to her. "I'm so happy for you, Sarah, truly. We'll plan a celebration for when Robert gets home. Hopefully, then he can tell us about Ander."

Sarah nodded and slipped the paper back into her pocket. "I was almost afraid to tell you about it," she admitted.

"Why?"

"It just seems so unfair for me to be happy when you're still afraid."

"Nonsense." Mary hugged her. "Your happiness is our happiness, and I know that soon we'll be celebrating Ander's return, as well. Then we can look forward to having those grandchildren we like to talk about so much."

"And life will go back to normal again," Sarah said.

"How wonderful that will be." They finished their walk home laughing and planning their future as grandmothers in a world where brothers no longer fought brothers, and where there was no more talk of secession. There would be plenty of food to eat and no need to sleep with a loaded gun within reach.

A WEEK LATER, MARY was hoeing her garden on a hot, cloudless afternoon when Sarah's wagon pulled into the yard. Next to her sat a scruffy looking young man Mary would know anywhere.

"Earl, they're here! Sarah and Robert are here!" She dropped her hoe and ran for the wagon. Boone was close behind, eager to greet his old friend.

Earl poked his head out the barn doors. He broke into a run when he saw it was true. "Welcome home, son." He grabbed Robert's hand and shook it heartily.

"Thank you, sir."

Mary crowded Earl out of the way. "Tell us. What do you hear of Ander? Is he well? Will he be home soon, too?" she asked, one question tumbling over another.

"Mary!" Earl laughed. "Give the boy a minute, and I'm sure he'll tell us."

"Will Ander be home soon, too?"

Why wasn't he answering her?

Sarah choked back a sob. It was then Mary saw her friend had been crying, and on Robert's lap sat a bundle.

"No! No! No! No!" The cry that rose from deep in her center and filled her throat was a pain she never imagined possible. It was the sound she'd heard so many times before, except now it was coming from her.

"I'm so sorry, Mrs. Bishop." Robert's voice caught as he tried to hand her the bundle.

She backed into Earl's arms. If she accepted Ander's personal belongings it would be final. He would be dead. But if she didn't take them, it was not true.

She stumbled and Earl caught her. She turned to him and he held her close. He dropped to his knees with her clasped tight in his arms. Boone whimpered. He licked her face, drank her tears, and howled out his own grief. She pulled him in and kissed him, their valiant hero who once saved Ander was powerless to save him a second time.

Sarah rushed to their side, but Robert remained seated, his head hung, chin to chest. His shoulders shook. Ander was his best friend. The two of them had gone off together with big plans to change the world, a belief in a better system, but only one returned, and the world was not a better place.

Mary accepted Ander's belongings. "Thank you," she whispered. "Were you with him?"

Robert nodded. She was numb while he told her about Ander's final moments, about his death on a battlefield in Gettysburg, Pennsylvania. She was grateful to hear this news from someone who cared about their son, not a stranger. She was relieved to learn that Ander died quickly, with little pain and a friend to hold his hand.

Robert handed her a letter. It was addressed to them in their son's fine penmanship.

Ander's pack clutched to her chest, close to her heart, and his final letter home held tight in her hand, she turned to Earl.

"Ander's dead."

Earl nodded.

There, she said it. It was real.

"He's not coming home."

"No."

The world closed in around her and everything went black.

CHAPTER 22

VIRGINIA: MAY 1866

The War ended as it began—one day it was there, the next gone. Mary and Earl lived each day in a fog of silent grief and pain.

The entire country was relieved but nothing was won. Not for anyone. Especially not the South. For them everything was lost. Their animals, their food, their husbands, sons, and brothers, all gone. Union soldiers roamed back roads looking for stragglers who still held out for the Confederacy. Men in fancy big-city suits rode in carrying their carpet bags, hoping to make a profit off grief-burdened backs.

Many of those who survived the fighting, the illnesses, the starvation that claimed untold numbers, packed up their meager belongings and left. They went far from the stripped fields, the burnt buildings, and the rows and rows of fresh graves. All the bleak reminders.

The slaves were worse off than any of them. Even though they were freed men and could go out into the world to make something of themselves, no one told them where to go, what to do, or how to be on their own. Some headed north, believing the promises of their Great Emancipator, believing a wonderful future lay ahead. Others headed west, knowing any fortune would have to be earned by their own hands. Still others stood and stared at the bearers of what was supposed to be welcomed news, frozen by uncertainty.

"We'll be all right," Earl assured her. "I still have a job. People are going to be needing wood to rebuild."

What they soon learned was no one had the money to pay for the wood. Earl came home earlier and earlier every day. Then that, too, was gone.

"Clay sold the mill to some Englishman." He dropped into the closest chair, then got up again to pace the floor. "Clay's going west to Oregon, where there are so many trees you couldn't cut them all down in ten lifetimes."

Mary wiped her hands on her apron. "Couldn't you work for this new man? He's going to need someone who knows how to run a lumber mill."

"Oh, that he will," Earl nodded. "But I'm not working for some dandy, and that's what he is. A dandy. He comes strutting in wearing his shiny shoes and a strange little round hat, carrying a walking stick. Not a cane, mind you, but a walking stick. He said he wanted to help 'rebuild our noble little country.'"

Earl mimicked the Englishman's mannerisms, making her laugh.

"What he wants to build is his own pocketbook. He's just looking to make a quick dollar. He doesn't know the first thing about cutting down a tree or sawing it into boards. He's going to get himself killed, and I'm not going to be a part of it. Although, I admit it might be fun to watch."

"Don't say that. There's been too much death already."

Earl teared up as he gazed at their children's picture on the mantel. He reached out as if to touch it but dropped his hand away at the last moment. "Yes, there has."

"So now what do we do?" Her voice cracked, sounding small and hollow. "Is there anyone else who might hire you?"

"No. There's no one left. Everyone's dead or gone. Anyone of any worth, that is. Clay's right. We have to leave."

"Oregon?" She panicked. "We don't have to go as far as Oregon, do we?"

"Not Oregon, but what would you think of Wisconsin?" He faced her, smiling.

"I don't know. I never thought about it. What would we do in Wisconsin that we can't do here? Besides, Wisconsin fought for the Union. What makes you think they'll even want us there?"

"They won't have any choice. We're all supposed to be one country again."

"They can't send us away, but they don't have to like us. At least here we know people. They're our people."

"Look around you." He pulled her close and pressed his cheek against the top of her head. "Our people are all gone. Your family . . . gone. This isn't our home anymore. Not the way we remember it. And it never will be again."

She tried to hold back the tears but failed. Earl was right. Everyone was dead or presumed dead. Lucy first. Her parents passed before the fighting even began, but her brothers, her nephews, even Ander, gone to the cause. George's wife Mae died in childbirth back in '62. It was thought they would finally have the family they so desired, but God saw fit to take Mae and their angelic little son straight to his side. Harlan's Isabel remarried soon after his death, to a Union officer no less, and took Harlan's youngest and still unmarried daughter Elizabeth with when she moved north to Boston to live in his family's home.

Even Sarah was gone. After Robert and Amy Lynn married, they all went north to St. Paul looking for work. Mary cried for days after they left. The familiar faces were gone. Only strangers walked in their place. And ghosts, so many ghosts she sometimes feared to close her eyes at night. They haunted her every dream.

"What would we do in Wisconsin?" she asked.

"I can easily find work with a lumber mill. Northern Wisconsin's covered in trees."

Mary took a handkerchief from her pocket, blew her nose, and nodded.

"All right, then?" he asked. "Wisconsin?"

"Wisconsin."

It didn't take them long to pack their few belongings. They managed to sell their house and land to the Englishman who bought the mill. He called it quaint and then started talking about how easy it would be to expand and build himself a truly grand house worthy of a man of commerce. Earl was right. That man didn't know the first thing about operating a lumber mill and would be lucky to survive long enough to draw up the plans on his grand new home.

They left early in the morning when even the birds were barely awake. They had many miles to cover, and the only people they wanted to stop and say goodbye to were buried in the local cemetery.

Earl followed as Mary silently walked from stone to stone, stopping briefly to touch each one, closing her eyes to see a face, hear a laugh. She remembered the way her brothers glared at Earl when they emerged from the woods ruffled, blushing, her hair full of grass the day before their wedding. She remembered when George broke down, fell to his knees, at Mae's grave the day they buried her with tiny Geoffrey Alan in her arms. They didn't see much of him after that. He kept to himself. Then one day he up and joined the Confederate Army. Harlan, ever the true brother and friend, went with him.

Then there was Ander, her sweet boy. George and Harlan and Ander died on the battlefield and were buried there with all the others. For them there was only a memorial to visit. Ander's was a small, simple stone to match his sister's and placed at her side.

On his other side rested Boone. He never overcame his grief for his master and slowly faded away. They had a special stone carved just for him. *Here lies Boone, loyal friend and companion to Ander.* She stood in front of those three stones the longest. Ander was there in spirit to keep his sister warm, and Boone to protect them both.

Earl slid his arms around Mary and looked over her shoulder at the small stones. There were no more tears, only acceptance of what once was and now would never be again.

"It's time," he whispered in her ear.

She nodded. "I know."

Mary glanced back at the wagon bed. "They're safe? You remembered to pack it, didn't you?"

Earl retrieved her box of treasures and laid it in her arms, squeezing her hand and smiling. "The safest place they could be." He helped her up to her seat. They rode out of town as the first of their few remaining neighbors came out their doors to face the new day.

CHAPTER 23

WISCONSIN: DECEMBER 1880

The days following Earl's death dragged into weeks. Weeks of sameness. Weeks of silence. Mary started and ended each day with the animals. She learned to ignore Earl's presence, his spectral eyes following her, watching her every move, from the end of that rope. In between, she slept or sat and stared into the fire, trying to push down her pain and anger. She didn't want to hate him but sometimes she did. Sometimes she hated him with a heat greater than the fire before her. She couldn't understand why he chose to leave her alone in that way.

Why hadn't he been stronger?

How many times had she asked herself that very question over the years? "Every time you succumbed to the temptation of drink," she answered aloud to his ghost.

The day the Reverend's wife, Frances Clark, paid her promised call, the weather had given them a brief reprieve from the bitter winds that had blown steady since the day of Earl's funeral, making the day almost spring-like in comparison.

Mary was returning from the barn with a basket full of eggs when Frances' buggy pulled up to the front door. "Good morning, Mrs. Clark."

"Good morning, Mrs. Bishop." She stepped down and took Mary's hand, holding it between both of hers. "I was so sorry to hear about your husband's . . ." She hesitated, clearly searching for the appropriate word. ". . . passing." Not suicide, not death. Frances Clark chose the gentler, almost pleasant, passing, to describe Earl's betrayal.

"Thank you." Mary gave the socially accepted response. The Reverend's new wife was young, at least fifteen years his junior. She was no more than twenty-five years old by Mary's estimation. "I see you're feeling better," Mary said, eager to change the subject. "The Reverend said you've been under the weather."

"Yes, thank you, much better."

The two women stared at each other in silence. Each at a loss for what to say next.

Frances' eyes lit up. "I almost forgot." She retrieved a blanket-wrapped bundle from the seat. "I brought cake," she said, producing a napkin-covered plate from under the blanket and holding it out proudly. Mary remembered she still had Frances' plate from the funeral, embarrassed that in her grief she had neglected to return it with words of proper appreciation.

"It looks delicious. Come in. I happen to have a fresh pot of coffee on the stove. I'll put these eggs in the kitchen and bring us each a cup." Mary set the cake on the parlor table and took Frances' coat. "Please, have a seat by the fire, Mrs. Clark, and I'll be right back."

"Call me Frances. Such formalities seem foolish, especially when it's only the two of us. May I call you Mary?"

"Yes, of course." It had been a long time since Mary sat and exchanged pleasantries with another woman, and it felt awkward to her. *A couple of hens clucking*, as Earl always said. Not since Irma Polk had Mary had a proper friend with whom she could sit and pass the time.

"You have a lovely home, Mary. Such a cozy room, perfect size to tuck in for the winter."

Mary placed a tray of coffee next to the cake while Frances looked over the many books shelved against the back wall.

"I don't think I've ever seen so many books in one place, outside my husband's study, that is."

"Most of them belonged to Father, but some of them are mine," Mary explained.

"I understand your father was a minister."

"Yes."

"Have you read all of them?"

"More than once. I must confess, I like Shakespeare best." Mary ran an index finger down a worn leather spine.

"Oh, I envy you. I never could understand what he was trying to say with all those odd old-fashioned words. Nonetheless, they are beautiful words. My strong subject was mathematics. I love numbers. Numbers make sense to me. I think they must be as beautiful to me as Shakespeare is to you."

Mary had never heard it expressed that way before. "I think you're probably right."

They sat in front of the fire. Mary poured the coffee and handed a cup to Frances.

"Thank you."

"How are you settling in?" Mary made an attempt at small talk. "Is it very different here from your home?"

"Actually, it's much the same," Frances replied between sips.

"Then you're adjusting to your new life, as a minister's wife."

"Yes. I think I'm getting along quite well." Frances blushed.

She's so young. Mary could hardly remember when talk of being a new wife made her blush.

Had it ever?

Being married to Earl, sharing his bed, had always felt so natural. From the day they first met, it was like they'd known each other forever.

"And you're keeping busy?" she asked.

Frances set down her cup. "Yes. I've been helping Mr. Polk with his store accounts. I understand his wife used to do his books before she fell ill. He's been doing them ever since, but doesn't much enjoy it."

"I think Irma was a lot like you when it came to numbers."

"So, you knew Mrs. Polk?"

"She was my dear friend. The two of us used to go fishing. We'd take a picnic lunch and make a day of it. She loved to fish but couldn't bring herself to touch them. I had to take them off the hook and clean them for her." Mary smiled, remembering how Irma would laugh and squeal as the fish flopped on the end of her line, then look away with a grimace when Mary slit them open and scooped out their insides. "I miss her," she sighed.

"I wish I'd had the chance to know her, but enough about me. How are you getting along, Mary?"

Mary gazed deep into the flames, away from Frances' eager face. There were no words to describe how she felt.

Frances reached out and touched Mary's hand. "Yes, well, perhaps time will make things easier."

"Perhaps," Mary said, but didn't believe it possible.

They finished their cake in silence. Frances fidgeted with her napkin and occasionally glanced toward the door, clearly uncomfortable with the lack of conversation.

Mary, on the other hand, preferred the quiet. She could almost make herself believe it was Earl sitting with her on that cold winter day instead of a young woman struggling for something to say. She could sit with Earl for hours, neither one speaking. They'd read, or contemplate the day, and be perfectly content.

"I suppose I should get back home." Frances set her cup and plate on the tray. "Would you like me to take this into the kitchen for you?"

"Thank you, but I can get it." Mary picked up the tray. Frances followed behind, still talking.

"I hope you don't mind if I stop by again sometime, and you're welcome to stop at the parsonage any time."

Mary moved a couple slices of cake to one of her own plates and handed the remainder back to Frances. "For your husband." She retrieved Frances' other plate from a shelf. "And I apologize for not getting this one back to you sooner. I hope it wasn't an inconvenience. I just wasn't much in the mood for a trip to town."

"I completely understand, and it was no inconvenience at all."

Mary helped Frances with her coat. Once settled in her buggy, she held out a hand. "I heard about your troubles, how the townspeople treated you and your husband. I don't blame you for staying away." She squeezed Mary's hand. "Shameful."

Mary cut her off, unwilling to have that discussion. "Yes, well, you'd better be on your way."

"Good-bye, Mary. I hope to have the chance to visit with you again soon." Frances snapped the reins, turned the horse around, then abruptly stopped. "I almost forgot. Mr. Polk asked me to give you his regards and remind you to feel free to call on him any time you need help."

Mary waved as Frances took the bend in the road leading back to town. Only after she disappeared did Mary return to her quiet parlor and pull a volume of Shakespeare's sonnets from the shelf. The leather was cool against the palm of her hand. She opened to the inscription and read: *To my eternal summer, Love, Earl.*

CHAPTER 24

WISCONSIN: CHRISTMAS Eve 1880

Without Earl to share the season, Mary wanted to skip everything Christmas. She prayed to fall asleep the night of the twenty-third and not wake until the morning of the twenty-sixth. She didn't want to think about all the celebrations being planned in the houses in town. Didn't want to be reminded of all she had lost and how little she had to celebrate. But as the days led up to Christmas, like Dickens' ghosts of Christmas past, those dreaded memories came to her in flashes.

"Remember what Christmas was like before?" she asked. Earl's presence was never far away, and she often found herself talking to him as if he was still alive and sitting next to her. All she had to do was close her eyes to feel him, smell him, almost touch him. "Remember what things were like with Mother and Father, George, Harlan, and Lucy? Ander?" Mary closed her eyes and let the memories wash over her, embracing the pain along with the joy.

Growing up, Christmas always began with church, but it didn't truly start for her and her brothers and sister until Mother's Christmas feast was laid before them in the afternoon. The whole house smelled like heaven, and the memory still made her mouth water. There would be a turkey roasted to a crispy brown, golden yams swimming in butter, carrots baked in a honey glaze, fruit compote, and sweets the likes of which they never saw any other time of year.

After dinner, their bellies nearly bursting, they'd take turns being blindfolded and see who they could capture first. No one ever captured her, and she laughed now at the thought. Not a tap of the foot or a creaking floorboard betrayed her position, nor did she give into the temptation to giggle, like Lucy, when their brothers' hands came a little too close. Then their parents would join them for a game of charades. Mother was the best at that one.

No one could pantomime a bible story the way she could. Mary still missed her and it made her heart ache.

After games, they would receive their gift. Lucy would get a length of cloth for a new dress, or a delicate piece of lace to replace an old tattered collar. Mary, once she outgrew her dolls, received a book. She remembered her joy the year it was a collection of colored drawings of the flowers of North America, many recognizable from the surrounding fields and forest. The book, its binding crumbling from use, held a prominent position on her shelves.

As the sun set to end the day and their eyes grew heavy, Father would read once more the story of the Lord's birth while they sat in front of the fire and sipped hot cider. Christmas always began and ended with a reminder of the true reason for the holiday.

Mary continued those same traditions after her marriage to Earl and the birth of their son, adding some of their own as the years went by. There were the candy sticks Earl handed out to all the children after the service. Although much smaller, and the decorations not near as grand, there was the tree with its beautiful candles and decorations modeled after the illustration of Queen Victoria and Prince Albert with their children. Ander spent hours searching the woods for anything he could fashion into an ornament. A pinecone or an abandoned bird's nest, long lengths of ivy to drape around the branches, clusters of berries to tie to the ends, anything to brighten their holiday found its way onto the family tree.

The pain of loneliness washed over her once more, and her tears left fresh hot trails down her cheeks. She was alone, she reminded herself.

Mary wiped her eyes. She could see no reason for a feast only she would eat, and no reason for a tree only she would gaze upon. Still, there were the children. She knew Earl's candy sticks were the only Christmas treat some of them received, and she couldn't bear to disappoint. The children played no role in their parents' behavior. They didn't strip Earl of his dignity one little piece at a time. They were innocents. She would go into town and buy not one but two candy sticks for each child. Then she would attend service Christmas morning and, afterward, hand out the candy with her head held high. She'd be damned if she'd let them drag her down, too.

Mary gathered a basket of eggs, setting aside a few for her breakfast. She wrapped some fresh-churned butter in cheesecloth and prepared to go into town.

People on the street stopped and stared, while others stole side-long glances when she drove by, no doubt thinking she wouldn't notice, and they wouldn't appear openly rude. Mary tethered Sophie and Max in front of the mercantile, took a deep breath, and walked in as if she had every right to be there, which she did. She walked up to the counter, ignoring Miss Booker and Miss Webster when they whispered to each other over a bolt of blue satin.

"Good afternoon, Mr. Polk. How are you today?" Mary greeted her friend, placing the basket of eggs and butter between them. She spoke loud enough so the two young eavesdroppers heard every word. She wasn't going to let them think she was ashamed or intimidated by them. She was neither.

"Good afternoon, Mrs. Bishop. I'm doing well. You?" He leaned forward. His brows knitted in concern.

Mary changed the subject, afraid of tears if she voiced her grief. "And how are your lovely daughter and her family doing out in South Dakota? Have you heard from her lately?"

He straightened, shoulders back, and grinned. "I got a letter from Emma Rose just the other day."

Mary knew he loved to talk about his daughter, son-in-law, and grandchildren. Who could blame him?

"She tells me my grandchildren are growing fast as prairie grass after a summer rain. They hope to come for a visit in the summer."

"How wonderful for you. It's been a long time since they were last here. I know how you miss them."

He nodded. "I do miss having them closer. Now, what can I do for you today?" He uncovered her basket and inspected the contents. "Very nice." He held an egg up to the light. "Very nice, indeed." He smelled the butter and smiled.

"I've come for candy sticks, Mr. Polk."

"I was hoping you would say that. How many do you want?"

Mary studied the jar of red and white striped sweets on the counter behind him. "I'll take them all," she decided with a nod. "That is, if you can spare them."

"I can. The children are going to be so happy." He carefully placed them in a sack so they wouldn't break. "I know how they look forward to the treat each year and I was afraid maybe now . . ."

Mary interrupted, hoping to ease his discomfort. "While I'm here, I also need some coffee and sugar."

"Of course."

Mary opened her reticule. "And I'd like to settle our account."

"One moment, Mrs. Bishop." Mr. Polk frowned and glanced over her shoulder.

Mary followed his gaze. Miss Booker and Miss Webster had inched a little closer. No doubt so as not to miss a single word.

"Is there anything I can do for you ladies this afternoon?" he asked. "Any last-minute holiday purchases perhaps?"

The two looked at each other, and then at Mary.

Miss Booker gave her friend a side-long glance. The girl's cheeks were a little brighter than they had been before being caught eavesdropping. Miss Webster shifted from one foot to the other and fiddled with a button on her glove.

"You know, Mr. Polk, I think I'm all set with my Christmas gifts, but thank you so much for asking," Miss Booker responded.

"Good day and Merry Christmas," they said in unison, hurrying out into the street, letting the door slam behind them.

He shook his head. "Now that we're alone, we can drop all the formalities and get back to the matter at hand. Mary, your account is paid in full. Earl came in the week before . . ." he hesitated, then his face lit up. "That reminds me." He hurried to the back room and returned with a wrapped parcel. "He also ordered this. He gave me a letter to put inside and asked that I wrap it for you when it arrived. I was planning on delivering it after I locked up this afternoon, if you didn't stop in before."

At a loss for words, Mary eased the package from his hands.

He leaned forward and said, with a slight shake of his head, "You needn't worry. I didn't read the letter. It's all sealed and tucked safe inside."

"Thank you, Oliver," Mary gently set the unexpected gift from Earl on the counter with her coffee, sugar, and candy sticks. "How much do I owe you for today?"

"Not a penny. Your fine eggs and exceptional butter more than cover the cost."

"Surely not!" she gasped. "They can't possibly."

"Oh, yes," he assured her. "Eggs and butter of this quality are in high demand with all the holiday baking. I'll see the balance is placed as a credit on your account."

She didn't know what else to say, so she thanked him again as he arranged her packages in her empty basket.

"And, let me say once more how sorry I am for everything that happened. I know what you're going through. When Irma passed . . ." He let out a long breath before continuing. "If there's anything you need, any way at all I can help, just let me know."

Mary held up a hand to stop him. It had been five years since Irma's death, but the loss of her friend was as keen as if it was yesterday. "You've never been anything but kind to us, Oliver. I know Earl counted you as his closest and dearest friend."

"And I, him."

Mary was struck by the softness in his eyes, the true compassion, and was reluctant to return to her empty house. She forced herself to leave the store and go back out into the cold. The bell over the door rang a sad good-bye behind her. She was barely out the door when someone called out.

"Mary! Mrs. Bishop!"

"Hello, Frances." Mary set her basket in the wagon and climbed onto the seat.

"I was on my way home for a cup of Christmas tea. The Reverend and I would be so pleased if you would join us."

"Thank you, but I need to get home. Perhaps another time."

"Well, then, can we at least expect to see you at service tomorrow?"

"I'll be there." Mary directed the team back onto the road.

"And one other thing."

Mary stopped the horses.

"Can I convince you to join us for Christmas dinner after? It's nothing fancy, but I'm told I'm a very good plain cook. It would only be the three of us."

There was nothing Mary could do but accept the invitation. Frances was well-intentioned, if not a little over enthusiastic, in her attempts to help. "I'd like that. Thank you."

"Wonderful! We'll see you tomorrow, then. Good afternoon, Mary." Frances turned with a wave and was gone.

AFTER UNHITCHING THE wagon and feeding the horses, starting a fire and putting a kettle on to boil, Mary sat and stared at Earl's package on the kitchen table. She could no longer put off opening it. Her hands shook as she untied the string, easing back the brown paper, flattening it as she went, until she revealed the book within. *Walden* by Henry David Thoreau.

Earl's letter was tucked inside the front cover. Heart racing, and light-headed, she broke the seal.

My Dearest Mary:

> *I have always felt bad for what happened to your father's copy of Walden all those years ago. I know how much you treasured it and should have been more careful that afternoon by the river. I know you said you forgave me but it always was one of your favorites and I see how you still stop and sigh as you reach for it on the shelf only to discover, once more, it is gone. And I see the pain on your face, even fleeting, that says you feel the loss all over again.*
>
> *You, my dear wife, have always been the one shining star, the one unchanging light, in my life. I'm sorry for the pain you are feeling this Christmas because of me and want you to know I loved you from the moment I first saw you lying in the grass on a hot Virginia summer afternoon watching the bees in the clover. Love, Earl*

So, he'd known even then what he planned to do and would not be there to give her the gift himself. He knew he would leave her alone this Christmas, and every Christmas to come. She held the book close.

Her grief, once held in check, burst free. Shoulders shaking, she wailed like a wounded animal until there was nothing left. After which, she sat empty, hollow, as the shadows crept across the floor. In time, she forced herself to get up and finish her day.

CHAPTER 25

WISCONSIN: CHRISTMAS Day 1880

Mary woke early Christmas morning, a sick knot in her stomach. It would be so easy to stay home, hide herself from everyone, but that would be the wrong thing to do. She had to go to town, make her presence seen at the church. Not merely for the children, who were accustomed to receiving their sweets after, but for herself. She couldn't let their parents do to her what they had done to Earl. She couldn't let them drive her to despair, make her hide as if she'd done something wrong when she hadn't.

They had been no different than thousands of others living in the south before the War. Their lives centered on an institution which, right or wrong, had been in existence since biblical times. Slavery. People did what little they could. Some, like Earl, did more than others to fight against it, but more often than not people turned their heads and looked the other way. There was little else they could do when the laws, and those who wrote them, held all the power. Now things could be different, but only if people allowed themselves to look forward rather than back.

Mary smoothed the skirt of her best dress, pinned her best hat in place, and checked her appearance in the mirror. Though graying at the temples, her hair still had that auburn shine her mother loved so much.

Remembering her promise to eat Christmas dinner with the Reverend and Frances, and not wanting to arrive empty-handed, Mary chose three jars of jam from her pantry—wild plum, raspberry, and blueberry—to offer as a gift. She placed them in a basket, then wrapped the basket in an old horse blanket to protect the jam from the cold during the service. She placed her Bible and the bag of candy sticks in the basket of jams on the seat next to her, took a deep breath to bolster her courage, and snapped the reins.

SHE HEARD THE CHURCH bells calling the faithful to worship even before she reached the first little houses on the edge of town. The cold morning air carried the pure, joyful sound up out of the valley to the hilltops and into the clear blue sky where it mixed with the threads of white clouds. It was as if the angels were singing, heralding the birth of the Savior. Their song filled her with hope.

Based on the number of wagons and buggies parked outside the church, she was the last to arrive. Mary stopped inside the door and scanned the crowded room for a place to sit. All those who didn't feel the need to attend any other Sunday of the year were certain to be there that morning, so she wasn't surprised the only open spot was in the very front pew.

Heads turned and a buzz spread through the crowd. Miss Booker and Miss Webster, together as always, leaned in to whisper and giggle. Perhaps it was time for another sermon on the evils of gossip. Mary would have to remember to recommend it to Reverend Clark. Though she doubted it would make a difference.

"Merry Christmas, girls." Mary greeted them as she passed. The two fell silent.

Frances smiled from her place across the aisle. Mary nodded in return. She shook as she struggled to remove her gloves. A man's hand reached over and squeezed hers. It was only then Mary noticed Oliver Polk seated next to her.

"Merry Christmas," he whispered and withdrew his hand.

"Merry Christmas." Mary returned his smile as they rose to sing the opening hymn.

THE LAST HYMN FILLED the little church with a resounding note of praise and promise. Mary looked up to the rafters and wiped a tear. Oh, how Earl loved to sing. She could still hear his off-tune voice rise above all others. When did all that promise of hope and salvation leave him? The darkness had overtaken him so gradually Mary couldn't name any one thing that had changed his heart. In time, there was just so much darkness he could no longer find the light.

Reverend Clark stepped down from his place behind the pulpit. He stopped, as was his practice, to offer a hand to his wife so they might proceed together to greet their departing parishioners. Then he surprised Mary by turning to her next.

"Would you like to join us, Mrs. Bishop? I see you have brought a little something for the children." Cries of excitement, mixed with some clapping, erupted from the younger congregants only to be abruptly halted by their parents. Mary stood and followed Reverend and Frances Clark down the aisle to wait at the front door.

Eager children held out their hand as they passed. They squealed with delight when she surprised them with two candy sticks, rather than the usual one. Each said a polite *Thank you, Mrs. Bishop*, or *Merry Christmas, Mrs. Bishop*, before being hurried out the door. Children didn't care about such things as North or South, Yankee or Confederate. They were pure souls filled with the joy of the season.

But from their parents Mary received only stares and the occasional muttered, *Rebel! Slaver! Traitor!* It wasn't always possible to determine who the offender was, but it didn't matter. Mary chose to ignore them for the sake of their children.

Oliver Polk was the last to leave the church. "You're a good woman, Mary Bishop." He took her hand in both of his. "You've made the children very happy. Merry Christmas!"

"Merry Christmas, Mr. Polk. Candy stick? I have more than enough."

"Thank you. I believe I will." Oliver let go of her hand after one last gentle squeeze, popped a candy stick into his mouth, pulled his collar up against the cold, and headed for home.

"She has some nerve," Maud Henry said to her friend, Gladys Olson, as Mary passed them in the churchyard. The two were co-owners of the town's seamstress and millinery shop. Neither of the women had ever been a friend of the Bishops. But after they had learned Ander died fighting for the Confederates, while their sons died for the Union, they became outspoken enemies.

"You'd think she'd have gotten the message," Gladys responded.

Agnes Schmidt joined the two. "What message?" she asked.

"Should have hung herself right next to that slaver husband of hers," added Maud. Gladys and Agnes nodded.

Mary gasped and the Reverend spun around to face them. "Ladies! I believe your husbands are waiting for you. I suggest you go home and celebrate with them, remembering the reason for this happy morning."

The three women scattered like grouse flushed by the hunter's bird dog. "Merry Christmas, Reverend," Agnes said as she scurried off.

Mary was shaken by the virulent nature of their comments. It wasn't the first time she'd been called ugly names, or faced such hatred, but the thought that her own neighbors, friends or not, wished her dead, was more than she could bear.

Frances put her arm around Mary. "Pay them no mind. Come and feast with us. Let's celebrate our Lord's birth with joy and forget all that nonsense."

"I think I'll go home after all," Mary whispered, pulling herself up to the wagon seat.

"Don't go," Frances pleaded. "Don't give them the satisfaction of chasing you out of town."

Mary glanced over her shoulder. Not everyone had left. Those who remained pretended to talk among themselves while watching her with great interest. Their children huddled under blankets in the wagon beds, sucking on their candy sticks. In the background, Oliver stood vigil on the stairs leading to his rooms above the store. One hand on his hip, he shifted his weight and stepped down to the street. Mary focused on his face. A schoolgirl blush spread across her cheeks. He smiled and tipped his hat, giving her strength.

"Oh, I'm not leaving," Mary assured Frances, loud enough for her audience to hear. "I was merely retrieving a gift I brought for you." She folded back the blanket, exposing the basket of home-made jams.

"Oh, Mary, thank you. What beautiful colors." Frances held the jams up to the sunlight one at a time, admiring their shining gem-like brightness.

The Reverend took one of the jars and examined it for himself. "I remember Earl always bragged about your preserves. We will certainly enjoy these. Let me help you down so you two ladies can get inside where it's warm. I'll see your horses stabled." He handed the jam back to his wife.

"Have you ever considered selling your preserves at Oliver Polk's store?" Frances asked. "I'm certain he'd have no problem finding interested buyers."

"Actually," Mary whispered with a smug conspiratorial grin, "I already do."

Frances' eyes grew wide when she realized what Mary was saying. "Are you talking about Althea Smythe's Homemade Jams and Jellies?"

Mary nodded. "I use my mother's recipes, so I put her name on them."

Frances linked her arm with Mary's as they headed to the parsonage. "We can hardly keep them in stock. Word spreads fast when a fresh batch arrives on the shelf." She hesitated, then giggled. "If only they knew," she said with a quick side-long glance toward the women who had lost interest and were starting for their own homes. "Those three are some of our biggest customers."

Mary knew it was unchristian of her but took pleasure in imagining the looks of consternation on the faces of those hateful people as she was escorted into the parsonage for Christmas dinner. She took one final look back to see if Oliver was still there, but he had gone up to his rooms.

CHAPTER 26

WISCONSIN: JANUARY 1881

Winter settled in hard after the New Year, but it was nothing the residents of Deer Creek weren't accustomed to. Like it or not, cold and snow and isolation were to be expected. Mary spent each of her days the same—up early to tend the animals, clean and cook, read and nap, tend the animals again, then go to bed so she could get up and do it all over again. It had been the same winter routine she followed every year, but without Earl beside her there was no peace in the solitude. She found herself alone with her thoughts for far more time than was good for her sanity, alone to replay the echoing taunts of *rebel, slaver, traitor*. Haunted by the memory of Earl's face as he became more and more withdrawn. Remembering the pain in his eyes when he had to tell her he lost his job at the mill because of pressure from some of the customers. He had so much hope for the future when they moved north, only to have it gradually whittled away to nothing, leaving an empty shell of the boy she fell in love with all those years ago.

Mary dozed in front of the fire one particularly bleak and quiet evening. She'd been mending a pair of stockings worn through at the heel, but the warmth of the flames and silence of the falling snow lulled her to sleep. The stocking she'd been working on hung precariously down one side of her lap.

She'd been dreaming. They were back in Virginia, the three of them. Earl was young and handsome, Ander not even school age yet. Her two boys had been fishing and returned home with more than enough for their little family. They laughed when Mary accused them of fishing the river empty. Ander said, *You're silly, Mama*, the way he so often did. She'd held out her arms and he ran to her.

The sound of horses and sleigh bells woke her just as Ander was about to wrap himself around her legs. Mary jumped to her feet, grabbing at the empty air in front of her, knocking her knee against the parlor table.

"Ander?" She spun around, searching the shadows that spilled from every corner. "Earl?"

She choked down a sob and dropped back into her chair. A dream. Ander was gone. Earl, too.

A heavy knock at the door brought her back to her feet. Horses stomped and snorted in the snow, setting sleigh bells ringing in the cold night air.

Mary picked her mending up from the floor and put it back in the basket by her chair. She wiped away the tears. It had all been so real.

Another knock.

"Coming." She smoothed her skirt and took a deep calming breath before opening the door.

"Oliver, what are you doing out and about at this hour?" She hustled him inside and closed the door.

"I couldn't let such a beautiful winter night go to waste, so I hitched the team to the sleigh and rode right out to ask my friend if she would like to go for a ride."

Mary stammered, attempting to find the right words. Only moments before she'd been dreaming about Earl and Ander and their home back in Virginia. Yet, now her heart fluttered like some young thing whose beau was asking her to the dance. She was reminded how it felt when Oliver's hand squeezed hers in church Christmas morning, and how he stood guard across from the churchyard, ready to come to her rescue when those hateful women suggested she should have hung herself next to Earl.

"I'd like that," she managed to say.

"Well, hurry then." Oliver waved his hands at her. "It's cold, so bundle up. I have plenty of blankets for our legs and hot bricks for our feet."

Mary grabbed her coat from the peg by the door, wrapped her head in a scarf, and pulled on her boots and warmest gloves. Excitement about the idea of a sleigh ride flared to life.

It wasn't long before they were skimming across the open fields under a bright full moon and a broad sky awash in stars. The rush of the blades and the muffled rhythmic drumming of the horses' hooves combined with the ringing of the sleigh bells. Mary laughed for the first time in months. A snowy owl flew across their path with an unfortunate small creature squirming in its talons.

Oliver stopped the horses at the top of a hill. They took in the scene of the valley below. The new snow sparkled like pieces of fine polished glass. A white blanket as far as the eye could see was broken only by shadowy groves of trees and the occasional farmhouse until it reached the smooth ribbon of the St Croix River. The constant motion of the water kept parts of the river from freezing over. Tiny lights glowed from inside each house, and curls of smoke rose telling them someone was warm and snug inside.

"I don't know that I've ever seen so many stars." Mary smiled at Oliver.

"My mother believed each star is one person lost to us on earth," he said, tipping his head to the heavens. "Whenever I find myself missing Irma, or our son, William, I look to the night sky and there they are looking back down on me."

Mary looked up to the stars, then over at Oliver. He rarely mentioned William, and never talked about how he died. She didn't ask. "That's lovely. How wonderful to think Earl, our children, my parents, brothers, and sister are still so close." Silence wrapped its arms around them as they watched their loved ones wink and blink at them from above. Peace filled her heart for the first time in years.

"You're shivering." Oliver broke her reverie.

She was having such a nice time she hadn't noticed the cold night air seeping through her coat.

"We'll head back." He called to his horses, shook the reins, and they were off, headed toward home in silence.

"Thank you, Oliver," she said as he pulled to a stop in front of her door. "It's been ages since I rode in a sleigh."

"I'm glad you enjoyed yourself." He laid his hand on hers.

His warmth seeped through their gloves. Her breath caught in her throat. "Would you like to come in for a cup of coffee?" Her voice cracked. She tried to cover it with a cough.

"I would love to."

Mary rushed about the kitchen getting the coffee ready and hunting down the last half dozen cookies in a tin she had buried at the back of the pantry shelf to keep herself from eating them all in one sitting.

She set the tray on the parlor table. "It's not much, but it should be enough to take the chill out."

"It's perfect. Sad to say, but I haven't had a homemade cookie since Irma died. I can cook, at least enough to keep myself alive, but I don't bother with the baking." He reached into his pocket. "I almost forgot. I brought you a little something."

Mary pulled the string securing the mouth of the bag. "You shouldn't have." She didn't know how she felt about receiving a gift from a man other than her husband. Should she refuse the gift or accept it so as not to offend? After all, it was only a little gift between friends.

"They came into the store this morning, and I thought of you."

"Oh, my! Thank you." A handful of dried apricots were nestled at the bottom of the bag, their dark golden skins and sweet aroma made her mouth water. She took a bite from one and held out the bag. "Would you like one?"

"No, no." He waved away her offer. "Those are for you to enjoy."

She tied the bag shut and slipped it into her skirt pocket while he poured them cups of coffee. "Can I ask you something, Oliver?" Mary took the cup he held out to her.

"Of course. Anything." Oliver picked up the other cup.

"Not to put a damper on our evening, but . . ." Mary hesitated. "How long was it before you stopped mourning Irma?"

"I still mourn her. It's been five years, yet sometimes it seems like only yesterday. It does get easier, though, and the memories grow sweeter, if that's possible."

"In my head I know that's true, but in my heart, it feels like the pain will never end."

"I remember." He sipped his coffee.

"Earl's not the first person I've loved who has died. I lost my parents, my sister and brothers, and, as you know, my Ander and tiny Lillian."

"A mother should never outlive her children, yet, so many do."

She thought about Irma, unable to stop the tears tracing paths down her cheeks. Her hands shook. Oliver took her cup before she burned herself with the splashing coffee.

Mary reached into her pocket for a handkerchief but came up empty. "Sorry," she sniffed. She wiped at her tears with the back of her hand. Oliver gave her his. She didn't know why, but Mary was surprised it was a crisp, fresh square. Earl's was always a rumpled mess.

"Most everyone in town lost someone to the War," he said.

Mary was fully aware of the other sons and brothers who fell. The local young men who sacrificed themselves did so for the Union, unlike her son and brothers and nephews who all died for the Confederacy. Traitors, they were called. Not patriots.

"You're right. I'm not the only person, the only parent, to lose someone. It's just that sometimes the pain is so great I'm afraid I can't bear it. I pray every day for the strength to look the other way from the taunts, but certain people make being a good Christian nearly impossible."

"Those women could try the patience of Job," he said. Their laughter broke the tension in the room. "I must be going." He stood. "My team will want to get settled into their warm stalls for the night."

She walked Oliver to the door. "Thank you, again, for such a wonderful evening. It was just what I needed, an excuse to get out of this house for a while. And for the dried apricots," she added, patting the bulge in her pocket. She held up the soggy and not so clean handkerchief. "I'll wash it and return it freshly pressed."

"That's not necessary."

"I insist."

"Very well. If you insist." Oliver took her hand in both of his and caressed the back with his thumb. "Good night, Mary." He slipped on his gloves and left.

Mary leaned against the closed door, heart thumping, lungs breathless, as the ringing of the sleigh bells faded away into the night.

"What is wrong with you, Mary Bishop?"

CHAPTER 27

WISCONSIN: JANUARY 1881

Sleep was impossible after Oliver left. Mary paced, her mind a jumble of emotions, questions she couldn't quiet long enough to attempt rest. Wrapping her shawl tight around her shoulders, she walked to the window. The night was cold, still. The sleigh ride had been a delightful surprise, a kind gesture she could have attributed to a dear friend wanting to cheer her in her grief and loneliness if it wasn't for the way he touched her when they said good night. She stared at the back of her hand where Oliver's caress lingered. Her heart raced and her face flushed with—what—passion?

His smile made it clear it was the reaction he had hoped for. "Nonsense!" she scolded herself. She couldn't love another man. She would love Earl until the day she died and was buried next to him. Was it wrong for her to react to another man's touch? And so soon after Earl's death?

Mary pulled the old hat box from under her bed. Safely tucked inside were all her most precious keepsakes. There was a deep blue swatch from her wedding dress and a tiny baptismal gown hand-sewn by her mother and worn by both her children. There were two small packs of letters and three tarnished photograph cases.

The first pack of letters was from Ander during the War. He couldn't often find paper to write, or a way to post them, but he got word to her whenever he could. Sometimes it was only a couple of quickly written lines as they passed through a town, but next she'd get pages of details about life in camp, perhaps a crude sketch or two. The last was hand-delivered by his friend, Robert. It was written on a scrap of butcher paper. Robert, in his kindness, had stopped to hastily gather what he could of Ander's few personal belongings as they were being forced to retreat by the advancing Union forces. Mary carefully unfolded the paper now crumbling with age.

Dear Mother:

> *We are in Pennsylvania near a small town called Gettysburg. This will certainly be the battle that decides the fate of our great Confederacy and I know we will soon return the victors. I will post this after. Perhaps I will return before you get this. Love, your son, Ander.*

She held the letter close to her heart and took a deep breath before returning it to the box.

The second pack of letters was from her dear friend, Sarah. She'd gone west to St. Paul, Minnesota, with Robert and his new bride, Amy Lynn, after the War. It had been years since Sarah's last letter.

She set Sarah's letters aside and wondered what had become of her friend. Was she still alive? She'd write her first thing in the morning and tell her about Earl, and perhaps Oliver. Sarah could be the only link Mary had left to Virginia, the only one who understood what it was like for them during the War.

Most dear of all were the three tarnished cases. Inside each was a daguerreotype. When they first moved to Wisconsin, Mary displayed the pictures with pride. Then one day Maud Henry came to visit and saw the picture of Ander in his uniform. That's when all their troubles began. Maud couldn't wait to tell Agnes and Gladys how the Bishop's son fought for the Confederacy. They, in turn, were quick to tell anyone in town who would listen. Heartbroken, Mary hid the pictures away.

"No more."

She set the pictures aside. But, before she returned the box to its place under the bed, she added one last letter. Earl's.

Back in the parlor, Mary opened each picture case and smiled at the people looking back at her, touching each one. The first was taken on their wedding day. How fortuitous as it would prove to be the last time her entire family would be together. No one could have known then this baby would live and Lucy would be gone three months later.

The second picture was of Mary's precious babies. Ander, a somber four-year-old, sat next to his sister, Lillian, as she lay peaceful, surrounded by flowers, in the tiny coffin Earl had made for her. Ander held her hand when Earl lowered Lillian into the ground. *Don't cry, Mama,* he had said. *You still have me. I'll always be your baby.*

The last picture was of a tall, proud, Ander standing next to Robert. The two posed in their Confederate gray before leaving with their friends to fight.

If anyone other than herself survived, Mary didn't know who or where. For all she knew, she was the last and when her time came there would be no one. Her mind returned to Oliver.

"How could it be wrong if I were to find happiness with someone else?" she asked Earl's likeness staring back at her.

She stood the pictures back on the mantel where they belonged, where anyone who came into the room could see them. She would not be ashamed. Her losses meant no less than the losses of any other woman in this town.

And she was no longer afraid. She would no longer allow a few narrow-minded people to drive her into despair and isolation. Mary sat back in her rocking chair, smiled up at her family, and closed her eyes.

THE MANTEL CLOCK STRUCK one. She must have dozed, the comfort of her memories allowing her to let go of all her anxiety and worries. The fire had burned itself out, and the room grew cold. It was time she went to bed. She stood and stretched, stiff from sitting so long.

A horse whinnied not far from the house. Mary looked out the window. Two men, mere shadows until they cleared the trees and stood in the light of the full moon, walked toward the barn. One stopped moving long enough to light a torch.

Mary grabbed her Colt revolver from the desk drawer and checked the chambers. Loaded. Thank God Earl had taught her to shoot. She stepped into her boots and out into the open yard, oblivious to the cold wind as it cut through her nightgown and shawl.

She aimed her gun. "Stop right there!" Her voice carried loud and clear through the winter air.

They turned.

"I am an excellent shot and I am not afraid to prove it!"

One dropped his torch in the snow. The flame sputtered and went out. He must have burned himself because he howled, shook his hand, and cussed in pain. The other took a shot at her before they bolted for the tree line.

The bullet took a chink out of the house several feet to Mary's right. Her gun held two-handed, feet braced, as Earl taught her, she followed the one who shot at her, keeping him in her sights. When she was certain of her shot, she pulled the trigger. Acrid black smoke exploded from the barrel as it kicked back in her hands. She didn't want to kill him. She just wanted to show she was serious. He screamed and stumbled in his tracks, holding his shoulder.

"Damn it! She shot me." It was Augustus Henry, town butcher and Maud's husband. His deep, heavy, German accent was unmistakable.

"Shut up!" Karl Olson, Gladys' husband, growled.

Mary scanned the tree line, looking to see if Agnes Schmidt's husband, Norbert, was hiding anywhere, but she didn't see him. As the local tavern owner, he was likely still busy in town. Perhaps he felt he'd done his part with all the alcohol he sold Earl.

"I know who you are, and I'll be paying Deputy Mueller a visit in the morning. Get off my property or I will shoot again, and I promise one of you will die this time." She pulled back the hammer and a second loaded chamber clicked into place.

"The bitch is insane." Augustus said to his friend.

She aimed toward the sound of their voices, the slight movement of shadow.

"Rebel trash, this ain't over." Karl yelled. They mounted their horses and rode away.

Mary stood ready should they double back or have any friends hidden in the trees. She had only five shots left and hadn't thought to grab extras.

The night was still once more. She lowered the gun. Her hands shook, either from the cold or the shock of having just shot at two men who tried to burn her barn down. She released the hammer, pulled her shawl tight, and walked over to Karl's dropped torch. She buried the hot end deep in a snow bank. It sizzled, smoked, and went dead. Luckily, they didn't get close enough to the barn to cause any damage. It was a good thing she didn't go to bed at her usual hour or she would have lost the barn and all her animals.

She went back into the house and reloaded the one empty chamber. She dressed, pulled on a coat, filled her pockets with extra rounds, then sat by the window. Popping another dried apricot into her mouth, she prepared to keep watch the rest of the night. If they returned, she'd be ready for them.

CHAPTER 28

WISCONSIN: JANUARY 1881

Mary eased open her eyes and tried to lift her head. She'd fallen asleep with her chin resting on her chest. She rubbed the back of her neck and turned it from side to side to release the tension.

The sun glared off the new snow covering her yard. She covered her eyes with one hand and squinted between her fingers until they adjusted to the bright light. Her other hand remained across the handle of the Colt revolver on her lap.

She shook her head to clear the fog making last night's events hazy. It was supposed to be another quiet evening home alone. She was mending her stockings in front of the fire. The basket remained by her chair. Then Oliver came by with his sleigh, and they'd gone for a ride. Her hand tingled at the thought of his touch. Her fingers stroked the back of her hand where his had rested.

But it was what happened after Oliver left that brought Mary to her feet, her stiff muscles forgotten.

She saddled up and rode into town with the cold torch strapped to Sophie's side. Her revolver holstered at her waist. Her hair was uncombed and wild, her eyes heavy from a night of watching the barn and little sleep, but her anger fueled any fatigue that threatened to overcome her. She must have made quite a formidable sight because, rather than merely stare at her passing, people scuttled back into doorways as if afraid she might shoot them next. She glared back at any who dared to make eye contact. Perhaps word of last night had already spread. She probably resembled a Wild West desperado who rides into town hell-bent on causing trouble, like the villains in those dreadful penny novels Earl loved to read. She wanted them to know she would no longer back down. She would not slink back to her house and hide from their hate.

She tethered her horse outside the local sheriff's office. Deputy Dieter Mueller sat with a mug of coffee and a newspaper, oblivious, or so it seemed, to the fact someone had entered the room. She waited, but when he didn't acknowledge her presence, she tossed the torch on his desk with a thud. The wet end left a black ashen smudge across the newspaper torn free from his hands.

"God damn it!" He jumped to his feet. "What the hell do you think you're doing?" When he saw it was a woman, he stopped short and removed his hat. "Pardon me, Mrs. Bishop. I didn't realize."

Mary took a deep breath. *He'll be on my side,* she told herself. "Good morning, Deputy Mueller," she said, keeping her voice controlled.

"What seems to be the problem?" He sat down, lifted the torch from his desk, and looked for a place to set it. It was then he saw her gun. "I'd appreciate it if you'd hand me that weapon."

"I'll just leave it in its holster, if you don't mind," she said.

Or even if you do.

He looked her in the eyes for a minute, no doubt assessing whether or not she was of any great risk, then sighed. "Again, what seems to be the problem? And start from the beginning."

"That." She pointed at the torch. "That's the problem."

"Looks like a torch."

"That torch belongs to Karl Olson. He used it in an attempt to burn my barn late last night. Luckily, I was still awake and able to stop him."

"Karl Olson tried to burn your barn? You said it was late. It would have been dark. Are you certain it was Karl?"

"Yes. There was a full moon and I could see their faces quite clearly. They also spoke, and I'd know their voices anywhere. It was Karl Olson and Augustus Henry."

"Augustus was with him?" The deputy leaned back in his chair and took a long swallow of coffee.

She didn't like the way he kept repeating her words in the form of a question. "Mr. Henry had a gun. He took a shot at me when I stopped Mr. Olson from lighting the side of my barn."

"Did he hit you?" He took another swallow of his coffee and looked quite amused by the whole story. Despite her best intentions, her outrage began to spill over to include the good deputy.

"Deputy Mueller, are you going to write any of this down?"

He shook his head. "No. I can remember it. So, you say Augustus shot you?" He took another long drink from his coffee.

Now he was mocking her. She never said any such thing. Was it possible he played a part in their scheme?

"No, he shot *at* me." Mary's voice rose in pitch with her frustration. "He's a rather poor aim, apparently, as I was certainly close enough that he should have been able to hit me. But he did take a chunk of wood out of the side of my house. You can ride out and see for yourself, if you like."

"And what did you do?"

"I shot back," She said matter-of-factly, rather pleased with herself, and watched the deputy's amused smirk disappear. He would have to take her seriously now.

The deputy's mug hit his desk with a clatter. Coffee sloshed over the sides and onto the back of his hand and the smudged, ripped, newspaper, to form a brown puddle on his desk. He cussed and put his hand to his mouth. Mary was glad to see the coffee was still hot enough to sting a little. He wiped the hand dry on his pant leg.

"And, Deputy, I am a good shot."

"Are you saying you shot Augustus Henry?"

"I winged him. A flesh wound. But I promised him then, and I promise you now, next time I will shoot to kill."

"Sit down. I'm going to bring in Karl and Augustus. We'll get to the bottom of this."

Finally, she felt vindicated knowing she would soon see those two locked in a cell where they belonged and, hopefully, an end brought to all the harassment.

"I'm telling the truth. You'll find Mr. Olson has a burned hand from when he dropped the torch. Mr. Henry, of course, will have a gunshot wound to his right shoulder."

Deputy Mueller stopped, held his breath, and closed his eyes. After a moment, he sighed, and headed for the door, hat in hand.

Alone, Mary studied the county and state maps hanging on the wall. She was still too angry to sit.

Oliver rushed in, slamming the door behind him. "Mary, what happened? Word has it you came riding into town with a gun. Are you all right? Are you in some kind of trouble?"

"I'm fine. I had a couple of late-night visitors, that's all. Long after you left. Karl Olson attempted to burn my barn down, and Augustus Henry took a shot at me."

Before he could reply, Deputy Mueller returned with the two men. They stood in the doorway, staring, jaws clenched. Time had left them no less angry than they were when she'd last seen them. But, then again, neither was she. As she'd predicted, Mr. Olson's right hand was bandaged, and Mr. Henry's right arm was in a sling.

"Good morning, gentlemen," she said. Now she would see some form of justice.

"Mr. Polk, is there something I can help you with?" Deputy Mueller asked. "I'm kind of in the middle of something here." He sat behind his desk. Augustus and Karl stood on the far end facing her.

"I came when I heard Mrs. Bishop might be in some kind of trouble, but now I hear it's these two who are in trouble."

"No one's in trouble, at least not yet. I suggest you go back to your store and let me straighten this all out. I'm sure it's nothing more than a misunderstanding."

"I'm not going anywhere." Oliver stood by Mary.

"Suit yourself, but I must ask you to be quiet and let me do my investigation. If everyone would pull up a chair and sit down so we can get to the bottom of all this, I would appreciate it."

Karl and Augustus set their chairs near the deputy, facing her, like they were judge and jury and she was the one on trial.

Deputy Mueller motioned to the one remaining empty chair against the back wall. "Mrs. Bishop." Oliver brought it over and held it while she sat.

"Now, as I was saying, I'm sure there's nothing more than a misunderstanding here."

"A misunderstanding?" She was stunned. That wasn't at all what she expected. "I assure you, there's no misunderstanding here. This man," she pointed to Karl Olson, "attempted to burn my barn last night. And this one," she pointed to Augustus Henry, "took a shot at me. I demand you arrest them."

"Mary Bishop's a lying rebel traitor, and everyone knows it." Karl Olson yelled.

"There's no need for name calling." Oliver sprang forward as if he was about to strike Karl.

"Mr. Polk, if you can't control yourself, I'm going to have to insist you leave." Deputy Mueller stepped between Oliver and Karl and pointed to the door. "Your choice."

Oliver returned to Mary's side.

"And it was she who shot me." Augustus Henry shouted over the growing ruckus.

"In self-defense," Mary reminded him, jumping to her feet.

"No, sir, that ain't true," he insisted.

Deputy Mueller held up a hand. "Sit down, Mrs. Bishop!"

She did as he asked, hoping to look like the reasonable one in the group.

Oliver's face turned red. She had never seen him so worked up before. "Mrs. Bishop is nothing but a good woman wronged. She wouldn't shoot anyone without cause, and she certainly wouldn't lie about it after."

"This is your last warning, Mr. Polk. Keep quiet or get out."

Mary put her hand on Oliver's arm. She didn't want the morning to end with the both of them locked up while the true criminals remained free. She hoped if she remained calm, so would Oliver.

Deputy Mueller turned his attention back to Augustus Henry. "Well, then, why don't you tell me what is true, Augustus." He leaned on the edge of his desk and crossed his arms.

"My wife's little dog ran off. Personally, I hate that little mutt and would love nothing more than to have it snatched up by some coyote, but you know how Maud dotes on that animal. There'd be no living with her if I didn't go find it and bring it back. Well, she sent me out looking for it, and I asked Karl to go along and help. That's all we were doing, Deputy. Looking for Maud's damned little dog."

"And that's why you were out by the Bishop place with a gun and a torch?"

"Yes, sir." Karl stepped forward. "I suggested Augustus bring his gun, in case we come across some wild animal. And I brought the torch to light our way."

"So, you're saying you were just passing by, looking for Maud's little dog, when Mrs. Bishop starts shooting for no reason?"

"That's exactly what we're saying." Augustus nodded.

"We were just passing by when she comes out of the house and starts shooting at us," Karl parroted back.

Mary couldn't believe what she was hearing. It was clear Deputy Mueller believed every word they were saying, adding to the story, even. And that was what it was, nothing more than a story.

Deputy Mueller turned his attention to Mary. "Like I said, it sounds like we have a simple misunderstanding here, that's all. I suggest the three of you go about your own business. And, Mrs. Bishop, please be a little more careful in the future or I'll be forced to bring you in on charges."

"Me?" She was stunned. "What charges?"

"How about attempted murder? Seeing as you've already stated your intent to shoot to kill the next time you see either of these men near your property, I might be saving their lives if I lock you up right now."

"I think that's a good idea, Deputy." Augustus stared her in the eye with a smug grin. "I think you should arrest her right now, before she has a chance to kill me."

Mary was back on her feet. "That's outrageous! That is not at all what happened. I insist you arrest these men."

"Go home, Mrs. Bishop." He paused. "Is that gun loaded by chance?"

She faced him. "Yes, it is, Deputy. And I intend it to stay that way." She looked at the two men now standing, facing her with their backs to the deputy. They were smiling, but there was a hard glint in their eyes. This wasn't over for them.

She knew it wasn't the first battle that determined who won the war. It was the final battle. She intended to win the final battle.

"Before leaving last night, these two threatened to come back and do me harm. I plan to be ready for them."

She let the door slam behind her and mounted Sophie as tears threatened to fall.

"Mary, wait." Oliver ran out to stop her.

"They were lying, Oliver. You believe me, don't you? They were lying and Deputy Mueller knows it." She was shaking.

"Of course, I believe you. Everyone in town knows what those two men are capable of doing, including Deputy Mueller."

"Yet no one cares. I don't know if I can ever feel safe here." She held her breath and closed her eyes.

Do not cry! Do not let these people see you cry!

"What can I do? How can I help you?"

"There's nothing you can do. There's nothing anyone can do. I have to deal with this on my own."

Mary rode away. At the edge of town, she turned left instead of right. It had been two months since Earl's death and past time she stopped to pay her respects.

CHAPTER 29

WISCONSIN: JANUARY 1881

There was nothing as sad and forlorn as a cemetery in winter. A handful of cold gray stones half buried in icy whiteness that spread as far as she could see. Drifts covered names, dates, leaving only anonymous sleep.

The snow cover was untouched, not a single footprint broke the surface. No one had been there since before the first snowfall. No one had been there since they laid Earl to rest.

Sophie carefully picked her way through the drifts, high-stepping and placing each hoof with uncertainty. Mary encouraged her, letting her choose her own path and pace until they reached the gate. Looping Sophie's reins over a fence post, Mary was relieved to see the wind had blown the gate open wide enough that she could squeeze through. She wouldn't have been able to open it otherwise.

Her hand went to the Colt still strapped to her side. She doubted Karl and Augustus had followed but couldn't be certain and couldn't take that risk. Unarmed and vulnerable, knee-deep in the snow with no quick way to her weapon, she would be an easy target. Considering the isolation of the cemetery in winter, she could lie there until spring before anyone found her.

A simple wooden cross marked Earl's grave for the short term. It leaned with the wind, almost flat. Mary lifted it and pushed it as far back down through the snow and into the frozen ground as she was able. Using both hands, she packed the snow high and tight to hold it in place.

"There," she said to Earl. "That should hold for a while. I'll return and check on it from time to time. I ordered you a nice stone. The undertaker tells me it arrived. He'll store it until spring when his boys can come out and place it for you. Then I can plant some flowers and do things up proper."

She stuffed her hands under her arms. They were almost numb from digging in the snow. Her fingers burned with a thousand small hot needles as the warmth slowly returned. She stared at the cross in silence. She had so much she wanted to say but didn't know where to start. Her mind raced, her emotions a jumble. Both sad and angry, she loved and hated him all at the same time. It was as if he died the day before instead of two months ago.

"Christmas wasn't the same without you. I didn't bake or cook, no decorations, but I did go to service and make certain the children received their candy. Oh, and Oliver Polk gave me your present. Thank you. I had dinner with the Reverend and his wife. They're good people, as you always used to say when someone paid a kindness." She paused. "Good people," she repeated.

"Oliver's been kind, too. Asks after me and makes sure I'm getting along, that I have everything I need. Last night he came by with his sleigh. Do you remember the last time we all rode in his sleigh?" Mary laughed a little at the memory.

"It was before Irma passed." Mary glanced at Irma's grave and her heart ached a little more. "It was so cold that night we thought Oliver was mad for even suggesting a sleigh ride, but the two of you insisted. We huddled under so many blankets I didn't know how the horses would manage the extra weight. The sky was smooth as colored glass. A million stars sparkled above us, and the full moon lit the fresh snow like a bed of diamonds below our feet. We laughed and sang and soon forgot all about the cold." Tears pricked at the back of Mary's eyes.

"It was a lot like that last night, except we didn't sing. We talked some, but mostly just rode in silence. I was happy, Earl. I was actually happy for the first time in a long time." Mary's heart raced when she thought of the way Oliver held her hand when they said good night. "I know some people in town will consider it too soon, but I think I might be spending more time with Oliver. I hope you understand."

She shivered in the icy wind and considered whether or not to tell him about the rest of last night. She decided not. His battle was over. This one was hers to fight.

"Well, I better be getting home. I need to get Sophie back to the barn and Max. She doesn't like to be away from him for too long. I know how she feels." Sophie whinnied and stomped her hooves back at the gate. "You were right about her. She's the best horse I could ever own." She took a few steps, hesitated, then turned back.

"I miss you so much, Earl. I know why you did this. I just wish you hadn't. I wish you could have trusted me enough to let me help you. I know what those people did to you, how they crushed your spirit with their cruelty, how it wore you down until you couldn't pick yourself up again. They're trying to do the same thing to me, but I'm staying strong. They may have started this fight, but I promise you, I will bring an end to it." Mary kissed the tips of her fingers and touched his cross. "Take care of the children for me. Tell Ander his mother misses him and give Lillian an extra snuggle from me."

Sophie headed for home without any encouragement from her rider. Mary didn't miss Oliver hiding behind the trees, watching over her, staying far enough back to give her and Earl their privacy, but close enough to come to her rescue.

"Thank you, Oliver, but you can go now," Mary called back over her shoulder. "I'll be fine."

At home, Mary took fresh sheets of paper from her desk, a pen and ink, and sat down to write a long letter to Sarah. She didn't know if her old friend would ever receive it, but just writing it felt like talking to her. Mary told her about Deer Creek, about the people and how they'd been harassed, and about what it did to Earl in the end. She told her about Irma, Frances, and Oliver. She wrote how she missed Virginia, her family, and their old life. She told her how much she missed her and how she hoped Sarah was doing well in St. Paul with Robert and his little family. She asked about her life and begged Sarah to write back soon and tell her everything.

By the time Mary finished writing and had sealed the envelope the sun was setting and long shadows reached across the room. It was time to tend the animals, have something to eat, and go to bed. She was glad to see the day come to an end.

CHAPTER 30

WISCONSIN: FEBRUARY 1881

"It's been two weeks since you stepped one foot off your property." Oliver accepted the coffee Mary offered him. "My sleigh is right outside. Let me take you for a ride."

"Sounds lovely, but I think it best I stay here." She poured herself a cup and sat opposite him, her feet propped up close to the fire. The heat spread through the soles of her shoes, surrounded her cold toes, and traveled up her legs to meet the hot coffee warming her insides.

"You don't think Augustus and Karl still plan on coming back, not after all this time?"

"I truly don't know what to think. You heard them in Deputy Mueller's office. They aren't going to give up this easily. So, in answer to your question, yes, I do believe they're coming back. If not today, then maybe next week, or next month, even." Mary wrapped her hands tight around her cup and let the porcelain warm her fingers until they were almost too hot to bear.

"Well, you can't stay imprisoned here indefinitely."

They sat in silence, enjoying the coffee, the fire, and each other's company. Mary's eyes drooped. She woke with a start when Oliver rescued her coffee from slipping into her lap. He set the two cups on the tray.

"I'll take this to the kitchen and then be on my way. Remember what I said, though. By hiding out, you're letting them win."

"I'm sorry, you needn't go." Mary stood and took the tray from him. "Give me that. I think I can honestly say I've never been so embarrassed. I can't believe I fell asleep."

"It's late," he said. "It's time we were both getting to bed."

Mary blushed at the carnal thoughts such a simple, well-meaning sentence brought to mind. Lord, you'd think she was fifteen again.

Oliver put on his coat and opened the front door. He turned back. "I'm not giving up on you. One way or another, I am getting you away from this house."

THE REVEREND AND FRANCES Clark came to see her on a quiet afternoon a couple days later while she sat reading in the parlor.

Mary opened the front door then stepped back with surprise. "What in the world?"

Frances pushed a squirming bundle into Mary's arms and a little gray head, looking more like a wolf pup than a dog, popped out.

"It's a puppy." Frances announced.

"I see that." The puppy fought to break free of his wraps and licked Mary's face, his tail wagging so hard she almost dropped him.

"He's for you," Frances said. They stepped past Mary and closed the door.

The Reverend explained. "One of our outlying members had a litter a while back. This was the last one in need of a home."

"And, naturally, we thought of you," Frances finished for him.

"Naturally," Mary said, somewhat bemused.

"With you living out here all alone, he'll make a perfect companion." Frances scratched the little guy behind the ears. She laughed when his head whipped around to lick her fingers.

Mary put the puppy on the floor and took their coats. He followed close on their heels as she led her guests into the parlor.

"He'll also be a good watch dog as he gets older." The Reverend gave Mary a knowing look. "His parents are both excellent watch dogs."

"We heard what happened." Frances' voice was full of concern. "The whole town's talking about it. How awful that must have been for you."

"And I have no doubt they're all saying they're not surprised, me being the evil rebel traitor they all know me to be."

"Well," she hesitated. "Some, yes, but not all. There are those who defend you."

"Yes," the Reverend assured her. "Mr. Olson and Mr. Henry have a reputation as troublemakers, and their wives' penchant for gossip keeps many at arms' length. However, no matter how justified you may have been in defending yourself, I feel compelled to urge you to find a more non-violent way to do so in the future." He looked at the gun on the table. "For your own safety."

Mary was not in the mood for a sermon on peaceful compromise. "Reverend, if they keep their attacks to mere words, I, too, will counter with mere words. But if they choose to use torches and guns, I will have no choice other than to reciprocate in kind." She let out her breath and attempted a smile. "I do promise to try, though. I'd love nothing better than to leave this whole ugly mess behind us."

Frances nuzzled the puppy and got a wet kiss in return. "We can't stay, but before we go, I must know what you intend to name this little guy."

"Boone."

Mary remembered when Ander finally got the dog he always wanted and named him Boone. At first, they were afraid a dog would give away their secret late-night guests, but when Boone saved Ander's life, they couldn't refuse him a home. She didn't know how they would have ever survived losing both their children so young.

"Boone. That's a fitting name." Frances gave Boone one last scratch under the chin. "You behave yourself, Boone, and I promise to come back and visit real soon."

Boone barked as if he understood, making them laugh.

After they'd gone, Mary turned to the excited pup. He wagged his tail and jumped up against her legs. "What am I going to do with you?"

Boone ran about the room, sniffing at every corner and crevice, stopping periodically to look back at her.

A wagon clattered into the yard. Boone ran barking to the door. Mary grabbed her revolver. Footsteps. A knock. Boone growled, already her stern defender.

"Here, boy!" She slapped her thigh. Boone returned eagerly to her side. She was glad to see he'd had some training. She cocked the gun.

"Who's there?"

"It's me, Oliver."

She eased back the hammer, set the revolver on the table, and opened the door. "What are you doing out here in the middle of the day? Who's manning the store? The Reverend and Frances left only a minute ago, so I know it's not her."

"I passed them on the road," he nodded. "I put up a sign saying I'd be back shortly and locked the door. Those women spend more time gossiping than they do buying. They can come back later if it's so important."

Mary laughed. He was right. She'd seen it herself on more than one occasion.

A sharp yip reminded them that Boone remained vigilant at her side. Oliver took a kerchief-wrapped surprise from his coat pocket and squatted down to hold out the peace offering. "It's only a bit of leftover beef steak from last night's dinner," he said. Boone snatched up the treat.

"I'd say you've just made yourself a friend."

"And that answers your other question, what I'm doing out here in the middle of the day. Frances told me they were surprising you with a puppy, so I couldn't wait to see him for myself."

Oliver ran his hands over the dog's body and down his legs, looked into his eyes and ears, pulled back his lips to see his teeth. Boone wriggled and nipped playfully at his hands.

"Yes, he's a fine dog. And I can see he's already taken with you. That's good. What's his name?"

"Boone."

"It suits him." Oliver scratched behind Boone's ears, gave him a pat on the head, and stood. The dog returned to sit at Mary's side. "You're happy with him?"

"I am." She smiled down at her new friend. "I already feel less alone and afraid." She picked up Boone and held him close. He licked her face, and she put him down again. She'd forgotten how nice it was to have a dog in the house.

"Good." Oliver hesitated, as if he was about to say something but wasn't certain he should. "As you know, next week is Valentine's Day. I would like to take you to dinner at Gretchen's Kitchen."

Mary couldn't help but chuckle. "Valentine's Day is for little girls and young lovers. Not for the likes of old people like us."

"Not so! Valentine's Day is for the young at heart, and my heart has never felt younger than it has this past month."

He was serious. Her heart beat a little quicker. She didn't know what to say. Boone scratched at the door. She distracted herself by letting him out.

"Gretchen Mueller will be making her famous Black Forest Cake in honor of the day," he added. "As you know, she's the best German cook in the county, and her Black Forest Cake is second to none."

Mary stepped to the window, pretending to keep an eye on Boone so Oliver wouldn't see her uncertainty. "Oh, I don't know." She hesitated, then turned to face him.

He took off his hat and held it in front of his chest, nervously playing with the brim. "Mary Bishop, will you go to dinner with me?"

Mary couldn't help but smile. How could she say no to him? He looked so much the part of the young suitor.

"Yes, Oliver Polk, I will go to dinner with you."

Oliver's eyes shone as he grinned. "Then I'll pick you up Monday afternoon at four. We'll want to arrive early, before the cake is all gone." He stopped at the door. Boone barked and Oliver let him in. "I'll bring the sleigh," he said. "We can go for a ride after. I won't accept no for an answer this time."

"That would be very nice."

He put on his hat and gave Boone one last pat on the head before leaving.

Mary closed the door after him, sat, and put her hands to her face. Her cheeks were burning as if she were a young girl again. "You're acting like an old fool." She laughed at herself. Boone barked and jumped against her until she picked him up.

"What do you think, Boone? Am I being an old fool?" Boone barked. "I think so, too," she whispered into his soft fur.

MONDAY CAME QUICKLY. Was she spending too much time choosing the right dress and pinning her hair with extra curls? She giggled and grabbed her reticule when she heard sleigh bells in the yard.

"Where's Boone?" Oliver asked, coming in the front door and looking around the room.

"I tied him up in the barn. He'll be plenty warm, and I won't have to worry about any messes on my floor."

"Puppies," he laughed.

"Puppies," she agreed. "But, other than the occasional over-excited mishap, he's settling in nicely."

"Good." Oliver nodded and fiddled with his hat.

The silence hung heavy over them.

"You look nice," he said.

"Thank you." Heat rose in her face as she touched her curls. "We should probably go," she prompted.

"Of course." Oliver held the door, then closed it tight behind her.

THE SUN HADN'T SET yet as they glided into town, sleigh bells ringing merrily. People stopped and stared as they rode by. She wasn't certain if they approved of her and Oliver or not, but she didn't care as much as she would have earlier.

Gretchen's Kitchen buzzed with conversation and laughter. Some couples were forced to wait at the door until a table became available, but Oliver had thought to make reservations so they were seated immediately. It was a cozy table in the back corner away from the draft of the front entry. Oliver took her coat and pulled out her chair.

Red cloth was draped around the edge of the ceiling and a small candle was lit in the center of each table. Cut-out paper hearts decorated by the local school children were affixed to the walls, giving the restaurant a festive appeal.

"Isn't it lovely?" Mary looked around the room. Oliver agreed.

Anna, Gretchen's daughter, fairly flew across the room with two steaming plates of chicken, mashed potatoes, and green beans.

"Good evening, Mr. Polk, Mrs. Bishop," she said, setting the plates in front of them. "I hope you don't mind, but we thought we'd keep the menu simple this evening and make everyone a chicken dinner."

"Your mother's a wonderful cook," Mary said. "How could we possibly complain when anything she served would be a feast?"

"I'll tell her you said so."

"How old are you now, Anna? Are you still in school? I don't think I've seen you in ages."

"I'm fourteen now, ma'am, and I help my mother full-time here in the restaurant. Can I get the two of you some coffee, or perhaps you'd prefer milk, or a red fruit punch Mother made special for today?"

"Coffee would be perfect," Oliver said. "Mary?"

"Yes, coffee for me, too."

Anna returned with two cups, somehow making it through the crowded room without spilling a drop. She had grown into a graceful and accomplished young woman. Mary suspected Anna would find a young man soon, if she hadn't set her eyes on one already.

"Thank you." Oliver took his cup from her and she placed Mary's on the table in front of her.

"Everything tastes heavenly, as always," Mary said.

"Thank you," Anna beamed.

Oliver looked up from his plate. "Please tell us you haven't run out of cake yet. I've been thinking about your mother's Black Forest Cake for days so don't disappoint."

"Oh, no, there's plenty. In fact, I wouldn't be surprised if we have some left for tomorrow."

Oliver's face lit up. "Then I will have to return in the morning to have a piece for breakfast."

"Please do. Now, enjoy your meal and I'll be back shortly to see if you need anything else." With that, Anna rushed off to help her younger brother, Claus, clear a table for the next guests.

Anna escorted Augustus and Maud Henry to the clean and vacant table. Maud stopped mid-way between standing and sitting when her eyes met Mary's.

"This table will not do, Anna," she declared, her voice rising above all the chatter. Maud looked around the crowded room. "Certainly, you have somewhere else we might sit, a table away from the stench of *traitor*." Oliver set down his fork and began to rise, but Mary squeezed his hand and shook her head.

"I'm sorry, Mrs. Henry, but this is the only available table. If you'd prefer to wait there will certainly be another shortly."

Mary felt bad for Anna. The poor girl's voice shook, and she looked around as conversations hushed and all heads turned in their direction.

"Sit, darling," Augustus urged his wife. He offered her the chair with its back turned to Mary.

"No! I want a different table."

"You can see for yourself, there are no other tables available. Sit. People are staring at us." Augustus tried to calm his wife while glaring at Mary with red-hot hate.

"That woman *shot* you, Augustus!"

Gladys Olson crossed the room from where they'd been sitting against the far wall.

"Augustus, Maud, come, you can have our table. We were just finishing our coffee and paying the bill." She threw a look, nose in the air, in Mary's direction before leading her friends away. Anna saw them situated with food and drink, as the room returned to its previous buzz of talk and activity.

Mary turned back to Oliver. "I'm sorry. Clearly this was not a good idea after all."

"Ignore them. Maud Henry made a fool of herself with that little public display of outrage. There is no doubt as many people talking about her as there are about us. Perhaps more. Now, are you enjoying your dinner? I believe, Gretchen has topped herself again."

"You're right. It is delicious."

"Look who's here, Reverend!" Frances Clark's voice carried across the room. "I thought I saw you two sitting over here."

"Good evening, Mr. Polk, Mrs. Bishop," the Reverend said with a nod and a smile.

"Come, dear, let's leave them to their evening." Frances winked at Mary, took her husband's arm, and led him to the table rejected by the Henrys.

Mary and Oliver finished their meal without another word about Maud Henry. Oliver was right, she told herself, not everyone in the room was gossiping about them. Several diners stopped to greet them on their way out. By the time Gretchen served their cake, they were back in high spirits.

"When Anna told me you two were here," Gretchen said, "I thought I'd take a break and stop out to say hello. Did you enjoy your dinner? It was good, *ya*?"

"It was wonderful! I wish I could cook a chicken as moist and delicious as yours."

Gretchen blushed. "You are too kind. Frances tells me your jams are the best. Maybe you can make some for me? With all my baking I don't have the time to make a good jam."

"Of course. I'll make extra this year, and I won't need near as much myself now that . . ."

Suddenly, Earl found his way back into her thoughts.

"I was sorry to hear about your husband, Mary. But now, you and Mr. Polk?"

It was Mary's turn to blush.

"*Ya*? Is wonderful, I think." Gretchen smiled at the two of them. "I must tell you, when I heard how my husband treated you when you were in his office, I gave him an earful, believe me. He will not be talking so rude to a lady, and a dear friend of mine, again. Now, I must be getting back to the kitchen. So many people! You enjoy. No hurry."

Gretchen returned to the kitchen in a heartbeat, leaving Oliver and Mary to exclaim to each other over her melt-in-your-mouth cake. Marvelous dark chocolate, cream, and cherries beyond compare.

And when they finished, Oliver took her on that promised sleigh ride through the starry countryside, ending the evening with an unexpected kiss, quick and light, on her cheek. His hot breath made her heart race and her knees go weak.

Oliver looked deep into her eyes. She could not look away.

"Mary Bishop, will you be my valentine?"

"Yes," she said, breathless. Mesmerized by the moment.

He kissed her again. This time soft and slow.

She didn't even notice the cold as Oliver drove out of sight.

CHAPTER 31

WISCONSIN: FEBRUARY 1881

The morning sun streamed in Mary's bedroom window and warmed her face. She smiled and opened her eyes. Her fingers went to her lips where the heat of Oliver's kisses still lingered. She swung her feet to the floor.

"Good morning, Boone. I imagine you're anxious to go out." Boone ran to the door, looking back to see if she was following.

After breakfast and all her chores were completed, Mary tossed snowballs into the air, letting Boone try to catch them with his teeth. Every time they broke, he was surprised and searched about his feet for the missing toy. Mary laughed at the truly bewildered look in his eyes. Even with the weight of the Colt strapped around her waist reminding her to be vigilant, she didn't think about Karl Olson and Augustus Henry.

Shortly after their noon meal, there was a knock on the door. Mary checked her hair quick in the mirror to see that each strand was in place, certain she would see Oliver waiting on her doorstep. Instead, she was shocked to see Maud Henry.

"Mrs. Bishop." Maud stood stiff and still, as if tied to a giant post and planted at Mary's door. Boone pushed himself beside Mary, a low growl rumbling from deep in his throat, ears laid back. "You have a dog," Maud said and stepped back. A hand flew to her throat.

"Yes, I do." Mary scanned the yard for any sign of trouble. "I also have a gun, as you may recall."

"I'm quite alone, and unarmed. I was hoping we could have a conversation that did not involve gunfire."

Boone stood firm in the doorway, blocking Maud's entrance. Mary didn't know whether to trust the woman's motives. She remembered the last time Maud paid her a visit, fourteen years earlier. She couldn't forget Maud's look of horror, the smugness, when she saw the picture of Ander and Robert posing in their Confederate gray.

"May I come in? It's rather cold today."

Mary ordered Boone back into his corner bed and let Maud enter. Boone's eyes followed Maud's every move, and she watched his.

"Why are you here, Maud? You certainly made your feelings quite clear at Gretchen's last night. I don't see where there's anything else to discuss."

Mary scooped up her letter to Sarah and hid it in her pocket. She had finished it days before but hadn't had a chance to post it.

"Actually, the reason for my visit is two-fold. First, I came by to apologize. I've given it a lot of thought since last night and have come to the conclusion that I was very rude to you and Mr. Polk. That was neither the time, nor the place, to air our grievances. I drew a lot of attention upon myself, which made everyone else in the room uncomfortable, including my husband, who doesn't embarrass easily."

Could Maud's apology be sincere? Mary was uncertain how to respond. She wasn't expecting an apology, but rather more accusations and threats. "Thank you. Apology accepted."

But I'll still be watching you, your friends, and your husbands.

Maud smiled.

"Would you like a cup of coffee?" Mary knew that being rude would only give Maud ammunition to use against her at a later date.

"Yes, thank you."

"I'm afraid it's my turn to apologize," Mary said when she returned with two cups. "But I don't have a single cookie or slice of cake in the house to offer with your coffee." Mary's blood ran cold, her heart raced. Maud was holding her picture of Ander and Robert. Mary wanted to snatch it back, but her feet wouldn't move.

"That's quite all right." Maud glanced over her shoulder and smiled. "I admit to having two slices of Gretchen's Black Forest Cake last night, and my dress is feeling a little snug today, as proof."

Mary's hands shook as she set the two coffee cups on the table, almost dropping one.

Maud turned her attention back to the photograph. "What was your son's name?"

"Anderson, but we called him Ander." Her voice cracked, and she cleared her throat.

"How old was he when he died?" Maud asked.

"Twenty-one. He was killed on the last day of Gettysburg. Your son?"

"Jonathan. He was just fifteen. Ran off in the night and enlisted without us knowing until after the fact. Had to lie about his age to get accepted. Shot down just six months later."

"I'm sorry." Mary wasn't lying. She understood the pain Maud would feel for the rest of her days.

"Me, too. The other young man?"

"That's Robert Shaw. He was Ander's best friend. They enlisted together. Two young men with a head full of ideas about war and glory."

Maud nodded. "Jonathan, too. No one could tell him different."

"But we tried," Mary remembered.

"Yes."

The two women stood silent for a moment, Maud starring at the photo.

"Did he return? Your son's friend?"

"Yes."

"I'm happy for his mother." Maud placed the picture back in place.

Next, she picked up the photograph of Ander and Lillian. Mary rushed to her side and snatched the picture from her hands.

"I apologize. I should have asked before touching such precious belongings. I assume that's also your son with a sibling."

"Yes." Mary ran her finger over Lillian's face. "Her name was Lillian. She was born too early and taken from us far too soon."

"As so many are," Maud agreed. "Then this one would be your wedding day, I presume." She looked at the last picture on the mantel, this time without touching. "You and your husband made a handsome couple."

"Thank you."

Mary found herself telling Maud about each person in the picture and what became of them. She didn't know why she was suddenly being so open with her. She knew better than to trust the woman. Maybe if Maud knew them as two people with families, two people who loved each other very much, and not just two Confederate rebels, then maybe all the hatred could come to an end. She didn't tell her about their secret night visitors, about the last two girls shot down as they ran through the woods. Nor did she speak of the young Confederate officer she'd been forced to kill to save Earl's life. Some things were better left in the past.

"You've suffered a lot of loss in your life, and for that I'm truly sorry. Unfortunately, we've talked so long I have to rush off now. I need to run a few errands before going home to make dinner for Augustus."

"You said the reason for your visit was two-fold," Mary reminded her. "What is the second reason?"

Maud turned and her smug smile returned. "Oh, yes. I just wanted to let you know people are talking about you in town this morning, you and Mr. Polk and your little appearance at Gretchen's last night. I wanted to warn you that your behavior was quite unseemly."

"Unseemly?" Mary was confused. "What could possibly be construed as unseemly about two friends having dinner together?"

"Oh, please, Mrs. Bishop! That was not just two friends having dinner together. The two of you were cooing over each other like a couple of love birds . . . and your poor husband barely cold in his grave. I can understand Mr. Polk looking for someone. Irma's been passed on for some years now and, besides, it's different for men. They need a woman to take care of them. But you . . ." She shook her head. "Very unseemly, indeed."

With those parting words, Maud Henry swept out of Mary's home as suddenly as she appeared. Leaving two full cups of cold coffee on the parlor table, and Mary stunned in the middle of the room.

THE NEXT MORNING IT was Frances who knocked on the door. Mary was baking bread and thinking about Maud's visit the day before.

"I'm not one to gossip, but there's something I think you need to know." Frances rushed in all breathless, her hair working free from the pins around her face. Mary wondered if Frances, too, had come to condemn her for her shameful Valentine's Day behavior.

She wiped her hands on her apron, took Frances' coat, hat, and gloves, and offered her a chair in the kitchen so they could talk while she worked her bread dough.

"What's got you all worked up?" she asked, hoping it was anything else.

"Was Maud Henry out to visit you yesterday?"

"Yes." Mary stopped kneading. As she feared, Frances had come to chastise her and insist she wear the appropriate widow's weeds. "She said she came to apologize for her behavior at Gretchen's."

"She's up to something." Frances leaned over to greet Boone with a scratch behind the ears. "*They're* up to something—Maud, Agnes, and Gladys. I overheard them talking while they cleaned the church. I guess they didn't know anyone else was there."

"What were they saying?"

"Maud was telling them all about some pictures of your family. Did you show her pictures? Did you tell her about your family?"

"She saw the photographs on the mantel of our wedding day, our children. She asked questions. I thought if she saw us as regular people, she'd stop harassing me."

"Well, Maud was telling them all about your family, and they were laughing. They said it was good to know there was only one Bishop left on this earth and that wouldn't be for long, if they had their way. They thought it a very good thing your family is gone, that you're all alone."

A pain shot through Mary's heart, almost dropping her to her knees. Maud did it to her again. She couldn't believe she was foolish enough to let her guard down like that with Maud Henry, of all people, a second time. She couldn't believe even someone like Maud could be so cruel as to say those things, and then laugh about it with her friends.

"You need to be careful. Don't let those women into your house again. I hate to say it, being a Christian woman and the wife of a minister, but those women are evil."

Mary pressed down hard on the springy dough with the heels of her hands, turned it, folded it over, then pressed down hard again.

"Just so you know, I stopped at the store and told Oliver on my way out of town. I felt he should know, seeing as he's sweet on you."

Mary blushed. "For heaven's sake, Frances, you make us sound like a couple of kids."

"He makes you feel young, though, doesn't he? I can tell."

Mary made herself busy and refused to look Frances in the eyes. Maud's words rang in her head. *Unseemly!*

Perhaps Maud was right. There was certainly something unseemly about Oliver's kiss. It promised more than a chaste good night.

No, there was nothing chaste about that kiss.

The memory made Mary blush.

"Yes, he does. I can tell," Frances said again.

"You don't think it's too soon? After Earl, I mean."

"Why do you ask?"

"An apology wasn't the only reason Maud came by." Mary stopped kneading her dough. Much longer and the bread would be inedible. It was probably already bordering on shoe leather. She wiped her flour-coated hands on her apron. "She wanted to tell me my behavior with Oliver was unseemly for a new widow and warned that everyone in town is talking about me."

"That's not true! I haven't heard a single unkind word said about you and Oliver. If anyone is talking, it's her little hen party. I never knew a group of women with so much time for gossip and so little compassion for a neighbor."

"I fear she may be right. I don't know what I was thinking when I accepted Oliver's invitation."

"Well, I think you and Oliver make a wonderful couple." She put on her coat. "I'm going to tell the Reverend about all of this as soon as I get home. I want you to know there are more people in town that are on your side, than those that are on hers."

"I find that hard to believe."

"Well, it's true." Frances picked up Sarah's letter from the sideboard. "Would you like me to mail this for you? I pass right by the Post Office."

"That would be nice," Mary said, handing her three pennies for postage. "I don't even know if Sarah still lives there. It's been so long."

"Old friend?"

Mary nodded. "From our years in Virginia."

"Then she'll be glad to hear from you."

Mary closed the door behind Frances and returned to the kitchen. Her holstered Colt hung from a peg within easy reach. She sighed. She had almost convinced herself it would be safe to put it away, that maybe they were finished with all the awfulness.

Perhaps not quite yet.

She put her bread in the oven, stacked her mixing dishes by the sink, and began scrubbing the table. She didn't stop cleaning until the kitchen was spotless, and she was too tired to be angry with Maud Henry and her friends.

CHAPTER 32

WISCONSIN: FEBRUARY 1881

"So, you're going to let Maud win." Oliver looked at Mary long and hard. She understood his confusion, frustration.

"No . . . well . . . no! I just happen to agree with her this time." She poured him a cup of coffee but almost spilled it down the front of his shirt when she turned and found him standing tight behind her. "Sit down, Oliver. You're making me nervous standing over me like this, following me around."

"I will not sit down until you give me a straight answer." He took the cup from her and set it aside.

He smelled of horse leather and sawdust. Mixed with the aroma of fresh coffee, it was comfortable, like they belonged together. Her breath escaped in a sigh. Her knees wobbled when he leaned in to kiss her. His lips were soft and tasted like desire. She slipped to the side, away from his grasp, while she still had the strength.

"I think maybe Maud's right this time. It's too soon after Earl. People will talk."

Oliver took a step toward her, and she took another step back. If he kissed her again, she'd lose all control. She couldn't let him get any closer. Since Maud's and Frances' visits, she had spent a lot of time thinking about what to do. She knew she was right.

"We need to take some time apart, time to decide what's best for both of us. Scandal is not, I know that much for certain. I've had enough scandal and gossip aimed my way to last a lifetime."

"I already know you're what's best for me," Oliver persisted, his voice rising. Boone stirred where he slept in the corner. "I know Earl hasn't been dead that long, but he stopped being a husband to you long before he hung himself." He was almost shouting. Boone barked a warning.

Mary trembled with her efforts to control her fast-rising temper. How dare he say Earl wasn't a good husband to her. "You can leave now."

"Mary," he reached for her. "I'm sorry. I shouldn't have—"

"Get out!" She shouted, reaching for the Colt. "Get out before I'm forced to use this on you."

They faced each other for a long moment.

"Mary, please," he begged. "I'm sorry—"

Mary's hand shook where it rested on her gun. "Go!"

Oliver sighed. His shoulders slumped. He picked up his hat from the table and walked to the door. But then he stopped, stood silent with his back to her for what felt like a lifetime.

Her anger began to dissolve. Mary raised one hand to touch him, then pulled back. She wanted to assure him it wouldn't be forever, just for a while. She needed to think, sort things out.

Oliver turned and drew himself up to full height. His stare hard and cold.

"I love you, and that isn't going to change because Maud Henry says it should. So, no, I won't get out. I'm not leaving until you admit you love me, too, and nothing anyone else says will change your mind."

There were no words to express how she felt at that moment. She did love him, but her shock and anger at what he said about Earl had robbed her of speech. The room spun with all the possibilities, all the *what ifs*. She gripped the back of the chair to keep from falling. Oliver dropped his hat on the table and strode across the room toward her. She rushed to the other side of the table, out of his reach, looking for something, anything, to throw. He followed her, steady and determined.

"I told you to leave my house, Oliver Polk!" She pulled her arm back to avoid his grasp, but she was too slow. She struggled to free herself.

"Stand still and talk to me, just for a minute. Then I'll leave you alone, if that's what you truly want."

She stopped fighting, and he let go of her arm. He was so close she could kiss him without having to lean in. She wanted to kiss him, more than she could have ever imagined possible, but she didn't dare. She knew if she did, she would never stop. She would want to spend the rest of eternity in his arms.

"Tell me you love me," he whispered, his face so close to hers she felt his warm breath on her cheek. "Just tell me you love me and I'll leave. That's all I need to hear. Then I'll give you all the time you need to sort this out."

"I love you." She barely heard her own words over the beating of her heart. They hung between the two of them like the scent of spring flowers.

Oliver kissed her again. He smiled, took her face in his hands and kissed her over and over. She knew she should stop him, tell him to leave, as he promised. She needed him, craved his touch, his kisses, the way a starving man craved food, the way a drowning man needed air. She was certain if she didn't have him, all of him, that very minute, she would surely die.

Mary pushed him back. "Not here." She took him by the hand and led him into her bedroom. Boone stretched and stood to follow.

"Sorry." Oliver stopped him. "Not this time." He closed the door.

WHEN MARY WOKE, THE afternoon light shone low through the window, throwing long shadows across the bed.

Oh, Lord, what have I done?

She tried to free herself from Oliver's arms, but he pulled her tighter. She shook him. "Wake up, Oliver. You have to go."

"Why?" He kissed her and held her close, not opening his eyes.

Mary slipped out from under his arm and gathered up the clothes they'd left strewn about the room in their haste to have all that they could of each other. She tossed his shirt and trousers at him.

"I said get up. You have to go. You promised." She stepped into her skirt and buttoned it tight. Boone snuffled beneath the door and scratched to be let in. "Stop that, Boone!" He whimpered. His nails clicked across the floor in retreat.

The bed creaked, and Oliver was beside her in two strides. Still naked, he slid an arm around her waist. She buried her face in his chest. The smell of his skin, its heat, made her want him again.

"No!" She pushed.

He fell back a step. "What's wrong?"

"Everything. This. Us. It's all wrong." She handed him his clothes. "Get dressed. You have to go."

She left the room before he could touch her again, kiss her, make her forget how to breathe. How could she let herself surrender so easily? What they had done was wonderful, no doubt about that. She hadn't felt passion like that in a long time, not even with Earl. But this was wrong.

Oliver's footsteps sounded behind her. She stepped behind the table and out of his reach.

"I don't understand." There was an edge to his voice she didn't like, but certainly understood. "Seems to me you enjoyed it as much as I did."

"Oh, yes. I can honestly say I can't remember the last time I enjoyed myself that much, but it can't happen again."

"I don't understand," he repeated. "First you tell me to leave, then you invite me into your bed, and now you tell me to leave again?"

"I know. I don't half understand myself right now. But I do know I need time to think."

Oliver stared, mouth open.

"Just go, Oliver, please." Mary's voice caught. A tear ran down her cheek. "Please," she begged.

"Fine." Oliver grabbed his hat and coat. "You know where to find me when you're ready to talk sense." He closed the door and was gone.

Mary stood where he left her and listened as he shook the reins and commanded his team to head back to town. The wagon creaked with the horses' first hard pull. They snorted and stomped at the ground for footing. It wasn't until he was gone that she finally moved to the parlor and dropped onto her chair. Her heart told her to run after him. Her head told her to stay put. She was filled with grief. Her heart weighted heavy in her chest as her world shattered into a thousand pieces. She knew he loved her, and she loved him, but could knowing that be enough?

He had no right to say what he did about Earl. Earl loved her and the children. No one could ever convince her otherwise. He was the best husband and father he knew how to be. It didn't matter that he was injured deep inside, or that every slight, every blow dealt him over the years chipped away at the cracks and left it harder and harder for him to stand. Taking his own life did not mean his love for her was gone, or weakened, only that he'd lost his sense of worth, what it meant to him to be a man, until he could no longer live with his own perceived failures.

When they met, she'd been a young girl in love and believed the poets who painted such glorious promises with their words—promises of happily ever after, promises of sunshine and rainbows until the end of time. She dreamt of growing old beside Earl, children and grandchildren filling their home with laughter. Yet here she was, just her and her dog, gray hairs at her temples, and a cold wind at her back.

Then there was Oliver. There was no denying her love for him was strong. It had begun so quietly she could hardly admit it to herself until she heard the words from her own mouth. He'd been Earl's friend, her friend, for years. Never once had she imagined being in his arms, kissing him. But now that seemed to be all she could think about.

Was Maud right? Was it too soon? Was she behaving scandalously? Probably. Earl hadn't been gone more than a couple of months, and here she was throwing herself into the arms of another man. Not to mention, that man was Earl's best friend. But she loved Oliver. She truly loved him. What could be wrong with that?

"Oh, Boone." She wept. "What should I do, Boone? What should I do?" Boone whimpered. She knelt down to hug him where he had come to sit at her feet.

"What should I do?"

CHAPTER 33

WISCONSIN: MARCH 1881

Mary looked inside the sugar canister.

"Empty." She sighed and replaced the lid.

She could no longer avoid Oliver. She was running out of everything. It wasn't only the sugar. There wasn't enough flour to bake even one loaf of bread, or enough coffee to get her through one more day. She used the last of her black thread mending the skirt she caught on a nail last week and now couldn't mend the coat hem she tore on that same nail. She really needed to remember to either pull that nail or pound it back flat.

But she couldn't seem to concentrate on anything other than the way it felt to be in Oliver's arms, the soft heat of his kiss. Her cheeks burned with the memory of what followed the kiss. Then there was the look on his face when he walked out her front door. Anger, pain, confusion, everything she was experiencing, too.

It had been a month but seemed like only yesterday.

She found a scrap of paper, made a list, and tucked it into her pocket.

"Well, Boone, I have no choice. I'm going to have to go to town for supplies or they're going to find my emaciated dead body dressed in rags. Now wouldn't that give Maud Henry and her friends something to talk about."

Boone barked and wagged his tail.

"I agree."

SPRING HAD STARTED its annual tease. Mary inhaled the rich dark smell of earth wet from snow melt. The first of the returning birds sang to each other high in the trees. She whistled back. A neighbor tapped his sugar maples. She made a mental note to be sure and buy a few jugs of syrup when he was done cooking. The weather had been perfect for sap that year, cold at night and warm during the day. He would have a good yield. Perhaps he'd barter some of her jam for his syrup.

He carried two more pails of sap out to his wagon and handed them up to his wife, who emptied them into the barrels before handing them back.

"Good morning, Alma, Thomas."

"Mornin'," Thomas grunted and walked away.

"Fine day, isn't it?" Mary looked at Alma, but the woman ignored her after a dark warning glance from her husband.

"Barrel's almost full, Thomas." Alma turned her back to Mary.

"Just two more pails and we're done," he replied.

"Yes, it is a fine day," Mary said. She looked up at the almost cloudless sky peeking through the still bare branches. She took a couple steps, then stopped and turned back. "Don't you let him work you too hard, Alma. Be sure and leave yourself some time to enjoy the day."

"Thank you. I will," Alma said.

"Alma, pay attention! We got too much work to do for you to be gabbing with Mrs. Johnnie Reb."

Alma took the pails her husband held up to her. "Sorry, Thomas, I didn't see you there." She handed him the empty pails. He tossed them into the wagon bed.

"Aren't you going to hang those again?"

"I'll do it later. All your talkin's wasted enough of my time. Now cover that barrel and sit down before you fall out." Thomas climbed up onto the seat and snapped the reins. Alma dropped back with a thud.

"You shouldn't call Mrs. Bishop that. It ain't Christian," Mary heard her say as they pulled away. "Besides, the war's been over a long time now."

Mary waved and Alma nodded back as the wagon disappeared around the turn.

She straightened her shoulders. Thomas' nasty words weren't going to ruin her beautiful spring morning. He always was kind of mean-spirited. Alma was the first to admit it when asked, but then she'd remind you how he'd lost his older brother to the fighting and hadn't been the same since. Mary could certainly understand that.

The streets were busy, and there was a line at Oliver's store. It seemed the weather had encouraged everyone to get out of the house—parents with errands to run, children chasing each other through the mud.

Oliver was busy helping one of the farmers with his wife's grocery list when Mary walked in. The man was claiming, loud enough for all to hear, that the fault was in his wife's handwriting. But it was well known he couldn't read and was too embarrassed to admit it. No one called him on the lie. Oliver took the list from him.

"Let me see if I can't read this chicken scratch," Oliver said with a kind smile. "Yes, I think I can just make this out. I'll take care of it for you." He collected various cans and jars and sacks from the shelves behind his counter and placed them in front of the man. "Does this look right to you?"

He handed the list back. The man pretended to compare it to the items in front of him. "Yes, yes, it does." He took one final look at the paper in his hand.

"Put it on your account?" Oliver loaded the items into a crate.

The man nodded, thanked Oliver, and carried his purchases out to his wagon.

A display of vegetable seed packets stood against the far wall. Mary occupied herself choosing what she would plant when it got a little warmer. Carrots, beans, peas, tomatoes, lettuce. She gathered the brightly colored envelopes in her hand. Squash, beets . . . and what else? Potatoes.

"Hello, Mary."

She dropped the seed packs on the floor. She was the last customer in the store. Oliver stood far too close for comfort. She longed for his touch, his kiss. Frances smiled, waved, and closed the door to the office, leaving the two of them alone.

She bent down to collect the fallen packets. "You startled me," she scolded. "I was so busy planning this year's garden I didn't hear your approach."

"Allow me." He gathered the remaining packets from the floor, his hand brushing hers. His touch like a candle flame against her skin.

Words escaped her as he stared deep into her eyes. He leaned in, slowly, and kissed her. She kissed him back. It was a bad idea, a dangerous one, but she couldn't help herself. She stepped back, her breath the only sound in the store.

"I have a list," she said, quickly changing the subject, and went to the front counter. "I brought a dozen eggs and two pounds of butter to help pay." She uncovered the goods in her basket.

"I've missed you." He stepped up behind her, placed his hands on her waist and leaned in to whisper, "I love you. Please don't send me away again."

His hot breath on her neck made her shiver. Her list crumpled in her hand. She tried to smooth out the wrinkles against the counter.

"Mr. Polk," her voice shook. "I must ask you to stop."

"I've given you time to think. I haven't come by, although God knows how much I've wanted to."

"Sugar," she read. "Flour." Her knees threatened to buckle along with her resolve. Her voice dropped to a whisper. "Coffee."

"Say it's all right, and I'll come by tonight, after dinner."

"I think that would be a very bad idea."

"We can talk, just talk, if that's what you like. I promise I won't kiss you." With that he let his lips brush lightly against her ear and her breath caught in her throat. "And I won't . . ." He let that thought hang in the silence.

She spun away, out of his grip and away from where he had her backed against the counter. "Please. I just need you to fill my list. Then I'll be on my way." She placed her seed packets on the counter next to the list.

He hesitated, walked around the counter, and quietly gathered her order. His manner stiff, he no longer smiled. She'd seen him treat a difficult customer with more courtesy than he was showing her.

"Can I put the difference on my account?"

"Of course." Oliver calculated the value of her eggs and butter against her purchase, wrote down the sum, and set it aside for Frances. "Good day, Mrs. Bishop."

Mary was stung by his formal tone, but why should she be?

Isn't this what I asked of him?

She fidgeted with her gloves. "I'm sorry. I just . . . I just need more time."

"I don't, but all right. More time." His voice was cold, distant.

Mary looked at the heavy box of groceries Oliver set on the counter. She hadn't considered how she would get them home.

"I walked," she said, almost a whisper.

"I'll arrange for someone to deliver them this afternoon. Good day."

"Good day, Oliver." Mary turned to leave, stopping in front of the sewing notions. She'd forgotten thread. She didn't want to go back. She needed the thread, but she'd been dismissed in no uncertain terms.

"Is there something else?" Oliver asked.

"I forgot black thread," she answered. "I meant to put it on my list, but I guess I forgot . . ." Her voice trailed off under his scrutiny.

Oliver came around the corner of the counter and placed a spool of black thread in her hand.

"Be certain to add this to my account."

"Consider it a gift." For a brief moment his eyes softened.

"Thank you." Mary left before she lost her nerve, dropped everything, and fell into his arms.

Out front, she almost knocked down Maud and Gladys in her rush to be gone. They looked from Mary to Oliver through the store display window, then back again.

"Unseemly," Maud said.

"Yes," Gladys agreed, and they walked away.

Before Mary could flee, Frances came out of the store, pinning her hat in place as she walked.

"I'm glad I caught you. I'm going to get a cup of tea at Gretchen's. Would you like to join me?"

"No, thank you. I have to get home."

"You're making a mistake. You know he loves you."

"I know."

CHAPTER 34

WISCONSIN: MAY 1881

Boone jumped about in the warm morning sunshine, enticing Mary to a game of fetch with the first muddy stick he could get his teeth around. He dropped it in front of her, stepped back, and wagged his tail, anxious for the chase. She tossed it. He bounded away, quick to return and drop it once more at her feet for another go.

The snow had been gone for weeks, but the return of the songbirds was Mary's assurance that winter was truly in retreat. She hadn't been to town in weeks, and no one, including Frances, had come out to see her. She had been left blessedly alone with her thoughts and had come to the conclusion that she was a fool if she let Maud Henry keep her from being happy with Oliver. He loved her, she loved him, and that was enough. She needed to tell him.

SHE DIDN'T KNOW IF it was her decision, the nice weather, or both, but Mary threw her shoulders back and, with a skip in her step, walked through town to Oliver's store. She hummed a favorite old song, the words long forgotten, whose melody came flooding back to her. People whispered to each other as she passed, but she didn't care. Not one little bit.

"Good morning," she said to each with a nod and a smile. They scurried away like night critters caught by the morning light.

"Good morning, Mrs. Bishop," a woman replied. She hesitated, mouth open to say more, but was stopped at the sight of Gladys Olson watching from the front door of her shop across the street.

"Good morning!" Mary shouted to Gladys. "Glorious day, isn't it? Don't you just love spring?" Mary smiled and waved. She laughed when Gladys ducked back into her shop with a quick worried glance up and down the street, in case anyone should notice and think they were friends.

Mary turned back to the timid woman, who, after watching Mary stand up to Gladys, stood a little taller. "I was sorry to hear about your little girl," she said, touching Mary's arm. "I lost twins like that, a boy and a girl. You never forget."

"A friend once told me that each star in the sky is a loved one gone before. They're always with us, just out of reach, patiently waiting, watching. Perhaps that will help when you're feeling lonely. I know it helps me."

The woman smiled and looked up over the roofs of the town. "Perhaps it will," she said. "Thank you."

Anna Mueller was sweeping springtime mud from Gretchen's front walk. Mary stopped to say hello.

"Something smells wonderful coming from your mother's kitchen."

"Apple kuchen," Anna said with a smile. "Warm from the oven. Would you like to come in and have a piece? The coffee is fresh, too."

The thought of Gretchen's apple kuchen made Mary's mouth water. Moist cake topped with slices of dried apple, brown sugar, and cinnamon. Mary glanced across the street. She wasn't the only person out doing her shopping on such a beautiful morning. Oliver's store was crowded with women. A couple of their husbands stood outside in hot debate over some topic or another. Mary couldn't decide who were the worst gossips, the women or their husbands. She would wait to tell Oliver her decision until there were fewer people around to eavesdrop. Not that she cared anymore.

"I believe I will," she said.

Anna leaned her broom against the wall inside the door. Mary took an empty table near the window where she could keep an eye on the store and know when it was quiet again.

"I'll be back with a nice big piece and a cup of coffee."

Mary had just enjoyed the first sweet bite when Maud Henry marched across the street, her eyes tight on Mary through the window.

"I was bound to run into her at some time," she said to herself, blowing on her coffee and taking a sip. "Might as well get it over with." She set the cup on the table and calmly took another bite of cake.

Maud sat down opposite her and gestured to Anna on the other side of the room.

The girl approached, obvious concern on her face. "Can I get you something, Mrs. Henry?"

"A cup of coffee, please."

"Kuchen? Warm from the oven."

"I whole-heartedly recommend it, Maud." Mary turned to Anna and smiled to set the girl at ease. "Tell your mother it's delicious."

"No, thank you," Maud said, ignoring Mary's cheerfulness. "Just coffee. I won't be staying long."

"And put it on my bill," Mary added.

Maud was clearly caught off guard by the generosity. "Thank you, Mrs. Bishop," she stammered. "But that wasn't necessary."

"Oh, but it is. I believe I still owe you a cup after our last visit was cut short." She paused to compose herself. "So, what can I do for you this fine spring morning?"

Maud gave an exaggerated sigh before proceeding. "What I'm about to tell you may be painful to start, but I feel in the long run you will thank me. I've given it a lot of prayerful consideration and I feel it is my duty, as a Christian and a fellow woman, to warn you Mr. Polk is deceiving you with any declarations of love he may have made."

Her concern was almost touching.

"I don't understand." Mary took another drink of her coffee, wiping her mouth on her napkin to hide her sudden wariness, uncertain of Maud's intent. Was this another trap?

"I know. He seems like such a nice man, and he is, to be sure, but it's true. In this case, his friendly exterior is a front for a malicious plot to hurt you." Anna set a steaming cup of coffee in front of her. "Thank you, dear."

Mary waited until Anna was out of ear shot before asking, "Why?" Maud had no reason to help her, as she claimed to be doing, so Mary did not trust her.

"Are you aware that Oliver and Irma Polk had a son?"

"Yes, I know about William. He died some years ago."

"But do you know *how* he died?"

"No. They never offered that information, and I have never asked. I saw no reason to pry into something so painful, as we are both aware from our personal experiences."

Maud waved at a friend passing the window. The woman looked at Mary, surprised, then back at Maud before crossing the street to Maud's shop. No doubt awaiting a full report.

Maud turned her attention back to their conversation. "He died in the War. A Union soldier."

"Many young men died in the War," Mary pointed out. It didn't make sense for Oliver and Irma to hide that about William, but it certainly didn't mean he was pretending to have feelings in order to hurt her. No doubt it was just too painful a memory to talk about. Some people kept such things close to their heart.

"He didn't perish in battle, as the rest of our sons did," Maud continued. "No, William Polk died a prisoner—at Andersonville, no less." Maud sipped her coffee and stared over her cup at Mary.

Mary gasped, almost spilling her own coffee. Andersonville was notorious for being brutal, for the inhumane way they treated their Union prisoners.

"He was beaten—tortured—starved." Maud paused between each word. They hit Mary like the blow of a hammer pounding a stake through her heart. "Until he was finally—mercifully—*allowed* to die—just a mere skeleton of his former self. His body tossed into an unmarked mass grave like some used-up Negro." She sipped her coffee. When the first tear escaped down Mary's cheek, Maud smiled, set down her cup, and stood to leave. "For a while we didn't know if Irma would ever get out of bed again. The only reason no one had brought this up to you before was our fear of what it might do to Irma. Then, by the time she passed away, well, by then there was no real reason to talk about it any longer. Until now, that is. Good day, Mrs. Bishop."

Maud stood and walked out with the same steady confidence with which she arrived. Gretchen rushed over to take Maud's seat. She held Mary's shaking hands and leaned across the table.

"I don't know what that woman said to you, but don't you listen to her. She's a mean old witch and nothing good ever came from her mouth."

"I have to go." Mary left some coins on the table and rushed from the restaurant, her half-eaten kuchen forgotten, her fork clattering to the floor when she accidentally knocked it from the table.

Her mind was a blur of questions, all screaming over the top of each other. Could it be true? Was Oliver and Irma's son tortured and starved to death at Anderson Prison?

"It must be true," she said to herself. It would be too easy to learn otherwise. Anyone in town could tell her if it were true or not. Maud would never put herself in such a position . . . unless she was certain Mary would believe her without question.

The sidewalks were crowded. People scattered from her path as she practically pushed her way through. A wagon pulled up short when she stepped in front of the horses without looking. The driver yelled something angry at her.

"Why wouldn't they have told us?" she asked herself.

"Excuse me?" a woman passerby asked. "Mrs. Bishop, are you all right? Can I help?"

Mary turned, confused. It was the same woman who spoke to her so kindly earlier. "What if Maud's telling the truth?" Mary asked herself. Asked no one in particular.

"The truth about what?" the woman called after as Mary rushed off again.

What if Maud was telling the truth and the Polks were never their friends? What if Oliver really was just biding his time, waiting for the perfect moment to spring it on her? What if he was part of the reason Earl killed himself?

Mary stopped. "None of this is true. It doesn't make sense. Oliver loves me. He said so." She would go to the store and ask him directly.

But . . . what if?

She stopped again. "You're an old fool, Mary Bishop!"

She almost ran Oliver down when he stepped out from the Post Office and into her path. He reached for her arm to stop her. She dodged his grip.

"Mary, I heard you were in town." His voice trailed off as she continued on her way home. "What's wrong?"

"Everything . . . nothing . . . I don't know . . . I have to think," she called back over her shoulder.

Mary didn't stop until she reached home and closed the front door behind her. She collapsed to the floor in a torrent of tears. Boone licked her face and rested his head in her lap.

"You would never betray me, would you, Boone. At least I'll always have you."

CHAPTER 35

WISCONSIN: MAY 1881

"At least we still have each other, Boone, and that will have to be enough."

Boone laid his head on Mary's lap and there they stayed, her back against the door. Mary scratched behind his ears, and Boone offered nothing more than his love in return. Her breathing slowed, and a semblance of peace returned in the calm of her quiet house.

"Perhaps Earl and I should have gotten another dog a long time ago, after the War was over and Ander was gone, or after we moved to this hate-filled little town. Perhaps Earl would still be with us." Boone licked her face. "Did I ever tell you about the first Boone? He was a very brave dog. He saved our Ander from drowning."

Her thoughts were interrupted by a commotion in the yard and a hard knock at the door.

"Mary?"

"Go home, Oliver!"

"Let me in. Tell me what's wrong."

She wasn't ready to talk to him, and there was nothing he could say that would make her feel any differently. She shared everything with him, all her pain over losing Lillian and Ander, and most recently Earl. Yet he kept something as monumental as William's death at Andersonville from her, from Earl.

"I know Maud's behind this. Gretchen told me you two had coffee, that Maud said something to upset you."

Mary debated whether to tell him.

"What did she say to you?" His voice was soft, pleading. "Talk to me."

The door shifted as he leaned against the other side. She could almost feel him touching her, his breath against the back of her neck, his arms around her waist, as if there wasn't a wooden door separating them.

"William. Andersonville." Mary's voice cracked with new sobs. "You should have told me yourself."

Oliver groaned. "Let me in. Let me explain."

She didn't answer. She didn't know what to say.

"I love you."

She loved him, too, but how could she trust him when he didn't trust her. Yet, he did deserve his say. She could give him that much.

Mary pushed Boone aside and he returned to his bed in the sunlight. Whimpering, he buried his nose in his paws. She stood and brushed her skirt clean, then ran her fingers over her hair, trying to force the loose strands back into place, aware that she must look a sight. Only then did she open the door.

Oliver stood, hat in hand, on her threshold. His eyes reflected the pain in her heart. She wanted to throw herself into his arms.

"Do you? How can I believe you love me when you clearly don't trust me?"

"Can I come in?" he asked.

Mary's resolve weakened, and she stepped aside to let him pass.

"Do you love me?" she asked again.

"With all my heart, Mary, and I know you love me, too." He stood close to her, caressed her arm, and leaned in close to kiss her.

Mary jumped back where his touch couldn't distract her. "Why didn't you tell me about William? About Andersonville? You know everything about me, yet, I didn't know perhaps the most important thing about you."

"When you first arrived in town his death was still too close. We didn't talk about William with anyone. Then, as time went on, there never seemed to be a reason, a good time, to tell you. We were afraid the news would be more upsetting than helpful, especially once everyone learned about your son and all your troubles began." He dropped into a chair and buried his face in his hands.

His explanation made sense, more sense than anything Maud said. "You didn't trust us," she said, aware how tenuous their friendship was in the beginning. "You didn't trust us to understand and still accept you as friends. Did you think we would turn on you the way the town turned on us?"

Her accusations must have stung, because when he looked up at her his eyes glistened with restrained tears. Her heart broke for him, for her, for all they stood to lose.

"Yes. I'm ashamed to admit it. Irma and I were afraid you would judge us, or think we were judging you. We were wrong. We saw that later, but by then it seemed too late, unnecessary even, to tell you. Talking about William would not bring him back to us."

Mary sat across the table from him. His explanation made sense. She wanted to believe him, saw no reason not to, except for what Maud said. And her reputation did not speak well of her honesty.

He reached across the table and took her hands in his. His were cold. She folded hers around them, trying to warm him.

"The War's been over almost sixteen years now," he continued. "Don't you think it's time we put it behind us, both as a nation and . . ." He pulled her hands to his lips and kissed them. "And as two individuals who suffered and lost so much?"

"It's hard to forget. Sometimes it feels like only yesterday."

Oliver stood, pulled her to her feet, and wrapped his arms around her. He smelled of wood and spices, tobacco, and horse leather. Mary closed her eyes and drew in a deep heady breath.

"But we must," he said.

His heart raced against hers, his fingers tensed against her back. She looked into his eyes, his gaze intense, drawing her in. He kissed her again. Not a soft, sweet kiss, but a hard kiss, hungry with passion. Her mind spun and breath caught. She was seconds away from complete surrender.

"Stop!" She pushed him away, held up her hands as a shield. "Please, stop." Her voice caught and tears trailed down her cheeks.

"Mary—"

"I can't do this. I'm sorry. I'm so confused. Just a little more time." She stepped back.

"More time?" His apology turned to anger. "I've given you weeks of time, months of time."

"You have to understand."

"But I don't. Tell me, why more time?"

"I don't know what to think, how I feel. I mean, I know how I feel, I just don't know how I feel about how I feel." Her heart told her to go to him, go into his arms and never let go. But her head was telling her to wait, to stop and think first, not be impetuous.

"Now you're talking in circles. Either you love me, or you don't. You said you love me. Do you really, Mary? Do you love me?"

"Yes. That is the one thing I do know. I just—"

"Just what?" he snapped.

"I don't know." Mary's voice caught. It seemed all she was doing lately was either singing with joy or crying. "You have to go, Oliver. Please."

"Oh, I'll go." He grabbed his hat and reached for the door. "But know this. My patience is running thin, and you're almost out of time."

He slammed the door and rode away.

"Oh, Boone, what have I done?" Mary dropped onto a chair and closed her eyes. "I went to town to accept Oliver's love, and then I sent him away again. He has every right to be angry with me. It would serve me right if he never forgave me this time."

The sound of a horse and a knock on the door brought her back to her feet.

"Oliver?" She threw open the door.

It was Frances. "We just saw Oliver riding hard for town. He looked angry. Did you two have another fight?"

A second woman stepped around from the other side of the buggy. Her hair was now more gray than blond, and her face as wrinkled as Mary's, but Mary would know her friend anywhere.

"Sarah?" She could hardly believe it was true.

"What happened, Mary? Did you let that temper of yours get the best of you again?"

"Oh, Sarah!" She threw herself into her old friend's arms and cried for joy.

Frances set Sarah's bag by the door and went home.

CHAPTER 36

WISCONSIN: MAY 1881

Was it really Sarah standing right in front of her? Mary pinched herself to make sure it wasn't a dream.

They hugged again, and their years apart were washed away. Boone barked and wriggled his way between them.

Mary held her out at arm's length. "How did you get here?"

Sarah freed herself from Mary's grip. "Easy. Train to Stillwater, then steamboat to Taylors Falls. I never imagined your river was so beautiful! The bluffs are inspiring, towering above the river, crowned in green."

"Good fishing, too," Mary said.

"Gosh," Sarah shook her head. "It's been years since I've been fishing."

Mary hugged her again. "Well, then, we'll have to remedy that."

"Anyway," Sarah continued, "from Taylors Falls I was able to hitch a ride with a traveling minister Frances knew would be passing this way. The Reverend Redmond Thorpe, a fascinating man full of so many stories of his travels." She shrugged. "Anyway, he dropped me at the parsonage and the rest you know."

A stray tear ran down Mary's cheek. She wiped it away with the back of her hand. "Sorry." Her voice cracked. "It's just, I felt so alone, and now I don't. Knowing you're still alive, having you here next to me, I feel young again. It's like we're back in Virginia with our husbands, that our sons will come running barefoot from the river any minute to show off their catch."

Sarah looked her up and down. "You haven't changed one bit," she said with a nod.

Mary laughed. "You're too kind. I've grown old and fat." She touched her hair where it was graying at the temples.

"We all do in the end."

"Not you. I'd know you anywhere."

"And I'd know you. Now, enough of this. Are you going to invite me in, or are we going to stand outside and exchange polite lies indefinitely?"

Mary picked up Sarah's bag and Boone led the way. "How long can you stay?"

"As long as you'll have me."

Mary opened the door and let her pass. "Careful. I might never let you leave."

"You have a beautiful home, Mary. And the porch is just like the one back in Virginia. Did Earl build it?"

"The house was already here, but Earl fixed it up and added the porch for me."

"And who is this that's been trying so hard to get my attention?" She leaned down to scratch Boone behind the ears and immediately gained a friend for life.

"This is Boone. He just recently joined my household. A gift from the Reverend and Frances." Mary set Sarah's bag aside for the time being and took her shawl and hat to hang on a peg by the door.

"Boone." Sarah sighed. "I haven't thought about him in years. Whatever happened to the first Boone?"

"He died not long after you left, never did get over Ander's loss. It's like he knew. Stopped eating, then he was gone."

They moved into the parlor, both quiet at the mention of Ander's name. "Robert speaks of Ander from time to time, always with tremendous grief." Sarah saw the picture on the mantel. Tears bloomed in the corners of her eyes as she gazed at it, held it to her heart for a moment, then set it back in place. "He blames himself, you know, for talking Ander into enlisting."

"You tell Robert it's not his fault. We never blamed him. The idea had been on Ander's mind for some time, and there was no stopping him from doing what he felt was good and noble—like punching another boy for making fun of a little girl's freckles." She sat and motioned Sarah to take the chair across from her.

Sarah laughed as she sat. "Oh, what a day. Mr. Nichols was a horrible man. Did you know Lucas went to the school board to try and have him dismissed for what he said about our sons?"

"No!" Mary put a hand to her mouth. "I never knew that."

"Oh, yes." Sarah nodded. "And Earl went with him."

"My Earl?" Mary leaned back and shook her head. She never imagined. He hadn't told her.

"Did you know another?" Sarah asked.

Mary sat up straight and waved a hand in the air. "Well, clearly it didn't work because that man was still teaching when we left for Wisconsin. And still terrorizing his students, from what I heard."

"So, tell me what's happening here. Imagine my surprise when I get two letters in the same day, one from a long lost, but never forgotten, friend, and the other from a minister's wife named Frances I'd never even heard of before."

"Frances wrote you? "But how . . .?" That's right, Frances had offered to mail Sarah's letter. "Was she the reason you came?"

"No, your letter was the reason I came." Sarah leaned over and took Mary's hand in hers. "Why didn't you write me sooner and tell me what was happening? You and Earl could have come to St. Paul. We would have helped you start over."

Mary shook her head. "We couldn't live in a big city. Earl needed room to hunt and fish. He was never happier than when he was out in the woods."

"There are sawmills in St. Paul, and always a need for good carpenters." Sarah stood and ran her hand along the carved mantel. "Earl did this, too, didn't he? I recognized his work the moment I saw it. Simple, practical, yet the center of the room."

"All the noise, all the people . . . no. We could never be happy living in the city."

Sarah faced Mary. "Come back with me. You can sell this place and use the money to buy a little house of your own with enough yard for a garden. We could see each other every day again. I know Robert and Amy Lynn would love to have you there. A second grandmother to the children. You've never met my grandchildren."

"We always talked about being grandmothers together. You're a lucky woman, Sarah."

"Two boys and a girl. They're a handful, but they're good kids, and I know they'd love you, too."

"I'll visit one day, I promise, but I could never live there. I have my horses, my animals, Boone. And what about Oliver?" Was that a coy look she saw flash in Sarah's eyes at the mention of Oliver's name?

"What about him? I know you love him but, according to Frances, you've rejected his love. It would be a fresh start."

Sarah was right, she had rejected Oliver's love, not once but three times. Yet, she found she couldn't even think of leaving him behind without her heart breaking.

"Unless you're reconsidering?"

There was that spark in Sarah's eyes again, and the little smile that said she knew what you were thinking.

"I don't know what I'm considering," Mary admitted.

"And then there are all these awful townspeople. The way they drove Earl to despair. The way they denied him his livelihood and taunted him. They destroyed him, Mary. You said so yourself. You could leave them all behind."

Sarah was right, but Mary didn't know how to respond. "Would you like some sweet tea?"

Sarah followed her to the kitchen. "I'm not trying to be cruel. You're my friend, and I'm worried about you in this place. Those men tried to burn your barn down. They took a shot at you."

"And I shot back, as you will recall. I can take care of myself."

Mary went out to the spring house, chipped ice into a pitcher, and filled it with cold tea from a jug she kept hanging from a rope down the well. When she returned, Sarah was setting out bread and jam on the table.

"I've missed your jam."

"I'll be sure and send some back with you. Don't let me forget." Mary poured tea into the glasses and placed the pitcher between them.

"So, was that Oliver we saw riding away earlier? He looked angry. Did you have a fight?" She took a bite of her bread. "This is even better than I remember," she said with a little groan of pleasure.

"Thank you." Mary took a bite of her own. "Yes, that was Oliver, and, yes, we had a fight. I just need more time. That's all. I don't know why men can't understand that, why they can't be patient."

"Did you need time with Earl? Did you have to think about whether or not to accept his love?"

"Of course not, but that was different."

"How? How was that different?"

"Earl didn't betray me the way Oliver did."

Sarah set down her glass. "Is there another woman? If there's another woman then there's nothing to think about. You don't need time. You need to put a whole lot of miles between you and a cheater. No man is worth that."

"No, it's nothing like that." Mary paused, then the whole story about William and his tortured death at Andersonville spilled out.

"And he claims he never told you because he didn't want to hurt you."

"Yes, but can I believe him? Maud Henry told me—"

"Forget about Maud Henry. She's the one you can't trust. Not Oliver."

"So, you believe him?"

Sarah was quiet for a moment. "Yes," she admitted. "I believe Oliver. That man clearly loves you. You said so in your letter, Frances said as much on the ride here, and the truth of that is written all over your face for the whole world to see. Except you."

Mary blushed and looked down at her glass, wiping condensation from the sides with her napkin. Sarah always could distill a problem right down to the simple heart of the matter.

"Enough about me," she said, changing the subject. "Tell me about Robert and Amy Lynn. Tell me all about your grandchildren."

They spent the rest of the afternoon and evening laughing at Sarah's grandchildren stories, comparing them to Robert and Ander as boys. It was good to have her friend back in her life. She would have to be sure and thank Frances for her meddling. And she'd have to find a way to keep Oliver in her life while she sorted everything out in her head.

CHAPTER 37

WISCONSIN: MAY 1881

The smell of biscuits baking and pork gravy simmering in a pan coaxed Mary from her sleep. Before she could answer the quiet knock at her bedroom door, a smiling Sarah came in and greeted her with a cup of fresh coffee.

"Wake up! Day's half gone. I never knew you to be anything but an early riser. What would Earl think of you sleeping to all hours?"

Mary was overcome by the sight of her friend. She had almost convinced herself it was all a dream until she smelled that familiar southern home cooking. Sarah had come back into her life.

"Oh, for heaven's sake. Tears again? I thought we were done with all that."

"You really are here." Mary wiped her eyes with the sleeve of her nightgown.

"Yes, I really am here. And I'm going to get you through this. I owe you." Sarah sat on the edge of Mary's bed and handed her the coffee. "You were there for me, all through my darkest days. You and Earl. Well, best he could in his own grief. And there was no one kinder to Robert than Ander." She wiped one last stray tear from Mary's cheek. "You will get through this."

"I missed you, my friend."

"I know you did. And you know how I know you did?"

"How?"

"Because you keep telling me."

Mary laughed. Sarah was right. She must have told her friend at least a dozen times since she showed up on her doorstep. "I guess I just want you to believe me."

"I do." Sarah patted Mary's leg through the blankets. "Now get yourself up out of that bed and dressed. I have the whole day planned. We are going to start Sarah's plan for healing Mary's heart with a hot breakfast, and it's almost ready. So, no dawdling." She took the coffee cup from Mary's hands and set it on the bedside table.

Mary dropped her feet to the floor as Sarah closed the door behind her. She knew they stayed up late the night before remembering all the old times, but she couldn't believe she'd slept that long.

Her stomach growled when she saw the steaming plate of biscuits and gravy Sarah set in front of her. "You didn't have to cook, Sarah. You are a guest in my home, not the hired help."

"I am not a guest. I'm family, remember? You told me that once, a long time ago, when I most needed to hear it."

Mary nodded. "I remember."

"I'll never forget." Sarah went back into the kitchen.

Mary wondered if Sarah ever found out the true nature of the extra deliveries their men took out of the county. Sarah never asked, and Mary never offered.

Sarah returned with a plate of food for herself. "Oh, and don't worry about the animals. They've been fed and their stalls cleaned." Sarah settled herself at the table after topping off both coffee cups. "It's been a long time since I've mucked a stall or milked a cow or gathered eggs, but I'm proud to say I still know my way around a farm."

Mary gasped, almost choking on a mouthful of biscuit. "Tell me you did not do my chores, too!"

Her mouth full of sausage gravy, Sarah nodded. She swallowed and pointed her fork at Mary. "I did, and I'm glad of it. The city's made me soft. I'm thinking I might just move back to the country. Robert's home is getting awful crowded as those children grow up."

"Where would you go?"

"Maybe here. Should I move to Deer Creek?" She finished her coffee.

Mary's fork clattered against her plate. "After everything I've told you about the people?"

Sarah set down her cup. "I could buy a little house with an acre of land. Someplace with room for a nice big garden and perhaps a few chickens. The more I think about it, the more I like the idea."

Why would Sarah even consider such a thing? "After how they treated Earl? How they still treat me?"

"We'd have each other. And Frances seems nice. She told me about Gretchen on the drive out of town. I like her already, and I haven't even met her yet. I think there are possibly more good people than bad in this town. I think maybe your grief at losing Ander, your family, your home, and now Earl, has caused you to include a lot of good people in with a few bad."

"Perhaps." Mary paused to think about Sarah's words. There was the woman who stopped her on the street to say how sorry she was to hear about the loss of her children.

"And Reverend Thorpe, that minister I rode with from Taylors Falls, he's a lonely widower. It's been a long time since I spent that much time with a man my own age, just talking and keeping company. He passes through here regularly. Might also be time I find myself a new husband."

"You aren't suggesting . . ."

"I'm not suggesting anything. I'm just saying I've been alone for too long, and I didn't realize it myself until you wrote me about Oliver. I need an Oliver of my own to keep me company."

Mary's heart quivered at the mention of Oliver's name.

"I saw that, the way your eyes lit up." Sarah shook her fork at Mary with a sly smile. "And now you're blushing like a schoolgirl in love with her first beau."

Mary stacked their breakfast dishes and took them to the kitchen, keeping her back to Sarah so she couldn't see her burning cheeks. She pumped water to heat for washing up.

"You said you have our day all planned?" Mary changed the subject.

Sarah took Mary's hand from the pump. "I'll do these later."

"But—" Mary never left dishes unwashed after a meal.

"No argument. We have much to do today, and barely enough hours to do it all. Get your hat. We're going to town."

"What are we doing in town?" What did Sarah have up her sleeve?

"You'll see. But on the way I want to stop at the cemetery. Pay my proper respects to Earl."

DEER CREEK'S LITTLE cemetery didn't look quite so forlorn in the springtime with the grass turning green and the leaves budding out. A few people had been out to clean their family plots from leftover autumn leaves and branches blown down by winter winds. There were even a few bouquets of flowers left as a hello. The undertaker's sons had been out to place Earl's new stone, which made everything final. Mary wanted to walk away, unable to bear the heartache, but Sarah wrapped her arm around her and held her tight.

"Stay with me," she whispered. "You're lucky to have Earl so close. Sometimes it feels like Lucas never existed, like our marriage was all a dream. If it wasn't for Robert, the grandchildren . . ."

"I know what you mean. Sometimes it's as if I've abandoned my children, my brothers, my parents, by leaving them so far behind. I wonder if anyone remembers us, stops to clear the debris from their graves, leave them flowers. Sometimes I have to speak their names out loud to feel like they're still with me."

"Twenty-three years. It will be twenty-three years this July since Lucas died. He's been gone more years than we were married."

"I remember. Every Fourth of July I live it all over again in my nightmares."

"Can I ask you a question?" Sarah gave Mary a quick glance. "About that day."

Mary's heart pounded, a drumbeat drowning out the birds singing high in the trees.

"A part of me doesn't want to know, but I need to. Is it true what Earl's uncle said about Earl and Lucas helping slaves run away?"

"Jackson was drunk." Mary stared over Earl's stone and out over the valley beyond.

"Is that why he shot Lucas? Because Lucas was helping slaves find freedom?"

Mary looked at her. There was a look of desperate need in her eyes.

"Shooting Lucas was an accident," she said. "The gun went off when Earl tried to grab it away."

"But, is it true?"

Mary paused, then sighed. Sarah had a right to know. "Yes." After all those years Mary finally said it out loud. "Yes, it's true."

Sarah turned back to Earl's grave, and after a silent moment, nodded. "I suspected as much. And you knew all along?"

"Only because I was there when the first family showed up in our root cellar begging for help." Mary told her about Cassius and Thomas, about Eliza and her little girl. She told her about how Cassius and Thomas had helped Earl after Mrs. Hollings had Uncle Jackson whip him for giving the children Christmas candy. She told her how Earl felt obligated to help them. How it just grew from there. How Clay Lund got involved and made all the arrangements. How her brother George was involved for a while. How she begged Earl to stop.

The entire story spilled out like an unexpected flash flood after a hard spring rain. Sarah stared at Earl's headstone, silent. "Forgive me, but I couldn't tell you. Not even Ander knew."

"It was too dangerous." Sarah agreed, finishing Mary's thought. "Thank you for telling me. Now I understand why Earl blamed himself, but it wasn't his fault. That's who Lucas was, someone who helped others, wanted to right all the wrongs in the world."

"Earl, too."

They stayed a few minutes longer. For the first time, Mary was free of her burden. Would Sarah feel the same relief from knowing the truth? She prayed it was so.

"Enough of the past. It's time to face our future. Your future. We're going to town." Sarah linked her arm in Mary's. Reluctant, Mary kept step with her friend, more than a little fearful of what Sarah had in mind.

CHAPTER 38

WISCONSIN: MAY 1881

"So, this is the famous Gretchen's Kitchen." Sarah stood in the doorway and surveyed the room. "I like it, from the white half curtains in the windows to the wildflowers on the tables. And whatever she's cooking smells wonderful."

Gretchen hurried from the kitchen, wiping her hands on her apron. Fine tendrils of hair had worked loose from their pins and stuck to her flushed and damp face. "You must be Sarah. Come, sit at my best table and I'll bring you each a plate. Today's menu is meatloaf with mashed potatoes and rhubarb pie for dessert. I picked the rhubarb myself this morning. And what would you like to drink? We have coffee, iced tea, lemonade."

"Iced tea would be perfect. Is it sweetened?"

"Of course. That's the only way Mary will drink it, so that's the only way I make it. Everyone else can learn to like it or drink coffee. Or, better yet, water. Might wash away some of the ugliness inside." She gestured to Anna on the other side of the room. "Bring Mrs. Bishop and her friend some iced tea." She turned back. "I'll be right out with your plates."

"What a lovely woman," Sarah said when Gretchen disappeared into the kitchen.

"Thank you, Anna," Mary said as the girl set glasses in front of them.

Sarah took a sip. "Perfect."

"We've heard so much about you, Mrs. Shaw. I'm glad you could come for a visit."

Mary set her glass down. "Where did you hear about Sarah?"

"Mrs. Clark stopped in yesterday. She told us you had an old friend from Virginia visiting."

"Of course, Frances," Mary said to herself.

"I understand you live in St. Paul now. I've never been, but I hear it's noisy and crowded and very exciting."

"Well, I don't know about exciting, but it's definitely noisy and crowded."

Gretchen returned carrying two steaming plates, using towels to protect her hands from the heat. "Now, if you need anything else you let me or Anna know." Gretchen returned to her kitchen while Anna went to greet more diners waiting at the door.

"Anna is Gretchen's daughter," Mary explained. "She's fourteen. Their son Claus is twelve and helps here when he's not in school."

"And you said her husband is the deputy sheriff?"

"Mmmm." Mary sipped her tea and nodded.

"The same deputy who—?"

"The only deputy."

Sarah took a bite of her meatloaf. "This is very good."

"Oh, yes. Gretchen is a wonderful cook."

They ate in silence, enjoying the food, enjoying the company, until Maud Henry spied them through the plate-glass window and stormed in to stand by their table.

"I heard you had a house guest, Mrs. Bishop, but I had hoped it was just an ugly rumor."

"And a good day to you, too, Maud." Mary forced a smile for their unwelcome visitor.

Sarah wiped her mouth with her napkin and placed it neatly back on her lap. "Now, why would Mary having a house guest be an ugly rumor?"

"Mrs. Shaw, I presume. May I call you Sarah?"

"No, you may not. Only my friends call me Sarah and you, Mrs. Henry, are not my friend."

Hiding a laugh, Mary coughed, choking on a bit of meatloaf that caught in her throat.

"I ask you again, why would my friend having a house guest be an ugly rumor?"

"It is not the fact that she *has* a house guest that is objectionable, but *who* that house guest is."

Sarah sighed and narrowed her eyes at Maud. "That house guest would be me. How am I objectionable? You've never even met me before today." Her tone made it clear she was losing her patience.

The entire room went quiet listening to the back and forth between Sarah and Maud. People weren't accustomed to anyone questioning Maud in such a manner.

"A Confederate rebel. There, you forced me to say it. A Confederate rebel."

"I see. Well, my friend and I are having a lovely meal together so if you would excuse us." Sarah went back to her food, ignoring the flabbergasted Maud Henry.

Maud took in a long, slow breath and turned her attention back to Mary. "Mrs. Bishop, I've heard another rumor, this one about you and Mr. Polk."

Mary hadn't expected this, although perhaps she should have. She forced herself to swallow what was in her mouth and set her fork quietly on her plate. "What about me and Oliver?"

"I've heard you are no longer seeing each other, that you sent him packing and broke his heart. Is that true?"

Mary hated Maud's smug little grin, the way she always took great pleasure in another's discomfort.

"Another ugly rumor and nothing more," Sarah responded. "You really should pay less attention to gossip and more attention to your husband because I heard an ugly rumor that he might be going to jail for attempted murder."

Maud gasped. "Good day, Mrs. Shaw, Mrs. Bishop."

"Good day to you," Sarah called out to the fast-retreating woman.

The room erupted in stifled giggles and a few outright belly laughs when the door slammed behind her. Maud Henry stormed across the street to her partners-in-crime waiting for their report.

Sarah scanned the laughing, whispering patrons. A few nodded with approval in return.

"I think you have more sympathy in this town than you realize. She's the one they're all afraid of, not you."

"And not Earl," Mary said to herself. "If only he could have seen this today, maybe it would have lightened his load a little."

Gretchen brought them pie and took a seat. "Anna, bring your mother a slice, too, and a cup of coffee." She turned to Sarah and pointed to her glass. "Never did get a taste for tea, that's just too sweet for me. I'll stick to my coffee. Don't care how hot the weather."

Anna set a plate and steaming cup in front of her mother.

"*Danke, Liebling*." She squeezed her daughter's hand, smiling. "I'm taking a little rest to get to know Mrs. Shaw, my new good friend, better. You can handle the kitchen for your tired mama, *ya*?"

"*Ya*. Enjoy your pie, Mrs. Bishop, Mrs. Shaw. Let me know if you need more tea." Anna disappeared into the kitchen and, with the efficiency of her mother, returned with pie for the couple at the next table.

"I'm so glad you came to visit, Sarah. Is it all right if I call you Sarah?"

"Most definitely, Gretchen."

"What you did to Maud Henry before . . . well . . . all I can say is someone should have put that woman in her place a long time ago." Gretchen took a bite of her pie.

"I admit it wasn't my proudest moment, but I couldn't help myself. I'll be asking God's forgiveness in my prayers tonight." Sarah shook her head. "Some people just have a way of making a body forget they're a Christian."

"Maud is definitely one of those people," Mary said, chuckling. "When she looks at me in that way of hers, I become all tongue-tied."

Gretchen finished her pie and washed it down with the last of her coffee. "I shouldn't eat so much pie. Every year my dresses get a little tighter and I have to let them out." She leaned across the table and added in a hushed tone and devilish grin, "But, my Dieter, he doesn't seem to mind himself a plump wife. If you know what I mean."

Mary grinned. "And I think it's fair to assume you don't mind a husband who's also growing a little, should we say, soft around the middle."

"You assume correct. That being said, I heard that rumor about you and Oliver Polk, too. I'm happy to hear it is not true."

"Actually—"

"No, it is not at all true," Sarah interrupted. "Just a little bump in the road, that's all, like any relationship. I am here to help smooth out that bump."

Gretchen smiled. "Good. Let me know if I can help because sometimes, I am sad to say, my friend Mary can be a very stubborn woman."

"Oh, I am well aware of that."

Arguing the point was useless because her friends were right. "Yes, I suppose I can be, when the circumstances call for it."

"Even when they don't," Gretchen added.

Mary blushed, and they laughed.

"You have no one to blame for your troubles with Oliver but yourself." Sarah shook her head. "Gretchen, I must say this has been a very enjoyable meal. Your rhubarb pie is easily the best I've ever tasted."

"I thought mine was the best you'd ever tasted." How had the conversation turned so quickly against her?

"It was, but now you must admit Gretchen's is just a little bit better. But don't worry. You still make the best jam."

Gretchen agreed. "Nothing like it."

"Well," Mary huffed in feigned indignation. "Now you're making more sense. I was beginning to think you'd both gone stark raving mad."

When was the last time she had so much fun? Then scenes of a winter sleigh ride, Oliver sitting beside her in the moonlight, came to mind, and she smiled to herself. The afternoon she spent in his arms, made her flush. Thankfully, no one was looking.

"We should let you get back to work." Sarah stood and reached out her hands to take Gretchen's. "It was good getting to know you, but we need to be on our way. I want to stop at the store on the way home and meet Oliver. See if he's worth all this trouble, or if he's really just a promise of future heartache that Mary doesn't need."

Mary's spine stiffened at the slight toward his good name. "Oliver's a wonderful man. There's no one better, and I will not tolerate my best friend saying such things about the man I love."

The two women looked at her and smiled.

"Of course, he is, Mary," Sarah said with a smile.

"I can't argue with you on that," Gretchen added. "But I'm glad to hear you say it."

Mary tried to hide an embarrassed grin and followed Sarah to the door.

CHAPTER 39

WISCONSIN: MAY 1881

The bell over Oliver's shop door announced their arrival. He came out of the backroom, stopped, and smiled.

"Good morning, Mrs. Bishop, Mrs. Shaw. I'll be with you in just a moment."

"How did he know your name?"

Sarah shrugged. "Small towns." She stopped to admire the rose-patterned china.

"Frances." Mary corrected her and turned her attention to the china case, as well. "Beautiful."

"Reminds me of the roses we used to grow back in Virginia."

Miss Booker and Miss Webster had been examining the display of ribbons but now had their heads together, whispering and staring in their direction.

"I'm sorry, ladies," Oliver said, going to them. "I thoroughly searched my storeroom but am all out of the blue satin ribbon. I don't expect to receive any more until next week. Would you like me to set some aside for you?"

"Oh." Miss Booker moaned and turned to Miss Webster. "And I was so looking forward to dressing up that old hat in time for church on Sunday."

"You could buy a new hat," Miss Webster suggested, eyes wide, clapping and nodding, her blond ringlets bouncing. "There's a darling straw hat with blue checked ribbon, wildflowers, and a bluebird in Mrs. Olson's front window."

"I saw it, but Daddy said I can't have another new hat until I've worn out my old ones." Miss Booker stuck out her lower lip in a pout.

"What if my dog accidentally were to get into your old hats and chew them all up? Then he'd have to let you get a new one."

"All of them? He'd never believe that. He'd make me go all summer without any hat at all."

Miss Webster gasped and put her hand to her mouth. "But your skin would turn all brown and freckled!"

Mary glanced around. Miss Booker's shoulders slumped with a deep sigh. Sarah stifled a laugh while they both pretended to be engrossed in the china display.

Oliver interrupted the inane chatter. "So, am I setting aside some of the blue satin ribbon when it comes in?"

"Yes, thank you, Mr. Polk," Miss Booker said with deep reluctance. "Two yards should be more than enough."

"Very good, then I'll see you next week."

"It's only one week," Miss Webster consoled her friend as they left the store. The bell rang and the click of the door latch cut off Miss Booker's reply.

Mary's initial discomfort at seeing Oliver melted away when the three of them burst out laughing. "Those two need to find some husbands," she said to him. "A couple of squalling babies and they won't have time to worry about new hats and blue satin ribbon."

"Mrs. Shaw." Oliver took Sarah's hand in both of his. "So good to meet you. Frances told me Mary had an old friend visiting. What do you think of our little town?"

"Interesting, I'll say that much. And you can call me Sarah."

"Call me Oliver. I'm hoping we'll become close friends."

"I know we will. I asked Mary to stop so I could invite you to dinner tonight. Nothing fancy, just some fried chicken and biscuits. And a chocolate cake, if you have cocoa in stock."

"I do, and I'd love to come to dinner." Oliver retrieved a can of cocoa from a shelf behind the counter. "That is, if Mary doesn't mind."

"Of course, you must join us for dinner," Mary said.

Oliver's eyes softened when he smiled at her. "I've missed you."

"I've missed you, too."

"We're settled then." Sarah grinned like the proverbial cat that ate the canary. "What time do you lock up?"

"Six o'clock."

"Then we'll plan for dinner at half past the hour."

The back door slammed, interrupting their discussion. Frances rushed in from the storeroom and stopped short when she saw them. "You two are the talk of the town," she announced. "Especially you, Sarah."

"Really?"

Mary wasn't surprised. Apparently, news of their little run-in with Maud had already made the rounds of the town gossips.

Frances unpinned her hat and set it on the counter with her reticule. "Did you really tell Maud Henry that she should pay more attention to her husband before he's arrested for attempted murder?" She laughed.

"I might have said something to that effect. That woman spends far too much time worrying about other people's business, and someone needed to tell her so."

Oliver looked at Sarah, astonished. "What happened?"

Sarah waved a hand. "I think you can guess. Besides, if I told you, wouldn't that make us no better than Maud and her friends?"

"Yes, it would," Mary agreed, although she had to admit she would enjoy hearing Sarah retell the story of Maud Henry's humiliation.

"Well, we have to get going if I'm going to get a cake baked, cooled, and frosted in time for dinner." Sarah handed the cocoa tin to Mary.

"I'll fill you in later," Frances whispered to Oliver.

Mary shook her head. "And you the minister's wife."

Frances blushed and shrugged. "Yes, well, doesn't mean I don't like the occasional little tale of revenge. The Bible's full of them, you know."

"What do I owe you for the cocoa?" Sarah asked.

"One chicken and biscuits dinner with chocolate cake."

"Well, we just happen to have one of those. Or, we will, come this evening."

"I'll be there."

The bell rang when they went out the door. "I like him," Sarah said. "If you don't want him, perhaps I do. As I've said, I've been alone too long." She stopped, looked Mary in the eye, and smiled. "Yes, you do want him. Don't try to tell me different." She linked her arm in Mary's and the two headed for home to start cooking. "I'll just have to find someone else to warm my bed at night."

"Sarah!"

"What?"

THEY SPENT THE EVENING telling Oliver stories about Virginia and laughing.

Oliver wiped the corner of his eyes. "So, Ander and Robert met during a schoolyard brawl defending the honor of a little girl."

"Amy Lynn is Robert's wife, now," Sarah added.

"And that's how the two of you met." Oliver pointed from one to the other.

"Yes," Mary nodded. "Standing behind our bruised and bloodied sons."

Sarah turned to her. "What did Mr. Nichols call them?"

"Truculent backwoods savages. It was all I could do to keep Earl from showing Mr. Nichols what a true backwoods savage could do."

Mary loved the way Oliver laughed. He threw his head back and roared.

"That's the Earl I knew," he said.

What was she thinking running away from him when she should be running into his arms? Loving Oliver didn't mean she had to stop loving Earl. She slid her hand from her lap to rest on Oliver's thigh under the table. He squeezed it and smiled.

Sarah rose to clear the dishes. "You two go for a walk, work off some of that cake. It's too nice an evening to waste indoors. I'll do the dishes, and by the time you get back maybe we'll be ready for a second slice with coffee."

Mary groaned. Another piece of cake? Thanks to Sarah's wonderful down-home cooking, she was certain her dresses would soon be too tight.

"How about it, Mary? A nice walk in the woods?"

Boone jumped to his feet at the word *walk* and ran to the door, tail wagging.

"You stay here with Sarah." Mary pointed. Boone looked back at Sarah, then at the door. He sat, refused to budge, hoping she would change her mind.

"Go lay down!" She pointed, again. This time Boone hung his head and sulked back to his bed by the fireplace.

As soon as they were out of sight, Oliver took her in his arms. She was hungry and it wasn't for a second piece of cake.

"I'm sorry, I've been so difficult lately," she said between kisses.

He eased her down onto the cool moss and dried leaves of the forest floor. His touch lit a familiar flame deep within her.

"Can you ever forgive me?"

Oliver stroked her cheek and pushed the loose hair from her face. She kissed his palm. He traced her lips with his finger.

"I love you, Mary. There's nothing to forgive."

"I love you, too." Her mouth searched for his, greedy for his kiss. Thirty years fell away and she was a young girl again. Their passion was unstoppable as the sky overhead turned from blue to pink to gray. After, Mary curled into him and they watched the sky slowly finish its fade to dusk. She didn't want to go back, but they needed to return before it got too dark. Oliver helped her up.

"Marry me."

She stepped back. This was something she hadn't expected, certainly not yet. "Don't you think it's a little too soon to be talking marriage?"

He pulled her close. His kiss buckled her knees. He held her close and she leaned her forehead on his shoulder.

"Too soon? After tonight, after what we just did? And it's not the first time, I might remind you. You still think it's too soon?" He chuckled, but then he stopped smiling. He took her face in his hands. "What are you waiting for?"

"I suppose you're right. It does seem kind of silly. I tell you what, I will think on it, and let you know my answer."

"Fair enough, but don't make me wait too long. I want to lie with you like this every night and wake up with you beside me every morning."

She gave him a peck on the cheek. "Now help me brush the leaves from my hair and clothes so we can head back. Sarah will be worried we were eaten by a bear."

IT WAS DARK BY THE time they got home. An extra horse was tethered outside the barn.

Who was visiting at this time of night?

Deputy Mueller sat at the table eating cake and drinking a cup of coffee. Sarah's pale face meant something was wrong.

"Oh, good, you're back," she said. "The deputy's been waiting to talk to us."

Deputy Mueller set down his cup, pushed his chair back, and stood. "Story goes, you two had a bit of a dust-up with Maud Henry at Gretchen's today."

"You know how she is, Deputy," Mary said. "She comes storming into the restaurant, calling us hateful names."

Why was she defending their side?

He put his hat on. "Maud is a difficult and opinionated woman, that's true. Point is, now you've made her angry. Word is she's feeling humiliated and plotting her revenge. I just wanted to warn you. Be careful, keep your eyes open, and if you see anything out of the ordinary, if she threatens you in any way, let me know. I'm going to put an end to this one way or another."

"Thank you, Deputy," Sarah said.

"And thank you, Mrs. Shaw, for the cake. It was delicious. Not as good as Gretchen's, but then, no one bakes quite like my Gretchen." He walked to the door. "Good night, Mrs. Bishop." He tipped his hat. "Oh, and you have something stuck in your hair." He smiled and closed the door behind him.

Mortified, Mary ran her fingers through her hair until she found the offending twig. Sarah looked away but not before Mary caught the little smirk that said she, too, knew what they had been doing in the woods.

"Would you like me to stay?" Oliver asked.

Mary picked up the deputy's cake plate and coffee cup and headed toward the kitchen, Oliver close behind. "Whatever for?" she asked. "Sarah and I can take care of ourselves. As you may recall, I have a gun and I'm rather good at using it."

"I do recall."

She set them by the sink for washing. "So, you go on home and I'll see you tomorrow."

"You'll consider my proposal?"

"Yes." She kissed him good night and hurried him out the door.

"Did Oliver ask you to marry him?" Sarah asked after he was gone.

"Yes." Mary walked by to her bedroom.

"And you didn't say yes?" Sarah followed, standing in the doorway, arms folded across her chest.

"Not yet. I told him I'd consider it and get back to him." Mary retrieved her hat box full of treasures from beneath the bed and brought them to the table. "I want you to know about these, in case anything happens to me. They'll be yours, along with the pictures on the mantel."

"Nothing's going to happen to you." Sarah sat across from her. "Don't even think that."

Mary opened the box and removed her memories one at a time and told Sarah about each one.

CHAPTER 40

WISCONSIN: MAY 1881

Mary cast the fishing line into the river and handed the pole to Frances. Sarah watched from her perch on a nearby rock, her hook in the water. The day was too nice to sit around home and worry about Deputy Mueller's warnings. To be on the safe side, though, Mary brought the Colt and kept it close at hand.

"I got something!" Frances tugged on the pole and slowly reeled in her catch.

"Already?" Sarah hadn't had a bite all morning. "You just threw in her line."

"That's it," Mary encouraged. Frances handled her catch like she'd been fishing for years. The fish splattered them as it fought to escape the hook. Mary wiped her face. "Get hold of it before it breaks your line and falls back into the water."

"Touch it? Oh, no, I couldn't do that." Frances scrunched up her face in disgust and held her pole out.

Mary grabbed the fish, freed it from the hook, and tied it to the string with the others she'd caught earlier.

"I give up," Sarah announced, pulling in her line. "I guess today just isn't my day to catch fish." She looked at the string of fish Mary held high to admire in the sun. "So, Frances, who's going to clean your fish for you?" Sarah asked with a teasing grin.

Frances looked from Sarah to Mary and back again. Her mouth hung slightly open, but no words came out.

"Don't worry." Mary laughed, patting her on the shoulder and taking a turn with the pole. "I'll show you how when I do mine."

"Or, perhaps Mary will merely do it for you," Sarah suggested with a wink to Mary.

"Would you?" Frances asked. "Please?"

Mary rolled her eyes. "First baiting the hook, now removing and cleaning the fish. Let me ask you this, can you at least cook the fish? Tell me you can cook fish and I don't have to do that for you as well, because I'm certain the Reverend is looking forward to a fish dinner tonight."

"Of course, I can cook fish." Frances defended herself, chin held high. "I just don't like the idea of touching their messy insides, that's all."

"Or, apparently, their scaly outsides," Sarah joked.

Mary pulled in another fish and tied it to the string.

Sarah shook her head. "Clearly, I was standing on the wrong rock. Oh, well, I didn't catch any, so I don't have to clean any. But I tell you what, Mary, you clean them, and I'll cook our share." Sarah set both poles aside while Mary washed her hands in the river. Frances spread out their basket lunch.

"I will clean all the fish," she agreed. "There's plenty for everyone's dinner tonight, including Frances and the Reverend."

They ate what was left of the fried chicken, biscuits, and cake from the night before. "Frances, did Mary tell you Oliver proposed marriage to her last night?" Sarah asked with a smug grin.

Frances pushed up onto her knees and reached out to embrace her friend. "Congratulations! I'm so excited for the both of you."

"I haven't said yes, yet."

Frances' face fell, and she dropped back onto her heels. "Why not? Oh, no, you two didn't have another fight, did you?"

"No, of course not." Mary offered her a slice of cake. "Sarah baked it. It's almost as good as Gretchen's."

"Thank you, Mary. I can accept that compliment," Sarah said with a slight nod.

Frances sat and took a bite of cake. "Why didn't you say yes? You love him, don't you? I know you do. And he loves you."

"Yes, why didn't you accept?" Sarah asked with her familiar Cheshire Cat grin. "And why did you come back from your walk with your hair all mussed and full of twigs? Not to mention the big grass stain on your back."

Frances gasped, her hand over her mouth. Mary blushed, and Sarah laughed out loud. Mary swore to herself she'd get her revenge later. It wasn't a conversation she wanted to have with her minister's wife.

"I told Oliver I would think on his proposal and get back to him—soon."

"You know," Frances whispered, leaning in to be heard, a rosy glow blooming on her cheeks. "I must admit, I've grown quite fond of the physical side of married life." She nodded, and it was Mary's turn to be shocked. Sarah choked on her lemonade at the unexpected announcement.

Mary held up her hand to bring a halt to the conversation before anything more was said. "All right, ladies, enough. You'd think we were a group of twelve-year-old girls whose mothers had just explained the duties of a married woman. Some things are better left unsaid." They burst out laughing.

"Oh, how I miss Lucas." Sarah said with a sigh after the laughter died down. "It's been far too long since I was *physical* with a man. I rather liked it, too."

Mary shook her head. "I did not ask to know all this about my friends' husbands, living or dead."

"It's also been a long time since I've gone fishing and had a picnic lunch with my friend," Sarah continued. She took Mary's hand. "Remember when we used to go fishing with Lucas and Earl? We'd take Ander and Robert and make a day of it. The boys would fish and sail their little wooden boats. It's how you got your first Boone. What a scare we had that day! I miss those times and think of them often."

"Me, too." Mary squeezed Sarah's hand. "But enough of this. We've gone from giggling over things way too personal, to crying over things that can never be again."

Frances set down her empty cake plate. "Not true. You can have those things again. You are right now. It's just a different time and place and some of the people have changed. Love and friendship are a gift from God."

"Why, Frances Clark, how very profound of you," Sarah agreed.

Frances continued. "And, the Reverend Thorpe spoke fondly of you before moving on to his next stop. He had dinner with us that night, and all he talked about was Mrs. Shaw this and Mrs. Shaw that."

Mary studied her friend. Was Sarah blushing?

They packed up their basket, and Sarah walked down to the river's edge for one last look at the beautiful St Croix before they left for home. "Mary, is that a cave over there?"

"Yes. Over the years the water has carved an opening in the cliff. It's not terribly deep but it does go a little way back in."

Frances walked down to have a look.

"Oh, I wouldn't go in if I were you," Mary warned.

Frances stopped and looked back. "Why not?"

"Bats."

They laughed when Frances ran back, shrieking and holding her hands over her hair.

THAT NIGHT, SARAH AND Mary quietly read in the parlor. June bugs clicked against the windows, drawn to the light. Boone stretched and yawned at their feet, as full and content as they were after their fish dinner. His belly rumbled, and he let go a loud and lengthy burst of gas.

"Boone!" Mary gasped and threw a hand over her mouth and nose.

"Oh, Lord help us." Sarah coughed, threw open a window, and fanned the air with her book. "Must be all those fish heads he ate."

"You're going out. You can sleep in the barn tonight." At the word *out* Boone got to his feet, stretched some more, and plodded to the door.

Sarah rose. "I'm going to bed, too. It was a wonderful day, and I'm exhausted. See you in the morning."

"You don't want to sit up to tell me more about you and the good Reverend Redmond Thorpe?"

"Not particularly. There really isn't all that much to tell."

"It didn't sound that way to me. What happened on that wagon ride up from Taylors Falls?"

"Good night." Sarah waved away Mary's questions and started back to her room.

Boone's ears went back and he growled, pawing at the door to go out.

"Stay!" Mary retrieved the Colt from the mantel. Boone crouched at her feet as she eased open the front door. A horse stomped and snorted near the barn.

"Mary?" Sarah stopped behind her. "Who do you think it is?"

"I don't know," Mary lied. Considering the deputy's warning, she had a pretty good idea who it might be. "Turn down those lamps and wait in here."

Mary stepped out the door, looking left, then right, to be sure no one was waiting in ambush. Boone stayed close to her side, his muscles tense. All she had to do was give the order and he'd attack. "Hang onto him. I don't want him getting shot," she whispered.

No one was in sight, but she sensed they were near. The hairs stood up on the back of her neck and along her arms. A shot rang out. She spun left, dropped her gun, and fell to the ground.

"Mary!" Sarah knelt next to her. Boone whimpered and licked her face.

"Stay back," Mary said with a groan, a searing pain in her left shoulder.

"All right, but you be careful."

Mary found her gun and struggled to her feet. A shadow moved through the moonlight along the barn. Mary fired blind in its direction. A horse whinnied somewhere in the trees beyond the barn. It was too dark to see the shooter's face, but a quick glimpse of a skirt told Mary it was a woman who rode toward town. Boone broke free and ran after the assailant. Mary and Sarah trailed behind. Whoever it was, she was riding too fast, giving Mary no chance for a second shot.

"Boone!" Mary called. The dog hesitated, then came back to her. "Good boy." She reached down with her left hand to pet him. Another pain burned through her. She grabbed her shoulder, dropping to her knees. The trees spun as her vision blurred.

"You've been shot." Sarah's voice was like listening through water.

Mary pressed her fingers through the tear in her sleeve. "I'm bleeding." She stared at her hand, red and slick.

Sarah helped Mary to her feet and into the barn. "Rest here. I'm going to chain Boone to the fence and close up the house. I'll be right back."

Mary leaned back against the wall, wincing. Her shoulder burned like a hot poker was being stabbed clear through. She fought to stay conscious, afraid if she passed out, she might never wake.

Sarah returned with the milking stool and helped her onto Sophie's back, climbing up behind to hold her tight. Oliver must have been working late because the last thing Mary remembered was stumbling into his store after he unlocked the door.

"We need a doctor." It was Sarah's voice, muffled and distant, then everything went black.

WHEN MARY REGAINED consciousness, she was on Dr. Hunter's examining table. Oliver stood next to her. She assumed the blood on his shirt and Sarah's dress was hers.

"It's definitely from a gunshot, Deputy," Dr. Hunter said.

"She shot me." Mary managed to utter.

"Mrs. Bishop, you're awake." Dr. Hunter smiled down at her. "Tell me, how do you feel?"

"Hurts."

"Yes, I imagine it does. But it's just a flesh wound. You should heal up nicely in no time."

"Did you say a woman shot you?" Deputy Mueller asked.

"Yes."

"Are you certain? Could it have been a man?"

Mary tried to sit. "Only if he was wearing a dress. I couldn't see her face, but it was definitely a woman." She winced and fell back on the bed.

"Rest." Oliver squeezed her hand. "Deputy, do you think it was Maud Henry? I know she's a vengeful woman, but do you really think she's capable of trying to kill someone?"

"Before tonight I'd have said no, but now . . . I don't know." He sighed and shook his head. "Mrs. Bishop, I will get to the bottom of this, and if it was Maud who shot you, trust me, she will see justice. Now, Mrs. Shaw said you shot back. Do you think you hit her?"

Her gun! What happened to her gun? She tried again to sit, hoping to see it somewhere safe. She didn't want the Deputy to take it. She needed it.

"Mrs. Bishop, do you think you might have hit the shooter?" he asked again.

"I don't think so."

Oliver eased her back down and leaned in to whisper, "Your gun's locked in my store safe."

She relaxed. The room spun, and she feared she might fall off the table with the slightest movement.

"Where's your gun now?" Deputy Mueller asked.

"We left it at the house," Sarah lied.

"Dizzy." Mary closed her eyes, but that made the spinning worse.

"That would be the pain-killer taking affect," Dr. Hunter assured her.

"Are you going to talk to Maud?" Oliver asked the deputy.

"I'm going to talk to a lot of people. But right now, Maud Henry is at the top of my list." He left.

Mary groaned. "I want to go home."

"You're in no condition to ride a horse," Dr. Hunter insisted.

"Stay here tonight, Mary," Sarah said. "I'll ride Sophie home, keep an eye on everything, and bring the wagon for you in the morning."

"I'm ready now." Mary sat, slower this time. Oliver helped her stand and caught her when she swayed.

"I'll take her home in my wagon, Doc. Mrs. Shaw and I can keep an eye on her."

"I'll send some more pills with you. They'll help you sleep."

The ride home was long and painful. Mary swore Oliver's horses took them over every bump and hole in the road. She leaned against the side of the wagon bed, clutching her gun in her lap and praying she wouldn't die before getting justice for Maud Henry.

When they finally arrived, Oliver helped her down and into the house while Sarah found a place for his team to bed down for the night.

"I'll sleep in the parlor so you can get some rest." He kissed her lightly on the end of her nose. "You're in no condition for the temptations of the flesh, as the Reverend would say in one of his sermons." He winked at her with a sly smile.

Mary laughed. She gasped as another pain shot through her shoulder and down her arm. "Sometimes I think you were sent by the devil himself to torment me. You shouldn't tease me when I'm in no condition to laugh."

"This seems the perfect time to make you smile. When is there a better?"

"Perhaps, but seriously, you don't have to stay at all. I'll be fine with Sarah here."

"That point, my dear, is not up for discussion. I'm staying. On the other hand, there is the matter of a certain marriage proposal. We could discuss that, or are you still thinking about it?"

"I'm still thinking about it."

He kissed her again, a lingering kiss on the lips. "Good night, Mary."

She kissed him back. "My gun?" He'd taken it from her when helping her down from the wagon.

"I gave it to Sarah for safe keeping. You won't need it any more tonight."

"Be careful. She never was a very good shot." She closed her eyes as sleep overcame her.

CHAPTER 41

WISCONSIN: JUNE 1881

Deputy Mueller stopped by a couple days after the shooting to update Mary on his investigation.

"I've questioned everyone in town, including Maud Henry. They all deny having anything to do with your shooting."

"You don't believe her, do you?" Mary refilled his coffee and held out a plate of cookies.

"No, thank you." He waved off the cookies and patted his soft belly. "Gretchen said I better not gain any more weight because there isn't even one extra inch to let out my pants."

"You know Maud did it," Sarah said, moving the cookies to the sideboard and out of reach.

"If she didn't, she at least knows who did," he agreed. "But without proof there's nothing I can do except keep my eyes and ears open." He stood and put his hat on. "I'll let you know if I learn anything new."

AS THE WEEKS PASSED, Mary's arm healed under Sarah's care. Oliver came by to check on her every day. Once in a while they even managed to sneak away for some time alone. Sarah smiled and looked the other way, pretending not to know about their clandestine lovemaking.

Since Deputy Mueller had no luck finding proof of Mary's shooter, the gun went everywhere with her. She took it with her when she went into town. It lay on her nightstand when she slept and was even with in her garden.

Mary stood and stretched her back. They'd been weeding for hours and the neat garden rows were evidence of all their hard work and, hopefully, an abundant harvest in the months to come. The sun was hot and the air still. She wiped her forehead with a sleeve and studied the dark line of storm clouds growing tall on the western horizon. Evening approached and there would be rain by nightfall. A good soaking rain, she hoped.

"I think we'd better call it a day." Mary picked up her hoe and headed toward the barn. Sarah followed, closing the garden gate behind her. "Come along, Boone," Mary called. "We need to milk the cow and secure the barn before the storm."

Boone wagged his tail and jumped to his feet, eager to follow. Movement, a snapped twig in the trees, made Mary stop. She wrapped her hand around the handle of the gun in her apron pocket. A doe with twin fawns stared at them from the edge of the woods. Boone barked and ran at them. The mama turned and crashed back through the brush, her fawns close behind, and disappeared.

"You know, Mary, you never told me how you came about getting that gun."

"Boone!" Mary slapped her thigh and he returned, stopping to look back and bark one final warning. "Good boy." She scratched his ears. "I'll be forever grateful if you keep the deer away from my garden. The fence can only do so much. I'm counting on you for the rest. And that goes for the raccoons and rabbits, too."

"I never asked before," Sarah continued, "because I sensed it wasn't good. But I'm asking now."

The approaching storm made the animals restless in their stalls. Mary used them as an excuse to ignore Sarah's question. She went from one to the next, stroking their necks and speaking a soft, comforting word or two.

Sarah followed behind. "Mary?"

She wasn't going to let it go. "Earl took it off a dead Confederate officer." Mary walked away, unwilling to say more.

"How did he die?" Sarah put out fresh hay for the animals while Mary pulled up a stool and sat down to milk. "Do you know, or did you find him already dead?"

Mary stopped milking, hesitated. Her eyes filled with tears. The boy's face still haunted her.

Sarah dropped the hay and went to her side. "Tell me."

"I killed him." Mary hadn't said those words out loud since the day she and Earl sat in their kitchen with Clay Lund. Sarah gasped and covered her mouth with her hands.

"I shot and killed him," Mary repeated. For the first time, she told the story, throwing off the weight she'd carried for twenty years.

Sarah held Mary as she wept. "How awful for you."

Mary used a clean corner of her apron to wipe her eyes. "Earl had it converted to shoot brass cartridges after the War, easier for me to load than the original ball and cap, quicker."

"So many secrets."

"I still see his face in my dreams. This gun is a constant reminder, no matter what a God-send it's proven to be."

The animals shuffled about and cried in distress. Boone growled and paced. He dug beneath the closed barn door, anxious to get out. Mary tried to restrain him, but he avoided her grasp and dug all the harder.

Lightning flashed. Thunder followed moments later. A commotion outside the barn made them stop and listen.

"Horses." Sarah said.

"I hear them." Mary grabbed Boone and tied him to a post, then double checked that all six chambers of her gun were loaded.

Sarah sniffed the air and spun around. "Is that smoke?"

Boone pulled at his rope.

"Stay! I've got this one," Mary said to him. "You keep the animals out of my garden, and I'll take care of intruders." He whimpered but stopped fighting. She turned to Sarah. "Wait here with Boone." Mary eased the barn doors open wide enough to get a look around the yard.

Another flash. Thunder followed immediately, making Mary jump. Fat raindrops spattered the yard.

Flames licked up the side of her house. Maud and Agnes stood nearby. Mary scanned the yard. *Where are you hiding, Gladys?* She was never far away when it came to Maud.

"Rebel trash!" Maud yelled above the storm's howl.

Mary stepped clear of the barn, aimed her gun, and took a shot. In her haste it went wide.

Maud laughed. She broke a parlor window and tossed her torch into the room, lighting the curtains. Agnes opened the front door and tossed hers inside. A sudden wind gust fanned the flames and they leapt higher.

The two women retreated into the shelter of the tree line. Mary ran after them, her skirts whipping about her legs. She took aim for a second shot, but something hit her across the back of the head before she could pull the trigger. She fell to the ground. The gun flew from her grip. She crawled around in the dimming light, searching, but couldn't find where it landed. The clouds opened up and the sudden down pour blinded her. The rain and wind plastered her hair to her face.

Sarah screamed.

Mary stumbled to her feet. Lightning flashed. Gladys and Sarah rolled around on the ground. If Gladys thought she could get the best of Sarah Shaw in a fight, she had a surprise coming. Sarah was on top when lightning flashed again. She broke free and got in a good kick to her attacker's ribs. Gladys cried out and curled up in the mud, coughing and gasping for breath.

Mary waited for another flash to search for her gun. She saw it lying next to the broken barn board Gladys must have used to hit her. Mary pushed back her wet hair, trying to blink away the haze clouding her vision. Her head throbbed. She reached back, flinching when she touched a good-sized knot already forming. She had to get up and retrieve her gun if she stood any chance of beating their attackers.

"I've got it." Sarah tucked the gun in her waistband. "Give me your hand." Mary reached up and Sarah grabbed her under one arm, helping her to her feet.

Mary struggled to stand but a wave of nausea brought her back to her knees as the yard spun. She squinted through the rain toward her house. Glass shattered. The porch roof sagged under the spreading flames.

"I'm going to get your photographs."

Was that Sarah talking? Mary wasn't sure through the buzzing in her ears. "No. It's too dangerous," she said, grabbing at Sarah's skirt hem to stop her.

"I'll be careful." Sarah stumbled through the rain and mud toward the house.

"My gun." Mary reached out, but it was too late. Sarah couldn't hear her.

Another blow sent Mary face first to the ground. She forced herself to roll over to face Maud standing over her with the barn board in her hands and a big smile on her face. Agnes stood behind, and Gladys pulled their wagon up next to them and jumped down. In the background, Sarah disappeared into the smoke and flames.

Maud threw the board to the ground next to Mary's head, splashing her face with mud. "Put her in the wagon." Maud's words came from somewhere in the haze threatening to envelop Mary.

"She's too heavy and slippery," Gladys complained and dropped her.

"Let's just leave her here." Agnes set her end of Mary gently on the ground. "Someone's going to see the fire soon and come to check."

"That's why we can't leave her." Maud grabbed Mary by the arm. "Get up!"

The three women yanked Mary to her feet. She leaned against the edge of the wagon bed for balance.

"Get up there," Maud said again.

Mary heard the frustration in her voice. She was not going to make this easy for them. If this was her day to die, Mary was going down with a fight. She just had to wait for the right time.

"Help her!" Maud hollered over the storm, stomping through the mud. She climbed up onto the seat.

Mary was in no condition to fight back. She needed to be patient and buy herself some time to get her wits back. She managed to get one knee up onto the wagon bed. As she lifted the second, the two women gave her a shove. She landed in a heap, scraping her hands and slamming her chin on the wagon floor. Agnes climbed up beside her.

Gladys sat next to Maud. "Where are we taking her?" she asked as Maud snapped the reins.

"I still don't understand why we have to take her anywhere. Can't we just leave her?" Agnes asked. "We've burned down her house, now she'll have to leave, like we planned."

"That was then, this is now. We have to get rid of her," Maud said. "She saw us. Do you want to go to jail, Agnes?"

"No."

"What about the other one?" Gladys asked.

Maud chuckled. "Let the fire take her."

Hot tears stung Mary's eyes. They'd just found each other again and now to lose Sarah like this. She wished she'd never written the letter.

SHEETS OF COLD RAIN soaked them, bringing Mary back to her senses. She kept quiet and listened. Maud fought to control her team. The rain had made the road a mire. Maud had to be getting desperate. All her careful plans were coming apart. She obviously hadn't counted on Mary getting a good look at them.

And she probably hadn't counted on Sarah's ability to fight back. While Maud and her friends had only read about the war in letters and newspaper accounts, she and Sarah had been living it. They learned years ago how to fight back for what was theirs. Now even the weather was working against her.

"I still don't like it," Agnes said.

It sounded like Maud was losing Agnes' support. Perhaps Mary could use that to her advantage.

The wagon stopped and the three conspirators got down. Mary stayed still, waiting for her chance.

"But, murder?" Agnes asked.

Murder? Mary had to act. The only one who could save her was herself. She jumped over the side of the wagon and ran. The road was slick. She fell, landing hard on her hands and knees. Maud stood over her and dug a foot into Mary's back, pressing a little harder every time she tried to free herself, making it more and more difficult to keep her face out of the mud. Maud's desperation was fueling her rage and making her more dangerous than Mary ever imagined.

"I can't breathe," she gasped.

"Stop fighting and I'll let you up. After all, I don't want you to die. Not yet, anyway."

Mary lay still, and Maud removed her foot.

After struggling to her feet, Mary tried in vain to wipe some of the mud from her clothing. Even the rain couldn't wash it all away.

"Grab her and follow me." Maud coiled rope over her shoulder and led the way.

Gladys and Agnes slipped and fell a couple times, pulling Mary down with them. Only Maud managed, somehow, to stay on her feet, keeping herself relatively mud-free. At least she was soaked from the rain. Maybe she'd catch pneumonia and die. Mary could only hope. It wasn't a wish she was particularly proud of, but it did seem like appropriate pay back.

"I think her rebel friend broke my rib when she kicked me," Gladys complained. Maud ignored her.

"Hurry up, you two. I want to get home and out of these wet clothes before I'm missed."

Mary kept her eyes out for any landmarks that might help her find her way home later. Rushing water. They were near the river. The women left the muddy path and proceeded across the rocks. It was her fishing spot, but where were they taking her? Gladys slipped again, catching herself but tripping Mary one more time in the process. She cried out, landing with her hip against the rocks.

All right, she'd have a knot on her head and a nasty bruise on her hip, but at least she was alive.

Maud laughed. "Did that hurt, Mrs. Bishop? I'd have Gladys apologize, but we're not sorry. Are we Gladys?" Gladys and Maud laughed.

"I'm sorry, Mrs. Bishop," Agnes whispered. "I'm sorry for all of this." Agnes helped her to her feet.

Maud handed Gladys the rope. "Put her in there and tie her up." Maud stepped aside and let the other two slog down through the rising river and into the cave. "Leave her where the water can reach her, but not right away. I want her to have time to think about this, think about how all this could have been avoided if she had hung herself with her no-good rebel husband. Or left town after he died. She had options, but she chose to stay and fight. Well, she lost. The Confederate rebel lost again."

Maud waited outside while they pushed Mary ahead and into the cave. They made her sit on a low rock nearly covered with water and bound her wrists and ankles.

"You don't have to do this." Could she convince them to help her? "The three of us together could easily—"

"Shut up!" Gladys slapped Mary across the face. "Do you think we'd betray a friend for you? Would we Agnes?"

Agnes hesitated.

"Well?" Gladys snapped. "Would we?"

Agnes shook her head. "No."

Bats circled not far over their heads, stirred up by the storm and the commotion below them. Agnes screamed and ducked when one brushed her ear. Her legs came out from under her, and she hit the cave wall.

"Agnes fell," Gladys called out to Maud, struggling to keep Agnes' head above water. "She hit her head. Out cold. I need help."

Maud came in to investigate. "Leave her."

"What? But—"

"Leave her." Maud helped Gladys prop Agnes against the cave wall. "Her soft heart has made her a liability. This way when someone finds them, *if* they find them, it will look like it was Agnes' plan gone wrong. And there'll be no one to tell them otherwise."

Mary struggled to free herself from her ropes.

Gladys slapped her again. "Settle down. You're not going anywhere."

Maud smiled. "Let's get going. I'm cold." She turned and disappeared into the storm.

"Sorry, ladies," Gladys said with one last look back. "But you heard Maud. Time to go."

Mary and Agnes were alone in the growing darkness, with only the bats overhead and the fast-rising river below.

CHAPTER 42

WISCONSIN: JUNE 1881

The heart of the storm was directly overhead. Lightning followed immediately by thunder. Impenetrable walls of rain blew sideways. Looking out the mouth of the cave, Mary couldn't see where the rain ended and the river began. But inside the river was rising fast. They'd soon drown if she couldn't free her hands and feet.

"Agnes." Her voice echoed off the walls. "Agnes, wake up! I need your help."

Agnes moaned, stirred, but didn't open her eyes.

"Help!" Mary screamed. She knew there wouldn't be anyone for miles, and certainly no one would be out on the river in such a storm, but she had to try.

"Help!"

She used her legs to push herself over to where a rocky ridge ran up the wall to the ceiling. Rubbing her ties against its sharp edge, she slipped and sliced the side of her hand. She was certain it was blood, not water, running down her fingers. A few more swipes and the rope broke. She was free. She massaged her wrists and flexed her fingers. Nothing was broken, but she might need a couple stitches on the cut. She tore off a strip of her petticoat and wrapped it around her hand, holding one end in her teeth to tie it as tight as she could. It wasn't clean, but it would have to do.

Agnes moaned again and tried to get up. Mary untied her ankles and used the rocks to pull herself over to where Agnes struggled in the rising water.

"Get up. We have to get out of here before we drown." Mary held Agnes above the water while the woman worked her way back to full consciousness.

The noise from the storm and the rushing river continued to stir up the bats. They circled overhead, flying ever closer. Agnes' eyes widened. She screamed and threw her arms up over her head.

Mary put a hand over Agnes' mouth. "No one can hear us, and you're only upsetting them more. Save your energy. You'll need it." She removed her hand when Agnes stopped struggling.

Agnes sobbed. "I can't believe my friends left me here to die."

"Why not? They left me here to die. Those are some friends you have. You might want to find yourself some new ones."

Agnes wiped her eyes. "I'm really sorry about all this. The plan was to burn your place down so you'd leave. You weren't supposed to die. No one was supposed to die." She looked around and shook her head. "I hope your friend is safe."

Sarah.

"I hope so, too, because if she's not, that's murder."

"If we get out of here, I promise I'll tell Deputy Mueller everything. How it was all Maud's idea, and how Gladys went along with it."

"And how you went along with it."

"And how I went along with it." Agnes nodded.

"But first we have to get out of here," Mary said. The water was up to their chins when they sat. "For your sake, I hope you can walk because I can't carry you, and I'm leaving while I'm still able."

They stood at the mouth of the cave and looked out into the rain. It had let up a little but not enough to see as well as Mary would have liked.

"How are we going to find our way back in this?" Agnes' voice cracked.

Mary turned and pointed a finger in her face. "Don't you start crying again."

Agnes took a deep breath. "I won't. I promise."

Mary turned back to the cave opening. "Lucky for you, this is my favorite fishing spot." She stepped out and leaned against the side of the cave. "Hang on to the back of my shirt and stay close."

They felt their way along the outside of the cliff. The water's surface pushed at their legs and weighed down their skirts. Once away from the cliff wall, she led Agnes into the trees and onto land. They were wet and the mud was like glue under their feet, but at least they were safe. The tree cover would help shelter them from the rain. They walked along the edge of the path, using tree branches to keep them upright. The slick mud sucked at their feet, making their shoes heavy. Their skirts stuck tight around their legs.

"Why are you helping me? Why didn't you just leave me there to fend for myself?" Agnes asked when they stopped to catch their breath.

"Because it was the right thing to do."

A flash lit the sky. Agnes cried out and hid her face in her hands.

"Let's keep moving. The sooner we get back, the sooner we find shelter." Mary doubted there was anything left of her home. She just hoped the barn was still standing. "Lord, if I can ask but one thing tonight, let my friend be safe and waiting for me."

"Did you say something? I couldn't hear you over the rain." Agnes leaned forward.

"Just a little prayer."

"For your friend?"

"Yes, for my friend."

"I'm sorry."

"I know. You said." Her words were cold and sarcastic, but she didn't particularly care if Agnes' feelings were hurt.

They continued in silence. The rain had finally let up, making it easier to see. The acrid smell of smoke burned her nose and throat.

"I think we're almost there," Agnes said, the fear in her voice easing.

Mary didn't respond. She would never forgive herself if Sarah perished in the fire. This was her battle, not Sarah's.

Agnes grabbed Mary's shoulder and turned her around. "I have to know if you can ever forgive me for my part in your troubles. I don't expect you to be my friend, but I need to know you forgive me."

Her plea seemed sincere. She had become Maud's pawn, caught up in Maud's twisted sense of blame and revenge. She wasn't much different than so many others in that way, except she recognized her wrong doings.

Before Mary could answer, a strong gust of wind bent an already battered tree, snapped it off at the fork, and brought one half crashing down in a hail of leaves and wood chips. Agnes screamed and disappeared into the falling branches.

CHAPTER 43

WISCONSIN: JUNE 1881

Mary threw her arms up to shield herself from the tree limbs. They tore her sleeves and left painful scratches on the skin beneath.

"Agnes, can you hear me?"

"Mary?" A voice came from somewhere behind her. A hand appeared through the branches.

"Can you free yourself?" Mary lifted the limbs between herself and freedom. It had stopped raining. Thunder rumbled in the distance. The storm had passed as quickly as it appeared.

"No," Agnes said from somewhere under the tangle of branches.

"Are you injured?"

"I don't think so. My skirt is snagged but nothing hurts. I just can't get enough leverage to pull free."

"I'm going to try and lift it."

"All right."

Mary picked her way through the branches until she found her footing. She wrapped her arms around the trunk and lifted. It barely moved, slipping from her grasp. Agnes cried out when it fell back onto her.

"It's too heavy. I can't lift it myself. I'll have to go for help."

"Don't leave me," Agnes pleaded. Her hand reached up through the tangle of smaller branches. Mary took it in both of hers and gave it a squeeze.

"I'll hurry," she said, turning to leave.

"Need some help?"

Sarah!

Mary threw her arms around her friend, heedless of the throbbing pain from her cut hand, not to mention the knot on her head from being hit twice.

"Careful of the lantern," Sarah warned. "We don't need to start another fire. Although I suspect everything's too wet now to worry about that."

Mary stepped back but didn't let go of the friend she'd feared dead. Sarah's face was smudged from the smoke. Her skirt suffered small burn holes, and the ends of her hair looked singed, but she was most definitely and blessedly alive.

Mary laughed. "You look a sight."

"I could say the same about you."

She probably looked worse than Sarah. From her wild hair pulled free of the pins and littered with leaves and broken twigs, to her torn, wet, and mud-covered clothes.

"Can someone help me, please?" Agnes' voice came from under the tree.

"So, who do you have under there? Are you sure you don't want to leave her there for safekeeping?"

"It's Agnes. Her skirt is caught." Mary went back to where she'd tried to lift earlier. "I think if I stay here and you stand closer to the end, we can lift it just enough for her to pull free and crawl out."

"Where are the other two?" Sarah set her lantern down and took her place where Mary suggested.

"Warm and dry in their own beds by now, I presume. Left us both for dead. On the count of three. One, two, three. Lift!"

Fabric ripped as Agnes crawled out. "Well, I guess this skirt is only good for the rag bag now," she said, examining the tear.

"Are you injured?" Mary asked. "Can you walk?"

Agnes stood and took inventory of her extremities. "A little scraped up, probably bruised, a cut or two, but other than that, I'm miraculously intact." She felt the back of her head. "Then there's this bump." She grinned and put her hands on her hips, chin held high. "Well, Maud Henry, I'd say Mary Bishop, Sarah Shaw, and I are a little harder to kill than you hoped."

Sarah retrieved her lantern. "I'd like to know what your role was in all this, why they'd turn on you all of a sudden, and why we should believe a word you say." She held the lantern up to Agnes' face.

The accused hung her head under Sarah's hard stare.

"Agnes has promised to tell Deputy Mueller everything as soon as we get to town. So, we'd better get going."

They looked again at the fallen tree.

"You're both lucky you weren't killed," Sarah said, with a shake of her head.

"I'd say someone is looking out for all three of us tonight," Mary agreed.

Agnes nodded, and they started up the road.

"Where's Boone?" Mary asked.

"I left him tied in the barn."

A few minutes later, they stood in Mary's yard. Her house smoldered off to one side. The rain had put out the fire before it was completely consumed, but what was left wasn't livable. To the other side stood the barn, fully intact despite the wind that should have carried the fire. She had the rain to thank for that, too. She looked at the smoking rubble of her house, then at her barn, then back at her house again.

"I'm sorry." Agnes touched her arm. "I truly am."

Mary shrugged off her hand. Little good an apology did her now.

"I'll hitch up the wagon." Mary opened the barn doors and was knocked off her feet when Boone jumped at her from the darkness.

"He must have chewed through the rope." Sarah laughed. "Looks pretty happy to see you."

"Are you happy to see me, boy?" Mary gave him a kiss on the head. "Are you? I'm happy to see you, too." She stood, attempting to brush bits of hay from her wet skirt. A fruitless effort, at best, and she gave up.

When Boone spotted Agnes, he laid back his ears and curled his lips, baring a row of sharp teeth. A growl rumbled deep in his throat.

"Boone, stop!"

Agnes jumped behind the barn doors as Mary pulled Boone back by the bit of frayed rope still hanging from his collar. Boone stopped growling. Agnes came out of hiding, but neither took their eyes off the other.

"Thank you, Sarah. I don't know what I'd do without Boone. I didn't realize how much I missed having a dog around for company until I got this guy."

Mary hugged Boone one more time. He licked her face and wagged his tail.

"Enough." She couldn't stop laughing. "I love you, too, but that's enough."

"I have something else for you." Sarah went into Earl's workshop and returned with Mary's hat box of treasures. "Your pictures are inside. I couldn't save anything else. I'm sorry. Your mother's wedding quilt, your father's books—there wasn't time."

"It's all I need." Mary reached for her box, then pulled back. "My hands are dirty." She choked back tears. "Thank you."

"Oh, and there's this." Sarah reached into her skirt pocket and pulled out Mary's Colt. "I kept it close, just in case."

"You better give me that before you accidentally kill someone. You can fight with the best of them, but you never were a good shot."

"Gladly," Sarah said.

Mary took the gun and put it in her pocket. "What about your things?"

"Nothing I can't replace at Oliver's in the morning."

Oliver.

Mary's heart raced. She needed to see him, couldn't go forward without him. It was all so clear now. Her past would always be in the past. Earl would always be a part of that past, but Oliver was her future.

Agnes interrupted her thoughts. "We have to get to town and talk to Deputy Mueller."

Sophie and Max were uneasy after all the commotion and the smell of smoke. It took a little doing to get them to leave their stalls and be hitched to the wagon. Mary gave Agnes one of the horse blankets to sit on in the back. She wrapped her treasures in a tarp to stay dry, should it start to rain again, and set them next to Agnes.

"I'm entrusting you with all I have left of my family. Earl, my children, my parents, brothers, and sister." Mary stared at Agnes long and hard.

"Thank you." She tucked it tight between herself and the side of the wagon. "I hope someday maybe you'll share them with me."

Mary glared at Agnes. She didn't know what to say. She turned back to Sarah.

"You'll have to drive. My hand's hurting something awful. I don't think I can handle the team." Mary sat next to her, her gun and bleeding hand cradled in her lap. In all they had to do to get free, she'd almost forgotten about the cut from the cave wall, and now the pain was almost unbearable.

"Let me see." Sarah unwrapped and turned it over to examine. "What happened to you out there?"

"I'll tell you all about it later. Right now, I think I might need stitches."

Sarah looked a little closer. "Get down. We need to wash it."

She dipped Mary's hand in the rain barrel. Mary gasped and her knees buckled when the cold water hit the open cut. Sarah ripped off a clean strip of her petticoat, soaked it in the water, wiped away the mud, then rewrapped it.

"I don't know if you need stitches, but you should at least have the doctor examine and bandage it properly."

"Come on, Boone." Agnes slapped her hand against the wagon bed. "You can sit back here with me." Boone leapt up next to her and laid his head in her lap. "I think he likes me, after all."

"Then you might be all right. Let's go, Sarah."

THEY MET REVEREND AND Frances Clark coming from the other direction. The Clark's buggy bounced wildly as he pushed his horse to go faster. He pulled back on the reins when he saw them. Frances jumped down and ran to their side.

"Thank God you're both safe. We came as soon as we saw the flames. I was so afraid those women had killed you this time." Frances stopped. She narrowed her eyes when she saw Agnes sitting in back. "What are you doing here?"

Agnes shrunk back. "We have to get to Deputy Mueller as soon as possible," she explained. "We must speak with him."

"Of course." Reverend Clark motioned to Frances to get back in her seat. "We'll follow you. And, Mary, you needn't worry about Oliver. Doc says he'll be fine."

"What happened to Oliver?" Her stomach tightened. She couldn't lose Oliver, too. Not after all they'd gone through to be together.

"Apparently those women knocked him unconscious and locked him in his storeroom so he couldn't follow," Frances explained.

Agnes shrank back from Mary's glare. "It was Gladys. I didn't know anything about it until after, when I heard her bragging to Maud."

"Be certain you mention that to the deputy, too. Don't leave anything out."

"Except for a beauty of a goose egg, he's just fine. He's been asking about you. Sounds like a desperate man in love, if you ask me." The Reverend smiled.

"If I were you, I'd marry that man before someone else does," Sarah said, again.

"Shush!" Mary's cheeks blazed under the cool rain that dripped from the overhead branches.

"You won't need that gun anymore." He indicated the weapon in her lap.

"If you don't mind, Reverend, I'll keep it with me for just a little longer."

THE STREETS WERE CROWDED despite the rain. Some pointed toward the smoke on the horizon, while others gathered around Deputy Mueller's office. The women's arrival drew their attention.

"Mrs. Bishop, I'm so happy to see you and your friend are safe," one woman said. Her face was familiar, but Mary didn't know her name.

Others greeted them as well, while some stood back to whisper among themselves. She was struck by how many voiced their relief.

Sarah helped her down from the wagon, and Agnes handed over her box.

"Mary!" Oliver pushed his way through the crowd and embraced her.

"How's your head?" Mary gingerly touched Doc's bandaging.

"Never mind me. I'll be fine. How are you? Deputy Mueller has Maud and Gladys down at the jail house with their husbands. He wants to talk to you, too, Agnes." His voice was as icy as his stare.

"I need to get over there." Agnes climbed down from the wagon bed.

"I'll go with you," Mary said.

"And me." Oliver took the box from her. "Your pictures?"

"Yes."

"And we'll take the gun." Reverend Clark held out his hand. "For safe keeping only." Mary hesitated, then handed it over. "Mrs. Shaw, we'll show you where to put your team and wagon, then we'll take Boone with us so you can join Mary and give your statement."

MAUD AND GLADYS WERE locked in one cell, their husbands in the other. Norbert Schmidt sat opposite the deputy answering questions to determine what role he may have played in all the trouble.

"Mrs. Schmidt, we've been looking for you," the deputy said when they entered.

"Are you injured?" Norbert Schmidt examined his disheveled wife, then hugged her. "We couldn't get these friends of yours to tell us what happened."

"They're not my friends, not anymore. And I'm not injured. In fact, I'm alive because of Mary. She saved my life tonight—twice—while they left us to die. I'll tell you everything Deputy."

Maud Henry paced the floor of her cell while Gladys glared from her seat on the bench against the back wall.

"Rebel traitor!" Maud screamed at Mary and spat through the bars. "That one's a rebel and a traitor, Deputy, and that one," pointing at Agnes, "is just a plain old liar. Are you going to believe them over me?"

"Sit down, Mrs. Henry."

"She's the one who ought to be locked up in here, not us!" she screamed, pointing again at Mary.

"Shut up, Maud, and sit down!" Augustus yelled. "It's over."

Maud sat on the bench next to Gladys. Agnes held her chin high and took the chair her husband offered.

Deputy Mueller pulled up another. "Have a seat, Mrs. Bishop." He pointed at her bundle. "Is that all you have left?"

"This and my barn. My animals were spared. Oh, and my gun." She looked over at the women. Gladys turned away, but Maud didn't flinch.

Except for the late Jackson Bishop, was there anyone as cold and mean as Maud Henry?

"I'm sorry. By the time I uncovered their plan it was too late. I caught them riding back into town looking like a couple of drowned rats."

Mary found the comparison amusingly appropriate.

"What will happen to them now, Deputy?" Oliver asked.

"There will be a trial, and if they're found guilty, they'll go to jail."

"What about me?" Agnes asked.

"That depends a great deal on the judge and what you have to say today."

"I'll tell you everything."

Agnes and Mary told their story. Sarah gave her side. The more they said, the quieter the four prisoners became.

When they were done, Deputy Mueller warned them, "I may need to talk to you three again, so make yourselves available. You'll also have to testify at the trial. In the meantime, I'll arrange for someone to take care of your animals until you decide what to do next."

"Thank you, and don't worry, Deputy, I'm not going anywhere." A blush crept up Mary's cheeks. "You see, Oliver and I are getting married."

Oliver smiled at her. Her cheeks grew hotter, and she had to look away to keep from giggling. What an old fool she'd become.

"Congratulations! And, I must admit, I'm not surprised. According to my wife, this has been a done deal for some time now." Deputy Mueller stood when the women rose to leave and held out his hand. "Mary, may I apologize, again, for the way I treated you that day you came in to report those two men." He looked at Augustus Henry and Karl Olson. "I didn't believe you, and I should have. It might have saved us all a whole lot of trouble today."

Mary nodded. "And maybe it would have changed nothing."

He turned to the Schmidt's. "Norbert, you can take your wife home, but don't go anywhere. There could still be charges, and I'm trusting you to bring her in if there are."

"Thank you, Deputy." Norbert put his hat on. "Come along, Agnes."

"Yes, thank you, Deputy," she said. "And, Mary, again, I'm sorry."

Sarah left shortly after for the parsonage to clean up. Mary and Oliver excused themselves to have Dr. Hunter check Mary's injuries first.

An hour later her hand was thoroughly cleaned, stitched, and bandaged. The lump on her head was declared minor. The storm had passed and the sky cleared. A million bright stars winked down on them. The crowds were gone and the streets quiet.

"Ask me again, Oliver." She slipped her arm through his.

"Ask you what? If I heard you correctly back in the deputy's office, I already have my answer."

"Ask me again, Oliver," she insisted.

He stopped outside the parsonage front door and took her in his arms. "Mary Bishop, will you marry me?"

"Yes, Mr. Polk, I believe I will."

Oliver's lips were soft and warm on hers. She stood at the front gate and watched as he strolled home in the moonlight. His happy whistle carried back to her on the night breeze. He stopped and waved from in front of the store. She waited until a lantern shone in his window before going inside.

CHAPTER 44

WISCONSIN: JUNE 1881

Mary slept late the next morning. When she finally woke, the sun was high and bright, and Sarah's side of the bed was empty. It took her a couple minutes to remember where she was, and why.

Frances' guest room. There'd been a fire. Maud and her friends had tried to murder her.

She tried to stand, but her legs rebelled. Every muscle in her body hurt. Boone, her ever-faithful protector, glanced up from his spot in front of the door.

"How are you feeling this morning?" she asked him. She cringed as she lowered her feet to the floor. He rose and sat by her side, placing his head on her lap. She scratched his favorite spot behind the ears.

"Don't you worry about me," she assured him. "I'm going to be fine, just a little sore, that's all."

There was a tap on the door. Sarah stuck her head in. "I thought I heard you up." She smiled and brought in a pitcher of fresh water for the wash basin and a cake of soap. A washcloth and towel were draped over her arm. "Frances is getting you something to eat."

Mary eyed the soap and water with a sigh. She'd washed off the worst of it the night before, but the idea of a real good scrub down sounded wonderful. "Almost seems a little pointless, though," she said, "when all I have to wear are the muddy, smoky clothes from yesterday. Thank goodness Frances had a couple extra nightgowns to lend us."

"I know what you mean, but donations are pouring in. Women from the church have been stopping by all morning."

"Not a bad fit." Mary nodded at her friend's dress. "I do question your color choice, though."

"Yes, well, I'm not normally a yellow person, but I didn't want to be ungrateful. A girl handed it to me herself. We saw her over at Oliver's the day we invited him to dinner. Miss Webster, I believe. Not the one worried about her hats. The other one, her friend."

Mary waved a finger at Sarah's bodice and sleeves. "That would explain all the ribbons and bows. We may have retained our girlish figures, or maybe not, but that doesn't make us one." Sarah laughed. Mary groaned when she stood.

"Speak for yourself. You might be feeling your age this morning, but I'm feeling just fine. Did you notice Gladys' black eye last night? I did that." Sarah set the water pitcher by the basin on the dressing table, gasped, and rubbed her shoulder.

Mary raised her eyebrows and smirked. "Just fine, are you?"

"That tree *was* terribly heavy," Sarah admitted. They laughed.

"As trees tend to be," Mary agreed. "Speaking of clothes." Her box was wrapped in the tarp and tucked beneath the chair where she left it, but her clothes were gone. In their place was a neatly pressed, cornflower print shirt and navy-blue skirt.

"There was no point trying to clean your old clothes, so we burned them. Those came from Agnes. She wanted to be sure you had something clean to wear when you woke up."

Mary was moved by Agnes' kind gesture. She hoped Deputy Mueller and the judge would go easy on her.

"Frances went to Oliver's store this morning and, between the two of them, picked out a few more things to get you started, including a dress that will make you the most beautiful bride in the state of Wisconsin—and Minnesota." She smiled.

"I can't afford all that," Mary said. "I have nothing but a box of photos and old letters, a barn with a couple farm animals, a garden, and a dog."

Frances joined them with a breakfast tray holding coffee and enough food to feed a small family. She set it on the bedside table. "And a man who loves you very much," she added, with a twinkle in her eye. "You owe him nothing but your love. He's going to be your husband. It's his duty, as such, to provide you with everything you need." She sat next to Mary and took her hand. "You are a very lucky woman."

Mary nodded. "Yes, I am. To have two men love me the way Earl did, and Oliver does."

Frances stood and poured Mary a cup of coffee. "And I didn't let Oliver send over half what he wanted. I told him your pride would never accept it all, at least, not until after the wedding."

"Thank you," Mary said. "For your help and this delicious coffee."

Frances held up a finger and smiled. "Remember, you do have one more thing you failed to mention in your little list of belongings."

"What's that?" What else had been saved from the fire?

Frances reached under the bed and pulled out the Colt. "A gun. And you know how to use it."

Their laughter filled the room.

A WEEK LATER, MARY put on her dove gray wedding dress. Sarah carefully pinned a cluster of white daisies in her hair. She turned this way and that in front of the mirror. While she didn't think Sarah was right about being the most beautiful bride in Wisconsin and Minnesota, she certainly felt like it.

"Are you ready?" Sarah asked.

Mary nodded.

Frances waited in the parlor. "Oh, my." She covered her mouth with a trembling hand.

"Do not cry, Frances," Sarah scolded, "or you'll have all of us crying before we get to the church. We can't have that. No bride is allowed tears on her wedding day."

Frances dabbed her eyes, blew her nose, and drew in a long, slow, deep breath.

"Are you all done now?" Sarah asked.

"Yes." Frances handed Mary a bouquet of daisies to match her hair. "To the church. Your groom awaits."

MARY STOOD IN THE CHURCH door. Oliver waited at the altar dressed in his best suit. His eyes reflected her happiness tenfold. She walked toward her future and placed her hand in his.

"You take my breath away," he said, before they turned to Reverend Clark.

The sun was shining, and a light breeze tickled the leaves. Spring flowers had been replaced by summer's vibrant blooms. Birds sang as the happy couple stood before Reverend Clark and declared their love for one another. Frances and Sarah were witnesses and showered them with flower petals when they left the church. It was a small wedding, only Sarah, Dr. Hunter, and Deputy Mueller and his family in attendance. Oliver's daughter telegraphed her blessings and promised a visit after the couple got settled. The children were anxious to meet their new grandmother, and Mary was excited to meet her new daughter's family.

She had a *family*. The word made her giddy. She hadn't thought she'd ever be able to say that again.

After the ceremony, Gretchen invited everyone back to the restaurant for lunch and a special cake she had baked and decorated for the occasion. Dr. Hunter brought several bottles of his homemade chokecherry wine. In all the years Mary lived in Deer Creek, she never knew the good doctor made wine. And a very fine wine it was.

"Your cheeks are quite pink, wife," Oliver said with a smile.

"I admit I am feeling a little tipsy." She giggled, much to everyone's amusement.

"It makes you look twice as lovely." Oliver kissed her hand. "And I didn't think that possible."

"Oh, stop. You're making me blush." She tried to gently push him away, but he held her tighter and kissed her on each cheek.

"How can anyone tell?" Dr. Hunter laughed harder than anyone at his little joke.

She thought he had been enjoying the wine a bit too much himself.

When the laughter died down, Gretchen came and stood before them. She took Mary's hands in hers. "So, now for the sad news. I heard a rumor the two of you might be leaving us. Is this true?"

"No." Mary smiled. "Just another ugly rumor. While there are those who would like to see me run, have done everything they can think of, including trying to kill me, in the hopes that I would run, I have no intention of leaving. Deer Creek is my home now."

"And that's a good thing," Frances said. "Because I won't be able to help Oliver with his books for much longer." She placed her hands protectively over her stomach. "The Reverend and I are expecting a child." It was her turn to blush.

The room erupted with applause and cries of happy surprise. Mary hugged her young friend.

"When?"

"Just in time for Christmas."

Everything was falling into place. Volunteers had already begun work clearing away what remained of her old house, and the plan for a new one was under way. With so many helping hands, it wouldn't be long before they would be able to move in. Mary even managed to salvage some of her mother's china from the debris.

In the meantime, they would stay in Oliver's rooms above the store. Sarah had set-up a cozy little corner of the barn where she could keep an eye on the animals and garden. Boone stayed with her for protection and company. And, as a little extra security, Mary was teaching her to shoot, although the only thing they had to be concerned about now was bears.

"It's been years since I've had to rough it," she said when Mary tried to talk her out of it. "Not since our journey to St. Paul. Besides, it's only temporary. By the time you and Oliver are ready to move into your new home, I'll have found a little place of my own in town, with a yard big enough for my own garden and perhaps a few chickens."

"So, you really are staying?" Mary's joy was boundless.

"I've already written Robert and Amy Lynn to send my things. It will be interesting to see how they respond. Robert will argue why I shouldn't go, but I'm guessing Amy Lynn will be more than a little relieved to have her mother-in-law out from under foot. Besides, I hear there may be a seamstress shop for sale. All I need is to find a milliner to partner with me."

"I've been playing around with my own hats." Anna's eyes lit up. "Mother says I'm quite good at it."

"Yes, she has the talent, our Anna does." Gretchen put her arm around her daughter's shoulders.

"Then I think we're all set, partner." Sarah shook Anna's hand. Anna squealed and Gretchen hugged her.

Deputy Mueller nodded, pleased. "If my daughter's half the business-woman her mother is, I'll never have to worry about her."

"But I will miss all her help here in the restaurant," her mother said.

Mary could hardly stop to think what the future held now that she was married to Oliver and her friend Sarah was staying. With so many changes, her heart raced, excited and fearful at the same time, but she knew with Oliver at her side all would be well.

What was to be a small luncheon had grown and continued all through the afternoon and into the evening as townspeople stopped by to wish them well. Most Mary knew by name, a few she only recognized in passing, but there was one man who was not familiar. He walked in and stopped, hat in hand. Tall and slender with silver hair, his posture reminded her of Mr. Nichols. Except, his features were softer, his eyes kinder. She assumed he was a traveler needing a meal, only to find the one restaurant in town full.

That was, until Sarah rushed across the room to greet him with a big smile. She appeared to stop just short of throwing her arms around him. He smiled, equally pleased to see her. Was he someone she knew from St. Paul? The two talked for a moment and then Sarah hugged him.

"Who's that with Sarah?" Oliver asked.

"I don't know."

Sarah ushered the man over. "Oliver, Mary, I'd like you to meet the Reverend Redmond Thorpe. He's the gentleman who so graciously gave me a ride from Taylors Falls to Deer Creek when I first arrived."

"Then I'll always be in your debt, Reverend," Mary said, "for bringing my dear friend back to me."

"Redmond, this is my friend Mary Bishop, now Mary Polk. I told you about her on the ride. And this is her new husband, Oliver."

"Congratulations and God's blessings on your marriage."

"Thank you."

How had Sarah and the Reverend Thorpe come to be on a first name basis so quickly?

"Redmond was telling me he's planning to retire from his traveling ministry and settle down right here in Deer Creek." Sarah's face glowed, her eyes sparkled when she looked at him.

First name again. Mary tried to read Sarah's eyes, but she blushed and looked away.

AFTER THE WEDDING CELEBRATION finally broke up, and Oliver and Mary had said their good-byes, they strolled arm in arm down the main street. The sky faded and the stars began to twinkle on, one by one. Many greeted them with congratulations and best wishes, but there were others who ignored her, even crossing to the other side of the street. She didn't care. She was happy in their new little world, and no one could hurt her ever again.

"What do you think of Sarah and Reverend Thorpe?" she asked Oliver.

"I think they seem very happy together."

"But she hardly knows him."

"Sometimes it works that way. I know it was like that with me and Irma, and you've said many times how you knew you loved Earl from the moment you met."

"Mmmm." Mary smiled and nodded. "That's true."

"But enough about them." Oliver stopped and pulled her into his arms for a kiss.

"Oliver! People are staring." She half-heartedly tried to free herself from his embrace.

"I don't care. I am in love with you, Mrs. Polk, and I want the entire world to know." He let her go after another kiss.

Mary took Oliver's arm as they strolled through town. They paused in front of the seamstress and milliner's shop. Normally a place buzzing with gossip, the curtains were drawn and the door locked, the owners sitting in a jail cell awaiting trial for arson and attempted murder.

"The shop will be a good fit for Sarah," she said.

"I agree." Oliver squeezed her hand. "And I'm glad Sarah's staying."

They continued walking.

"I actually feel a little sorry for Agnes, Gladys, and Maud," Mary said.

"That's because you're such a kind-hearted person. They shoot you and burn your house to the ground, you lose almost everything, including your life, and still you can feel sympathy for them. It's one of the reasons I love you."

At the end of the street they stopped and turned toward the cemetery gates.

"Do you want to go up?" Oliver asked.

She shook her head. "They're not there, you know. They're in our hearts, in the stars, so always with us. Someone told me that once, not so long ago." They stood quiet for a moment. "Do you want to go up?"

He shook his head. "Let's go home, Mrs. Polk."

"Let's go home, Mr. Polk."

Mary smiled to herself and didn't look back. She had everything she needed, her photos, her letters, and her Oliver.

About the Author

Jane Yunker is a poet and fiction writer living in northwest Wisconsin along the beautiful and inspirational St Croix River.

She is a member of the Wisconsin Writers' Association (WWA), Romance Writers of America (RWA), the Wisconsin chapter of RWA (WisRWA), and the Romantic Women's Fiction (RWF) online chapter of RWA.

Find her on her website: www.janeyunkerauthor.com. And at: facebook.com/JaneYunkerAuthor, and Twitter @poetryWI.

Made in the USA
Monee, IL
15 February 2020

21854903R00155